Pucking my Bad Boy Boss

An Enemies to Lovers Fake Relationship Romance

Livvy Stone

Join Livvy Stone's Readers' Circle!

SNAG *THOUSANDS* OF FREEBIES, bargains and sneak peeks, get the scoop on the latest releases, and be the first to dive into upcoming stories. Oh, and did we mention your welcome gift? Say hello to 'Pucking My Brother's Best Friend,' Livvy's FREE eBook crafted just for you!

Scan this QR code to join and download your free book!

Scan me

Contents

1. Isabella   1

2. Dom   9

3. Isabella   18

4. Dom   24

5. Isabella   29

6. Dom   35

7. Isabella   42

8. Dom   46

9. Isabella   56

10. Dom   64

11. Isabella   71

12. Dom   78

13. Isabella   87

14. Dom   93

15.	Isabella	100
16.	Dom	110
17.	Isabella	119
18.	Dom	127
19.	Isabella	133
20.	Dom	143
21.	Isabella	158
22.	Dom	169
23.	Isabella	174
24.	Dom	180
25.	Isabella	189
26.	Dom	194
27.	Isabella	200
28.	Dom	205
29.	Isabella	209
30.	Dom	214
31.	Isabella	219
32.	Dom	223
33.	Isabella	226
34.	Dom	232
35.	Isabella	237
36.	Dom	243
37.	Isabella	246
38.	Dom	249

39.	Isabella	252
40.	Dom	256
Epilogue		260
Epilogue 2		265
Pucking My Off-Limits Billionaire Boss		272

1

Isabella

"Jenna, these conferences could put a caffeine-addicted squirrel to sleep," I groan into my phone, swirling the olive in my martini. Neon Nights is humming with the seductive energy of New York City nightlife. A deep blue glow casts an almost dreamlike haze over the hip crowd, and the bar's modern aesthetics provide the perfect contrast to my day at the impossibly dreary NHL Annual Strategy Symposium.

Laughter dances from the other end of the call. "I can't even picture you, Miss Always-in-Control, at one of those things. All suits, ties, and puck dynamics. But come on, it can't be *that* bad?"

I roll my eyes, even if she can't see it.

"Imagine getting mansplained about the aerodynamics of hockey sticks," I say with a hint of dry humor. My feet ache in my high heels, longing for the comfort of my usual sports attire.

Jenna's laughter rings through the space. "I bet you were wearing your 'thoroughly unimpressed' face the whole time," she teases.

"Oh, absolutely," I reply. "But I'm really not a fan of this whole suit-and-heels thing. My feet are staging a full-on rebellion."

"Missing your comfy sneakers, aren't you?" Jenna asks knowingly.

"You have no idea," I groan. "And don't get me started on the hair. This power bun has been a nightmare." I reach up, letting down the tight bun that's been pulling at my scalp, and my hair cascades down in a wave of liberation.

Jenna chuckles. "Ah, the small joys of shedding the professional armor and coming back to your true self."

"Exactly," I agree, running my fingers through my hair. "Give me my team jacket and a pair of comfortable shoes any day. That's the real Isabella Carrington, not this suited-up, high-heel-enduring version."

"Well, suit or no suit, you're still the Isabella who's kicking ass and taking names," Jenna says supportively.

"Thanks, J."

As I vent, my gaze drifts across the bar, landing on a sight that stops me mid-sentence. There's a man, all sharp lines and brooding intensity, seated in a way that screams confidence. The tailored cut of his suit showcases broad shoulders and an athlete's physique. The dim lights catch the intricate tattoos that wind down his rolled-up sleeve on his left arm all the way to his hand, then back up along the same side of his neck, revealing tales I can only guess at.

"Earth to Izzy!" Jenna's voice snaps me back to reality.

Caught in my open admiration, I quickly divert. "Sorry, Jen. Just... surveying the room."

"Ooh, someone caught your eye?" Her voice lifts with mischief.

I smirk, keeping my voice casual while my gaze subtly follows the man across the bar. "Just a random guy. He's definitely hot, but I've got bigger fish to fry."

Jenna laughs. "Always business with you. Speaking of which, why'd you call?"

I sigh, tapping my nails against the bar. "Needed a break, and a momentary escape. But you know me, always finding a way to work."

Jenna's laughter rings through the phone, light and teasing. "Seriously, give me *one* good reason why-" There's a sudden pause, a muffled sound, then Jenna's tone shifts, more serious. "Oh, shoot, that's Dr. Reynolds calling from the hospital. Might be important. I gotta take this. Keep me posted, okay? And go conquer the world, or at least that bar."

"We'll see. Bye, Jen" I end the call, laying my phone on the bar. Fishing a sleek tablet from my bag, I pull up a few documents, figuring I can squeeze in some work while enjoying my drink. Then it's back home to Seattle in the morning.

I lose myself in reports and strategies, making notes and planning moves for my team, the Silver Blades. In the periphery of my vision, I occasionally notice the tattooed stranger glancing my way, his dark eyes intense. But right now, my focus is all on the game off the ice. After all, in the fast-paced world of sports management, every moment counts.

I don't know what hits me first—the potent warmth of the martini or the sultriness in the gaze of the tattooed man. It's a heady combination. I'm used to feeling eyes on me, especially in my line of work, but this? This is a different ballgame–or hockey game, in my case.

I glance up, just a cursory survey, but I'm not prepared for what greets me. Those intense eyes, exuding a primal, unspoken challenge. It's the kind of confidence you don't often see, the kind that says he's played the game—in more rinks than one—and knows how to win. That hint of a smirk, so infuriatingly arrogant, is enough to send a jolt straight to my core.

There's something else, too. The guy looks *familiar* in a way I can't quite place.

My cheeks flame. *Damn it, Carrington, pull yourself together.*

I quickly return my attention to the screen, telling myself that the bar's ambient temperature is the reason for my sudden warmth. I become engrossed in a particularly gnarly contract clause, letting its jargon and complications distract me from the man who seems to have temporarily short-circuited my brain.

A new email pops up, pulling my attention. Some update about the Seattle StarPucks, the newest franchise team to hit the ice. As I scan the lines, I make a mental note to respond later. My eyes flit over stats, percentages, margins—numbers and figures that ground me, making the world make sense again.

Around me, the bar comes alive. Glasses clink, laughter grows louder, and the sensual beats of 'Earned It' by The Weeknd begins to play. The seductive rhythm weaves through my consciousness, adding a layer of sultriness to the mundane data before me. And yet, even amidst all this, I can feel the weight of a particular gaze.

Resisting the temptation becomes a game. How long can I keep my focus strictly professional with the embodiment of temptation mere feet away? The more I dive into my work, the more my surroundings blur into indistinct chatter, shadows, and light.

The bustling hum of the bar, the background music, it's all become a comforting white noise. I lose myself in the drudgery, each line blurring into the next.

"You know, they say puck size matters," a voice rumbles suddenly, low and tinged with mischief, breaking through my trance.

Startled, I almost knock over my martini, catching it just in time. I slowly lift my eyes from my screen. No longer across the room, the mysterious stranger is now leaning against the bar beside me, all broad shoulders and simmering intensity. The close proximity sends a jolt of awareness down my spine. The heat he gives off is palpable, like standing too close to a bonfire.

"Excuse me?" I challenge, arching an eyebrow, my voice dripping with feigned disdain, though my racing heart gives away my surprise.

His lips curve into a teasing grin, green eyes dancing with amusement. "Just reflecting on a topic from the conference today. Interesting how such minute details can have such a significant impact on the game."

My cheeks blaze as realization dawns. He'd been at the Strategy Symposium too. No wonder he'd looked so familiar.

And yet, it's the man himself that truly captures my attention. Up close, his charm is practically an assault. Those expressive eyes, the texture of his short beard, his laugh lines—it's all intensely, impossibly distracting. And I've never been a tattoo sort of woman, but the way those designs look crawling up his ropey, thick forearm, vanishing underneath the tightly-rolled sleeve of his shirt, reappearing up above along his thick neck... *damn*.

As he starts to introduce himself, holding out a hand, I cut him off, "Dominic Steele. You're Dom Steele." The words spill out, the dots finally connecting. He's not just some hockey enthusiast; he's THE hockey legend.

That's why he looked so familiar. Not just because he was some guy who happened to be at the conference, but that he was a hockey god in the flesh!

For a split second, I feel like a rookie who's stepped onto the ice for the first time, disoriented and off-balance. The man beside me isn't just a handsome stranger; he's a monumental figure in the world of hockey, a living legend. And here I am, working on budget reports and getting tipsy in his presence.

A touch of pink colors my cheeks, but if he notices my embarrassment, he doesn't show it. Instead, with the smooth grace of someone who's been in the limelight for years, he replies, "Most people just call me Dom."

I'm too stunned to speak.

He gestures to the empty seat beside me. "Mind if I join you? I promise I won't critique your spreadsheet. Much."

His teasing tone, combined with that signature Dom Steele confidence, is utterly captivating. All I can manage is a sassy smirk as I motion for him to take the seat. Work can wait, but opportunities like this? They're as fleeting as a puck in the final seconds of a tied game.

"Go ahead," I say, trying to sound cool and in control. Still, my voice hitches just slightly, and inwardly I'm berating myself for it. The bar's ambient murmur seems to fade a touch as he settles next to me. I nod to the seat beside mine, a clear invitation.

Watching Dom move is like observing poetry in motion. For a guy built like a fortress, he carries an unexpected grace with every step. It's a strange juxtaposition—the raw power of an athlete combined with the fluidity of a dancer. As he takes the seat, there's a smooth pivot, an ease in his descent, the lean of his tattooed arm on the bar counter.

My eyes can't help but drift down, taking in the defined muscles of his forearms, and then, a bit lower, to his perfectly shaped behind. A playful, albeit inappropriate thought crosses my mind: I wonder what those arms would feel like wrapped around me—and just how firm that amazing butt really is, what it'd feel like bare underneath my hands...

Whoa, Isabella! Get a grip! But oh, what a deliciously sinful grip that could be.

"So, you were at the conference too?" I ask, hoping to steer my thoughts to safer territory.

Dom chuckles, his smoldering intensity momentarily replaced by amusement. "Yep, and it was every bit as riveting as watching paint dry."

I snort with laughter, nearly spitting out my drink. "Thank God I wasn't the only one stifling yawns! I thought I was going to be buried under PowerPoint slides."

His laughter is hearty and infectious. "And let's not even get started on those long-winded keynote speeches."

We exchange playful banter, tearing apart various elements of the conference, and it's evident we're on the same wavelength. It's surprisingly easy, this back and forth with him.

Dom arches an eyebrow, his magnetic eyes twinkling with mischief. "Anyway, did you catch that session on the evolutionary trajectory of the hockey puck? I mean, who knew there was a prehistoric age for those little rubber discs?"

I stifle a giggle. "Oh, absolutely enlightening! I was on the edge of my seat. And don't even get me started on the dramatic unveiling of the new puck design. I've never seen so much fanfare over a few added grooves."

He laughs, a rich, hearty sound that has a flutter running down my spine. "Oh, come on! That laser light show? The dramatic music? It was like witnessing the launch of a new iPhone—just rounder and... more slappable."

I feign a dramatic gasp. "How dare you! Pucks are the very essence of our sport! Next, you'll be making fun of the strategic placement of water bottles on the bench."

He leans in conspiratorially, voice dripping with mock gravity. "Ah, now that's classified info! But between you and me, I've always believed there's a secret society deciding the precise angles those bottles should face. I mean, it's the only logical explanation."

My laughter is genuine and unbridled. It feels like a release, especially after the stiffness of the conference. "Oh, please. It's all about the optimal squirt trajectory."

Dom chuckles, clearly delighted by my response. "Ah, squirt trajectory. Now that's a panel discussion I'd sign up for!"

There's a lull in the conversation, and right away I notice that it's not an awkward pause—not even a little. It's the kind of pause you have with someone you've known for a while, someone you're totally comfortable with.

Strange, considering I've just met the man.

"So, Isabella," Dom leans in, his voice dropping a notch, "what do you do when you're not suffering through tedious conferences? You mentioned the Silver Blades earlier."

"Ah, the Silver Blades," I say, pride evident in my voice. "I'm their Strategy Manager. I pretty much oversee the strategic planning and execution for the team. Makes me sound important, right?"

Dom's eyes light up with genuine interest. "That's impressive. Not just a pretty face then?" The flirtation is evident, but it's his playful tone that makes me laugh rather than roll my eyes.

"I like to think I have the brains to match," I retort, shooting him a sassy grin.

I can't ignore the electricity in the air, the tingling sensation whenever our hands brush, or the heat that rises in me every time I catch his gaze. It's been ages since I've had this much fun talking to someone, and for a fleeting moment, I forget who he is—forgetting the fame, the accolades, and the legacy.

For now, in this dimly lit bar in New York, he's just Dom. And I'm having the time of my life.

2

Dom

"I SWEAR, IF ONE more person tries to explain to me the aerodynamics of a slap shot, I might just spontaneously combust," I say, grinning devilishly.

Isabella throws her head back, laughing. "Oh, come on, Dom. Surely, after all these years on the ice, there's some hidden, profound mystery about it you've missed?"

I smirk, leaning closer. "The only mystery here is how I've managed to stay awake through half those sessions."

Her laughter gradually fades, and I take the moment to really look at her. Damn. Up close, she's even more striking. The dim bar lights catch the rich, raven-black strands of her shoulder-length hair, making them shimmer like the midnight sky. Her hazel eyes, framed by those sleek, black cat-eye glasses, have this intense yet playful glint.

It's as if they're challenging me, daring me to keep up with her sharp wit.

Her laugh, that genuine, soul-deep laugh, makes her entire face light up. The way her lips curve, full and inviting, has my mind wandering down paths it probably shouldn't. And it's not just her face. I can't help but appreciate her lean athletic frame, the unmistakable curves that her tailored pantsuit hints at. She has me wondering how those toned muscles would feel under my hands.

She's a blend of strength, beauty, and intelligence. It's a dangerously alluring combination.

"So, Isabella," I begin, my voice dropping an octave lower, involuntarily adding a sultrier tone. "Strategy Manager for the Silver Blades, huh? Sounds important. Do you, like, plan out how many left turns players make during a game?"

She snorts, her earlier laughter replaced with an amused smirk. "Oh, at least a hundred. It's a very scientific process. Mostly involves me spinning a wheel and yelling out directions."

I chuckle, leaning back and taking a sip of my drink. "I knew it! All those years wondering about the secret strategies, and it's just a glorified game of Twister."

She laughs again, and I'm caught in the melodious sound. I'm used to being the charmer, the one who has people hanging on his every word. But here, with Isabella, it feels like the tables have turned. Every quip, every laugh, every glance she throws my way—I'm hooked. And it's a feeling I'm not quite sure what to do with.

I let the moment linger, the atmosphere thick with playful tension. There's a magnetic pull between us, undeniable and strong. It's been a long time since I've felt this kind of connection, especially so instantly.

"So," I start, leaning my elbow on the bar counter, "how does someone like you end up in hockey management?"

She arches a perfectly sculpted eyebrow, her smirk growing more pronounced. "Someone like me? You mean a woman?"

I can't help but laugh, that smooth, self-assured chuckle that's gotten me out of more than a few tight spots. "Nah," I reply, my eyes shamelessly raking over her, "more like a *beautiful* woman. Someone who looks like you wouldn't have to work a single day in your life... unless you wanted to."

For a split second, I worry I might've laid it on too thick. But then, a delicate blush spreads across her cheeks, making her already stunning face glow. God, I could get addicted to that blush.

She rolls her eyes, though the smile tugging at her lips gives away her amusement. "Oh, please. That's your go-to line, isn't it? Well, for your information, Mr. Steele," she playfully stresses my name, "my love for hockey strategy isn't rooted in my looks. It started with my brother."

I raise an eyebrow in genuine curiosity, my previous cockiness momentarily overshadowed. "Your brother?"

She nods, taking a sip of her drink. "Mhm. He was obsessed with hockey. Played it all through school and college. I never really had the inclination to get on the ice myself, but I was always there, watching his games. The more I watched, the more fascinated I became with the strategies, the planning, the maneuvers. Not the physical side of the game, but the mental one."

Leaning in closer, her enthusiasm palpable, she continues, "I started seeing patterns, predicting plays before they happened. And when my brother moved on to a minor league, I began suggesting strategies. Turns out, I had a knack for it. From there, it was just a short leap to the management side of things."

She finishes her tale, looking a touch bashful. It's a new side to her, one that intrigues me even more. "So, you're the brains behind the operation," I muse aloud, genuinely impressed.

She shrugs modestly, but her eyes gleam with pride. "Someone's got to do the thinking, right?"

Chuckling, I nod in agreement. "True that. Many guys I know just skate around, hoping for the best. But I always believed in the power of a good strategy."

Her face lights up, pleased with the validation. "Exactly! It's an art, a game of wits. It's what makes it exciting."

As the night wears on, the atmosphere between us lightens, making it easy to forget the outside world. It's her turn to probe now.

"So, Dominic," she drawls out my name teasingly, the soft glow of the bar lights making her eyes dance, "I've always been curious. After such a legendary stint on the ice, where did you vanish to?" Her playful tone falters slightly, "Of course, I mean after... the injury."

Instantly, her cheeks redden, as if realizing she may have overstepped. "Sorry, I shouldn't have brought that up."

I wave off her concern, the memories of that day, though painful, having been dealt with a long time ago. "It's alright, Isabella. Ancient history." I lean back in my chair, the leather creaking softly under my weight. "You know, life has a funny way of pushing you in the direction you're meant to go. Sometimes it's a gentle nudge, other times it's a shove off a cliff. Either way, I believe it all happens for a reason."

She seems taken by my response, her tense shoulders relaxing. A smile graces her lips, one that seems both relieved and genuinely pleased. "That's a refreshing attitude," she remarks.

Under the table, my fingers drum a nervous rhythm. Few people know about my recent endeavors in the hockey world. I've been working in the shadows, letting others take the limelight. And while part of me wants to spill everything to Isabella, a gut feeling tells me it's not the right time. Some secrets need to remain hidden, at least for now.

However, it's as if she reads my mind. Her gaze sharpens, eyes narrowing playfully, "What are you hiding, Mr. Steele? You have that look. The one people get when they're sitting on a juicy piece of gossip."

Caught off guard, I'm saved by the bartender's timely announcement, his voice echoing through the now almost-empty establishment. "Last call, folks!"

She shoots me a mischievous glance, leaning in as if to share a secret, her lips just inches from my ear. "You got lucky this time, Dom. But I have a knack for uncovering secrets." Her warm breath sends shivers down my spine.

Pulling away with a smirk, she collects her things, ready to call it a night. And as she does, I can't help but think that life's little push tonight was leading me right to her.

As the atmosphere between us thickens, the pull becomes undeniable. In a bold move, I reach over and slide my hand onto her thigh, feeling the warmth of her skin even through the fabric of her dress. Our eyes lock, and for a moment, everything else blurs.

"You said you've got a knack for uncovering secrets," I murmur, my voice dripping with intent. "What else are you good at uncovering?"

A coy smile dances on her lips, and the glint in her eyes tells me she's picked up on my challenge. "Wouldn't you like to know?"

The next thing I know, we're rushing towards the elevators, barely able to keep our hands off each other. The world outside is a distant echo as our mouths collide, every touch a promise of the fire that's about to ignite.

The doors open to my penthouse hotel suite, and the sight that greets us is nothing short of breathtaking. But right now, New York City, in all its glory, plays second fiddle to the woman in front of me.

Clothes are discarded with haste, our urgency palpable. As I peel off the last of her garments, Isabella looks down with a hint of self-consciousness, a soft chuckle escaping her lips.

There's an energy between us that can't be ignored. As I lean into her, our foreheads touching, I can't resist teasing her just a bit more.

"So, Miss Strategy Manager," I say with a smirk, "got any tactics for this particular scenario?"

She chuckles, her eyes dancing with mischief. "Oh, I've got a few moves in mind. Care to see?"

With that, her hand darts down, reaching around and grabbing my ass, giving it a squeeze. She grips me hard, a soft *mmm* pouring form her mouth as she takes hold. No doubt she's a fine strategist in more ways than one."

When she's had her fill of my glorious glutes, she brings her hand towards the front of me wrapping her fingers around my manhood. The sensation is heady, causing me to groan as I press my face into the crook of her neck, leaving soft, wet kisses there.

"You're quite the multitasker, aren't you?" I manage to say between gasps.

She laughs, her breath hot against my ear. "You have no idea."

It's my turn to show her what I'm made of. Sliding my hand between her thighs, I relish in her sharp intake of breath. I know just how to touch her, and in mere moments, she's writhing under my touch. She's already wet and warm. I spread her lips and find her clit, teasing her.

Her hand bucks against me, guiding me to where she wants to be touched. I kiss her hard, nibbling her lip. Her eyes are winced closed, her breaths quick and sharp as I bring her closer and closer to orgasm. With a shriek, she releases, her climax washing over her. Her voice, a mix of moans and whispered curses, is the sweetest symphony to my ears.

Before she can catch her breath, I scoop her up effortlessly. She's light in my arms, her eyes wide in surprise. Without breaking eye contact, I pin her against the wall, her legs wrapping instinctively around my waist.

The world narrows to this single point of connection. With every breath, every touch, we push each other closer to the edge.

As I hold Isabella against the wall, the gravity of our situation sinks in. This passionate escapade, spontaneous and wild as it is, still needs a touch of responsibility. "Protection?" I pant out, my forehead resting against hers.

She gives a short nod, her chest heaving with every breath. "On the pill."

The relief I feel is palpable, not just because of the lack of barrier, but because this moment feels like it's meant to happen exactly like this. The world outside seems to blur as I align our bodies, and when I move inside her, it's a revelation. It feels as though our bodies were crafted to fit together, each curve and contour matching in a dance of perfect unity. She moans as I push inside, her walls stretching out around me as she takes my inches.

There's a synergy between us, a rhythm that amplifies with every thrust, every gasp. The world outside the windows of the penthouse fades into nothingness as we become the sole focus of each other's universe. Her soft moans in my ear become my guiding light, urging me on.

"I can't believe... how good this feels," she manages to say, her fingers digging into my back.

"Neither can I," I admit, my voice a low growl. I shift my angle slightly, eliciting a sharp gasp from her as I hit just the right spot. Watching her come undone beneath me once is breathtaking; watching it a second time is nothing short of a miracle.

"Please Dom," she moans. "*Please.*"

I know just what she wants. And with her feeling as good as she does wrapped around me, I'm getting closer and closer to the edge myself. I learn down, sucking on one nipple and then another, her arms wrapped around my neck and her breasts shaking with each hard plunge into her.

The intensity between us is so tangible, it's as if we're riding a wave that's destined to crash. And crash it does. With a final shared climax, we collapse into a sweaty, satisfied heap on the bed.

The aftermath is just as intoxicating. Lying next to each other, our limbs tangled, we watch the city lights twinkling like a million stars. The New York skyline offers a breathtaking view, but I find myself more entranced by the woman beside me.

Isabella traces patterns on my chest absentmindedly, her gaze distant. "This city," she murmurs. "It's so alive, even at this hour. Endless possibilities, endless stories."

I chuckle, pulling her closer. "You always this philosophical after sex?"

She laughs, a sound that feels like music. "Only when it's this good."

That earns her a playful nudge, and we fall into a comfortable silence. It's the kind of silence that speaks volumes, where words are unnecessary. As I stroke her hair, my thoughts wander. There's a secret, a piece of news that I've been holding back all evening. Now doesn't feel like the right moment to share it either. Instead, I want to bask in the afterglow of this unexpected connection.

"You're full of surprises, Isabella," I finally say, breaking the silence.

She tilts her head, meeting my gaze. "So are you, Dom. So are you."

***

The steady rhythm of my heartbeat and the soft sounds of the city lulled me into a gentle slumber. When I eventually stir, the first thing I notice is the warm patch of bed beside me, now vacant. Isabella is gone. There's a mixture of disappointment and understanding churning within me. After all, our connection, as fiery and intense as it was, started on a whim.

Blinking away sleep, my gaze settles on a small piece of paper resting on the end table. Picking it up, I can't help but smile as I read her neat handwriting:

"Dom, had fun. Maybe we'll find ourselves on the same rink again … or maybe not. Either way, I guess I learned that puck size *does* matter after all."

- Isabella"

I chuckle, folding the note and tuck it away in the drawer. This was a one-off thing—that's the message she was trying to get across. So be it. Not a bad way to spend the evening.

I roll onto my back, folding my hands behind my head. A grin forms on my lips as I remember my secret, the little detail about my work that I hadn't told her.

Maybe our fling wouldn't be so one-off after all…

3

Isabella

THREE MONTHS. THAT'S THE lifespan of a fling, they say. Or, in my case, the duration it takes to cement a one-night stand as a potent, lingering memory. Here I am at the rink, the echo of pucks and skates on ice barely breaking my focus. The Silver Blades are a cyclone of potential chaos, missing the finesse of my strategies like toddlers miss their mouths with spoons. No matter. It's my job to get them in line.

And I do my job well.

I blow my whistle, the sharp sound slicing through the chilly air. "Huddle up!" My voice rings out, authority woven through each syllable. They come to a sliding stop, sending a spray of ice shards into the air. Heads bowed, shoulders heaving. I step onto the chewed-up ice, tablet in hand, their attention now laser-focused on me.

"Gentlemen," I start, locking eyes with each player, my gaze landing on the captain last. "We're not dancing ballet out here. I want precision, I want speed, and above all, I want execution. You've got the plays, you've got the skill—now let's put the two together."

My finger taps on the screen, bringing up the latest play. I'm met with nods and the odd furrowed brow. Good. They're thinking, at least.

"Jackson, you're anticipating the pass two beats too soon. You need to watch for Darcy's cue. It's as if you're reading the last page of a book before even cracking the spine. Spoilers don't win games." A light-hearted chuckle ripples through the group, easing the tension. Jackson nods, a slight red tinging his cheeks.

"And Darcy, you're holding the puck like it's a newborn. This is hockey, not a nursery. I want confidence, I want decisiveness." Darcy, built like a tank with a gaze to match, doesn't falter under my stare. He nods once, all business.

I step back, satisfied with their renewed focus. "We're a symphony, not a solo act. Let's get that puck singing across the ice, not thudding. Capisce?"

"Capisce!" they echo, a collective force once again.

I send them off with a swift motion, my chest swelling just a tad as they set back to their drills with renewed vigor. It's like conducting an orchestra, each note having to hit just the right pitch, each player finding their rhythm. That's what I do—I create harmony from discord, symphonies from silence.

I'm still that girl who'd rather orchestrate the play than score the goal. Always have been. As they run through the drill again, nailing it with near perfection this time, I can't suppress the grin that spreads across my face. This is where I belong.

Behind the glass, I catch a reflection that isn't my own. A figure, leaning against the doorframe, watching the practice. Even from this distance, the stance is familiar—confident, cocky. Could it be...?

I shake my head. No time for distractions. There's work to do. After all, we have a championship to win, and I'm the one to lead them to it. Dominic Steele is just a memory, one that flickers like a candle in the wind, bright for a moment, then gone.

My brain plays an unsolicited highlight reel, the scenes vivid as if I'm back in that plush penthouse suite, where the city lights winked at us through the expansive windows, silently cheering on our carnal dance. I remember the weight of his gaze, heavy with desire, as if he could peel back the layers of my carefully tailored persona and see the raw, unedited version of me. I push the thoughts away, locking them up tight. Work is my solace, not memories of tangled sheets and whispered names.

A slick pass, a shot on goal, and finally—a cheer. I'm jerked back to reality by the satisfying clank of the puck hitting the net. The play works flawlessly. A surge of pride rushes through me, and I can't help but wear it openly. This is the product of my mind's workings, executed by the sinew and sweat of the players before me.

The sound of blades cutting the ice redirects my attention. Sam, my brother and the heart of the Silver Blades, skates over with that same boyish grin that's charmed our parents since he was in diapers. He's the one who drew me into this world, and I'll never let him forget it.

Sam skates up, his helmet crooked. "Hey, Iz, looks like your drills are finally, well, drilling some sense into them."

I laugh. "It's about time. I was starting to think I'd have to lace up and show them how it's done myself."

He chuckles and glances at his phone that's buzzed in his pocket. I watch him tap out a reply, his eyebrows raised in a way that tells me it's someone interesting. "Who's that?" I ask, half-curious.

"Oh, it's D," he says casually, slipping the phone back into his pocket.

"D?" I prod, brushing a strand of hair from my eyes, my brain too fried from strategy to dig through my mental Rolodex.

"Yeah, he's here for the game tonight. Got some business or other." Sam doesn't elaborate, and I don't press. Hockey is always full of people coming and going, names that ebb and flow with the seasons.

I should be more curious, but the name doesn't stick. It's just another initial, another meeting in the endless grind of the season. I'm more interested in whether the team can replicate that last play come game time.

"Cool," I reply, watching the Zamboni roll out onto the ice. "Maybe I'll catch him later then."

Sam nods, his gaze already on his departing teammates. "Yeah, you should. He's got some interesting ideas."

As I watch the team file out, the letter 'D' is already dissolving in my mind, just a drop in the day's ocean of details. There's no flicker of connection to that night three months ago, no shadow of Dominic Steele crossing my thoughts. Just plans for the next practice, the next game, the next win.

The echo of the last whistle lingers as Sam and I trade one last volley of jabs. "Hey, Iz, remember when you used to think a power play was a new move in chess?" he grins, his eyes twinkling with the shared memory of childhood games.

I shove his shoulder playfully. "Keep it up and the next power play will involve you sitting on the bench watching the chess pieces move without you." We laugh, the sound bouncing off the high ceilings of the arena before he skates off to join the team.

The buzz of my phone drags me back to reality. It's a message from the General Manager, Rick Hansen. "Come see me in my office when you get a chance." Rick's a legend from the ice—his hockey cards are still taped to the walls of die-hard fans. Now, he trades the stick for strategies and the skates for suits, but the commanding presence never fades.

I make my way up to his office, the familiar scent of chilled air and the faint musk of equipment filling the halls. Rick's office is perched like an eagle's nest above the rink, with glass walls that give him an unobstructed view of his icy kingdom. The walls are lined with memorabilia, each puck and stick a testament to the glory days of his career.

He's poring over a pile of papers but looks up as I knock, a smile crinkling the corners of his eyes. "Isabella! Just the wizard of plays I wanted to see."

I cross the room, my boots silent on the plush carpet. "Please tell me it's not another budget cut, Rick," I jest, sinking into one of the leather chairs across from his desk.

He chuckles, shaking his head. "No, quite the opposite. The plays you've been drilling into the guys—impressive work. They might just make athletes out of them yet."

His praise warms me, but before I can bask in it, he's moving on. "Now, there's something else. The owner is coming in."

I'm puzzled. "Owner? You mean Jack? He's here more than his own house."

Rick's expression is serious, a rare departure from his usual jovial demeanor. "No, Isabella. The owner. Above Jack. From the Hudson Sports Group. Owns several teams."

The Hudson Sports Group is a titan, their logo stamped across multiple leagues, an empire of athletics. And suddenly, the office feels a lot less cozy. "Here? Why?"

Rick's phone buzzes, and he reads the message, his eyebrows arching slightly. "He's here now, actually. Wants to meet."

I sit up straighter, my mind whirring. The owner of a sports conglomerate doesn't just drop by. This is big league. "Now?" I echo.

Rick nods, gesturing towards the door as footsteps sound in the corridor. "Now."

The question mark practically hangs in the air, visible as my breath in the cold of the rink. Who is this mystery owner? Why is he coming? The thoughts pace in my head like a penalty shootout—back and forth, back and forth.

Rick, leaning back in his chair, sees the play of emotions on my face and offers a half-grin that doesn't reach his eyes. "I know, Izzy, this is a bit left field."

I cross my arms, not bothering to mask my frustration. "A bit? Feels like we're playing a whole different sport here, Rick."

He nods, the picture of sympathy. "I get it. But this guy, he's been the boss for a good stretch. Just not a spotlight kind of guy, until now."

I frown. My world is the ice—clear and bounded, where everyone knows everyone and titles mean everything. "Why haven't I heard of him? I mean, a shadow boss?" I let out a laugh, but it's edged with uncertainty. "What is this, a spy movie?"

Rick's smirk widens, and he looks like he's enjoying this far more than one should. "Let's just say he prefers the strategy room to the trophy room. Likes to let his teams do the talking."

I shake my head. This isn't adding up, and the sense of not knowing the plays grates on me. I'm about to press further when there's a knock on the door.

Rick doesn't miss a beat. "Come on in, D."

D? My mind can't help but flick through the dossier of D-named possibilities. I roll my eyes, muttering under my breath, "What kind of high-flying boss goes by 'D'?"

The door swings open, and in strides a figure that sends a shock-wave through the room. My heart doesn't just skip a beat; it feels like it's been body-checked against the boards. It's him.

Dom.

Standing there, a smirk playing on his lips, eyes glinting with the same playful challenge they had three months ago. He looks every inch the confident leader—no trace of the bad boy who tangled the sheets with me. Well, aside from those tattoos, that is.

"Nice to see you again, Isabella."

The words hang in the air, a perfect slap shot that finds its mark dead center. I'm caught—pinned like a goalie at a breakaway, no defense, no warning. My mind races, every sense sharpening.

4

Dom

"Dom?"

The door closes behind me with a sound that resonates through the room like the final buzzer of a game. There she is, Isabella, looking as if I've just pulled off the most illegal of moves. Surprise etches her face, her mouth slightly parted, those sharp, intelligent eyes wide. It's a look I could get used to—Isabella caught off guard, all those walls down.

And damn, does she wear authority well. The business suit hugs her figure in all the right ways, managing to look both immaculate and inviting. The skirt flirts with her knees, and the jacket cinches at the waist, showcasing curves that have etched themselves into my memory. Her hair, that rebellious mane that refused to be tamed even in the throes of passion, is pulled back in a professional ponytail that screams 'I mean business.'

Rick's chuckle pulls me back from my visual tour. "Surprised to see Dom Steele in the flesh, eh, Izzy?"

I watch her recover, the professional mask sliding into place as she tries to transform her shock into something resembling nonchalance.

"Well, you don't expect a legend to just waltz in every day," she quips, but her voice has a tremor that betrays her.

I decide to take the reins before she finds her footing. "Let's get down to business," I suggest, and the way her brows furrow tells me she doesn't like being rushed. Good.

"Wait, we're doing a meeting *now*?" she asks.

"No time like the present," I continue, moving towards the head of the table with a confidence I've honed over years in the rink and the boardroom. "I like to see what I'm invested in up close."

Isabella stands her ground, though. "I was under the impression that this meeting was scheduled for tomorrow," she says, a challenging edge to her tone.

I lean forward, hands flat on the table. "In hockey and in business, Izzy, sometimes you've got to call an audible. Adapt and act."

Rick nods, understanding the play, but Isabella looks like she's about to drop the gloves. "This isn't a game, Dom," she fires back, "This is a professional team with schedules."

"And sometimes," I say, locking eyes with her, "the coach has to change the game plan."

She doesn't break eye contact, the ice of the rink mirrored in her gaze. "I'm not one of your players, Dom."

"No," I concede with a half-smile, "you're definitely not."

The air is charged with challenge, the kind that tells me we're both players who love the game. I can tell, this is a woman who doesn't just hold her own—she defines the game.

"So, shall we?" I gesture to the seats, not waiting for her response as I take my place at the conference table in the center of the room. I'm looking forward to this, the head-to-head, the strategic dance.

I can almost see the steam coming off Isabella as she reluctantly takes her seat across from me. Her frustration is palpable, a tangible thing hanging in the air, and I can't help but find it slightly amusing.

But as much as I might enjoy the fire in her, I'm here to play a bigger game.

"As much as I've enjoyed our previous... teamwork," I begin, watching her reaction closely, "let's not forget—I call the shots."

She folds her arms, leaning back in her chair, but there's a hint of acquiescence in the line of her shoulders. She knows the score.

"I'm shifting my base to Seattle for the season," I announce, letting the words settle over the room like a sudden change in play. "We've got potential here, and I want to tap it personally."

Rick nods, always the mediator, but Isabella's jaw sets. She's clearly not used to being micromanaged.

"About your strategies," I continue, flipping open the folder I've brought with me. "They're good. But 'good' doesn't win championships. You're playing with ideas when we should be playing to win."

She bristles, ready to defend her work. "Hockey's evolved, Dom. What won games ten years ago won't cut it now. We need to be ahead of the curve, not just riding it."

I respect her gumption, the way she stands by her decisions. But respect doesn't mean agreement. "There's a difference between being ahead and being out in left field," I retort. "And right now, you're not even in the ballpark."

Her eyes flash. "My plays are based on statistics, projections, player strengths—"

"And risks," I cut in. "Unnecessary ones. We've got a solid team, but they need structure, not stunts."

We're toe-to-toe now, our debate echoing the same intensity as a playoff game. The room's temperature seems to have notched up a few degrees with our back and forth.

That's when Rick clears his throat, a sharp sound that cuts through our standoff. "Okay, let's take a breather here. We all want the same thing—to see the Blades come out on top."

He's right, of course. And as much as I enjoy the head-to-head with Isabella, we've got a bigger opponent than each other—every other team in the league.

Isabella takes a deep breath, and I can tell she's reigning in her pride, her passion. "Fine," she says, her voice cooler now. "We'll discuss the plays, see where we can make adjustments."

"Good." I lean back in my chair, satisfied with the truce, however temporary. "I'll be around to oversee those adjustments personally."

Her gaze meets mine, and there's a promise there, a challenge that tells me she's not down for the count. Not by a long shot.

The sleeves of my shirt roll up with ease, the fabric a minor hindrance to the business at hand. I'm laying out the roadmap to victory, piece by piece, when I catch Isabella's gaze drifting. She's looking at my forearms, her teeth tugging at her lower lip in a moment of absent-minded temptation. It's a small victory, but I file it away, a smirk threatening the corner of my lips.

Still, I can't resist teasing her a bit. "Focus, Isabella. This is the part where we strategize."

Her eyes snap up, a flash of irritation there before she schools her features into professional indifference. It's a mask, but I can see the cracks.

I lean forward, elbows on the desk, interlocking my fingers. "Seattle's hockey scene is about to get more crowded. The StarPucks are stepping onto the ice, and they're independent. A wildcard. Unpredictable. Hungry." My voice drops a notch, the gravity of the situation settling between us. "They're not part of my domain. And that means they're going to be looking to make a statement. At our expense, if we're not careful."

The room is silent, the weight of a new rivalry hanging in the air. I've seen what the hunger for recognition does to a team—it either breaks them or forges them into champions. And the Blades? We're going to be forged.

"I want a game plan. I want innovation, but I also want feasibility. We're going to be facing them on the ice soon, and I want the StarPucks to remember the day they met the Blades as the day they met their match."

I see it then—the flicker of determination in Isabella's eyes. The spark that tells me she's as much in this fight as I am. We may be at odds at times, but we share the same goal: victory.

"I expect a full report on my desk. Strengths, weaknesses, opportunities to capitalize on," I command, standing to signal the end of the meeting. "And Isabella, this is where you show me those strategies of yours can stand up to the real test."

Rick nods, already thinking, always the strategist. But it's Isabella who holds my gaze, a silent promise that she's not to be underestimated.

"Understood, Mr. Steele," she says, her tone suggesting a salute.

As I leave, I find myself looking forward to seeing what she brings to the table. To seeing if that fire in her can melt ice. Because if it can, the StarPucks won't just be remembering us—they'll be reeling from us.

5

Isabella

I'M SLOUCHED IN MY office chair, a half-eaten turkey wrap in one hand, and my laptop open in front of me. On screen, Jenna's bright, mischievous face fills the window, her red curls bouncing as she laughs at my latest Dom anecdote.

"He did what?" she gasps between giggles, clutching her sides. Jenna always finds the humor in things that make my blood boil.

I roll my eyes, a rueful smile threatening despite my irritation. "He just commandeered the whole defensive drill, Jenna. It was like watching a five-star general storm the field. He's got zero boundaries. It's like he thinks he's the coach, manager, and the Zamboni driver all rolled into one!"

Jenna's still laughing, but her eyes are sympathetic. "And to think, just a week ago, you were still drooling over how he'd filled out that suit."

That gets a reluctant chuckle out of me. "Was not drooling," I protest weakly, but she knows me too well.

My gaze drifts past the screen, down to the rink where Dom is now animatedly gesturing to one of the players. The player nods, seemingly taking the impromptu coaching in stride. I should be down there. Those are my plays they're running, but Dom's the one in the trenches, dictating the flow.

"Looks like he's really getting into it," Jenna observes, following my gaze through the webcam.

"Yeah, into everything," I mutter. "He's like a—" I search for the right word, "—a tornado. Leaves a path of upheaval wherever he goes. It's exhausting."

Jenna's expression softens. "You're the best at what you do, Iz. Don't let Mr. Hotshot Owner throw you off your game."

I take a deep breath, drawing strength from Jenna's unwavering support. "Thanks, J. I needed that," I say with a renewed sense of resolve. I sit up straighter, pushing aside the lingering frustration. "Anyway, enough about Dom and his antics. How's the hospital? Any new drama in the ER?"

The subject change is a breath of fresh air, and Jenna launches into a tale about her latest shift. She recounts an incident involving a particularly clumsy intern, a hectic emergency case, and an untimely spill that almost turned into a disaster.

We're wrapping up our call when my eyes catch a moment down on the rink, one that encapsulates the infuriating enigma that is Dom Steele. He's not just barking orders. He's down on one knee, demonstrating a stance to a rookie who's all wide eyes and nodding head.

It's moments like this that throw me. For all his overstepping, there's a passion and a knowledge there that's... I shake my head. Respectable.

"I've got to go," I tell Jenna. "Duty calls."

She winks. "Go show that tornado what you're made of, Iz."

I end the call, take a final bite of my wrap, and toss it into the trash. Standing, I smooth out my blazer and head for the door.

Down on the rink, Dom's gaze lifts, and our eyes meet. There's a challenge there, an unspoken duel, and for a moment, I'm back in his penthouse with the city lights painting us in silhouette.

But that was another world.

This is my rink. My team.

With a determined stride, I head towards the ice, ready to remind Dom Steele exactly who calls the shots here.

The moment my heels click-clack onto the cold, hard surface beside the rink, I can feel the shift. Heads turn, eyes follow—my team, my territory. Dom's in the heart of a huddle, a general amidst his troops, but this army isn't his.

"Circle up," I call out, voice clear and resonant over the hum of the arena.

The interruption hits Dom like a slapshot, his head snapping up, surprise etching his features for a split second before his trademark smirk takes over. He straightens, turning to me, an unspoken challenge in the set of his shoulders.

"Keep going, Steele," I say, not missing a beat, "I'm sure the team was just getting to the good part of your... 'insights'."

The players exchange wary glances but re-form the circle, this time with me at the helm. Dom's presence looms at the edge, his energy a stormfront pressing against the calm I'm holding onto by a thread.

He interjects as I lay out the next drill. "I was just explaining—"

"But you're not the coach," I shoot back, not bothering to mask the ice in my tone. "You may own the team, but these guys? They respond to me."

His chuckle grates against my nerves. "Ownership has its privileges, Isabella," he says, voice low and taunting. "And instructing my team is one of them."

The 'my team' stings, a thorn in my side, but I don't let it show. "Your team," I retort, "performs based on a structure, a system. One that doesn't include an owner undermining—"

"Enhancing," he corrects, stepping into my space, asserting dominance.

The team's eyes are ping-pong balls, volleying between us. This isn't just about drills anymore; this is about respect, about the pecking order. If I flinch now, I'll be the one chasing pucks.

"No," I say firmly, meeting his gaze dead-on, "undermining. And if you think that buying a team gives you carte blanche to trample over protocols, then maybe you should stick to the boardroom."

Dom's eyes harden, the playful edge sharpening into something more cutting. "And if you can't handle an owner who takes an active interest, maybe you're not as tough as I thought."

The words are a red flag, a dare, and I rise to it.

"You want to run this practice?" I challenge, crossing my arms. "Fine. But don't think for a second I won't be here, making sure it's done right."

There's a beat of silence, the air crackling with our standoff.

Dom's posture relaxes, an unreadable shift in his stance. Then that sly smile creeps up, slow and deliberate, a silent tell that he's playing a longer game. The edge of it says everything without a single word—like he's humoring me, the indulgent smirk of an adult watching a child take determined, wobbly steps, bottle in hand, all the while ready to sweep it away.

His voice, when he speaks, is smooth, almost respectful, but there's a note in it that chimes with challenge. "Lead the way, Coach," he says, the words calculated.

It's a concession, one that doesn't sit right—a carefully wrapped gift that feels like a Trojan horse at the gates. It's too easy, too neat. I'm not just coaching a team; I'm being tested, I can tell. Is this a setup? A prelude to a fall he's too eager to witness?

The way he relinquishes control is almost theatrical, his hands spreading in a gesture of acquiescence, as if bestowing the rink back to me. It's a grant I never needed from him, but it's clear he wants me to think I did.

The practice runs like clockwork, my voice the one cutting through the noise, but Dom's presence is a shadow I can't quite shake. And as the players move, a part of me can't help but admit—his intrusion has sparked a fire, a burning reminder that in this game, on this ice, I can't afford to miss a shot. Not with Dom Steele waiting for any chance to leap off the bench and into the fray.

The Zamboni sweeps across the ice, an intermission in the day's tensions, as the sound of blades and pucks subsides into a rare moment of quiet. Dom's still there, an interloper in the stands, fingers flying over the keys of his laptop and his gaze fixed on the screen with that same intensity he applies to... well, everything.

As the players disperse, I run a drill critique in my mind, already recalibrating for the next session. The air is colder in the aftermath, my breath a fog of war that lingers in the space between my command and their compliance.

Sam skates up, still in gear, pulling off his gloves. "That was some faceoff with Steele," he says, a touch of concern beneath the ribbing tone. "What's the game plan here, Coach?"

I shrug, my eyes still on Dom's distant figure. "Just drawing the lines, making sure they don't get blurred. It's about respect, not just for me, but for the team's dynamic."

Sam's eyes dart to where Dom sits, then back to me. "I get that, but tread carefully, Iz. Dom's a heavyweight."

I let out a snort. "And what? I'm bantam?"

He chuckles, shaking his head, the bond of sibling shorthand clear in our exchange. "Just saying, it's delicate."

"I don't 'know,'" I say, perhaps a little too sharply. The complexity of it all, the lines of personal and professional so entangled, irks me.

He sighs, the sound carrying his resignation. "He and I go way back. The Wolverines, remember? Before his injury. Been tight ever since."

He pulls off his helmet, running a hand through damp hair. "Speaking of, we're hitting O'Malley's later. You could come—"

I cut him off with a wave of my hand. "Pass. You have your bro time."

He grins, unfazed. "Your loss. O'Malley's has the best wings in the city."

I watch him skate off, heading for the locker rooms, leaving me in the echo of the now-empty rink.

Turning back to the stands, I notice that Dom's attention isn't on his screen anymore. It's on me. Our gazes lock across the ice, a silent clash from a distance. I break it first, my focus not on this battle, not on this strange game of chess I've found myself in, but on the bigger picture—my team, my career, my life that suddenly has Dom Steele in the middle of it, like a stone thrown into a still pond.

How the hell did it come to this? How did my well-ordered world get flipped upside down by the sudden, whirlwind return of a one-night stand turned team owner, turned daily aggravation?

With a shake of my head, I gather my clipboard and notes, my armor against the chaos, and stride out of the rink. My heels echo a staccato beat that speaks of battles to come, of strategies to be formed, not just for hockey, but for dealing with the force of nature that is Dom Steele. Because one thing's for sure, I'm not the type to get checked into the boards.

I glance back once more, and he's still watching, that inscrutable smirk in place. Game on, Mr. Steele. Game on.

6

Dom

"Come on, Rangers! Don't let those assholes push you around like that!" I'm shouting at the screen, my voice drowning in the cacophony of the bar.

Sam, next to me, is just as animated, his eyes glued to the action. "Fucking hell, man! You'd think they'd have learned by now, right?" He throws back a gulp of his beer, the glass clinking as he sets it down.

The game is a nail-biter, the kind that keeps you on the edge of your seat, every play a potential game-changer. I love it.

We're at O'Malley's, the epitome of a classic hockey sports bar. The walls are adorned with jerseys and memorabilia, each piece telling its own story of game night glory. The air buzzes with the sound of lively chatter, punctuated by the occasional cheer or groan as the game unfolds on the numerous screens around us. It's the kind of place where the beer flows as freely as the hockey debates, and every screen is a portal to sports heaven.

During a lull in the game, Sam turns to me. "So, Mr. Hotshot from the New York City Penthouse, how's it feel being back in the real world, getting your hands dirty with the team?"

I can't help but laugh. Sam's always been good at keeping things light, even when he's poking fun. "I'll tell you, man, it feels damn good. Beats sitting in front of a screen all day, that's for sure. Nothing like the chill of the rink and seeing the guys in action up close."

Sam nods, a smile playing on his lips. "Yeah, I bet. Must be a nice change from the high life, huh? Getting back to the grassroots of the game."

I take a sip of my beer, the cool liquid a sharp contrast to the warmth of the bar. "Absolutely. There's something about being there, in the moment. The energy of the players, the sound of the puck against the stick. It's where I belong, man."

He chuckles, raising his glass for a toast. "To getting your hands dirty, then. Welcome to Seattle, D."

Our glasses clink. "Thanks, Sam. It's good to be here. And working with the Blades, it's... it's something else. Makes me feel like I'm part of the game again."

Sam's expression turns thoughtful. "You always were part of it, Dom. Just in a different way. But now, you're shaping the future of the game, and that's something."

I nod. "Yeah, it's a new chapter. And I'm ready to write it. These guys, the team, they've got potential. It's just about unlocking it."

The game picks up again, our attention drawn back to the screen. The energy in the bar rises, a collective anticipation as the players on the screen battle for control.

As the players on the screen clash in a flurry of skill and speed, I'm momentarily transfixed. A forward breaks away, slicing through the defense like a hot knife through butter. It's a play straight out of my own book, one that I'd executed countless times on the ice. For a split second, I'm back there, feeling the cold bite of the rink, the exhilaration of the chase, the puck at my stick, and the net in my sights.

The crowd in the bar erupts as he lines up the shot, the tension palpable. The puck flies, a blur of potential, and finds the back of the net. The bar explodes in cheers, but I'm lost in my own memories, the echo of the crowd blending with the ghosts of cheers from my past.

I shake my head, pulling myself back to the present, the nostalgia a bittersweet sting. That life, those moments on the ice, they're part of a chapter I've closed. But damn, they still burn bright in my memory.

Sam glances at me, an unspoken question in his eyes, but before he can voice it, he's distracted by the celebration around us. As the noise dies down, he turns back to me, a knowing look on his face.

"Buddy, you look like you're solving the world's problems over there," I rib Sam, nudging his shoulder. "What's eating you, dude?"

"Nothing. Just thinking about the piss-poor defense I just witnessed." I nod at the screen.

Sam chuckles, brushing off my teasing with an easy grin. But then his expression turns serious again. "How are you, really?" he asks, his gaze steady on me. "Come on—I've known you for years, brother. Obvious as hell to me when the great Dom Steele's got something on his mind."

I raise an eyebrow, caught off guard. "What do you mean? I'm good, living the dream." I take a swig of my beer, trying to brush off the question.

He leans forward, his tone earnest. "It's just... It's been a few years since your injury, and I remember how tough it hit you. Are you sure being this close to the game, not playing, doesn't mess with you?"

Fucking hell, am I that easy to read? Had I been watching the game with some wistful expression?

I shrug, feigning nonchalance. "Nah, man. I don't dwell on that stuff. I don't get all sentimental and shit. Being close to the game, it's different now, but it's still good, you know?"

Sam nods, seemingly satisfied with my response, but I can tell he's not entirely convinced.

"Seriously, D. I mean it," Sam insists, his tone a mix of concern and the usual brotherly ribbing we've come to expect in our friendship. "I was there when you were injured, I know how much it hit you. You can talk to me, you know."

I let out a short laugh, shaking my head. "Look at you, getting all Dr. Phil on me," I tease, trying to deflect. But deep down, I appreciate his concern. It's not every day you get a friend who sticks by you through thick and thin.

Sam's not letting it go, though. "Come on, man. We've been through a lot. Just want to make sure my bud's holding up alright."

I laugh. "You know, for a tough guy on the ice, you've got a soft side."

Sam rolls his eyes but grins. "Guess I learned from the best. But seriously, D. This new role with the Blades, being so close to the rink, the players... It's gotta stir up some old ghosts, right?"

I pause, considering his words. The truth is, being back in the rink, feeling the energy of the game, the players—it does stir something in me. The roar of the crowd, the chill of the ice, the thrill of the game. It's a world I thought I'd lost forever.

"Yeah, it stirs up some stuff," I finally admit, my gaze drifting to the screen showing a highlight reel of the game. "But it's not all bad. It's like... finding a new way to love the game. Coaching, mentoring—it's a different kind of rush."

Sam nods, understanding flashing in his eyes. "That's good to hear, man. You've got a lot to offer these kids. And hey, if you ever feel the itch to get back on the ice, I'm always up for a one-on-one – no-contact, course."

I chuckle, raising my glass. "You just want a chance to say you've beaten Dom Steele."

He raises his glass in return, the clink echoing our shared laughter. "I'd tell them that even if I lost."

That gets a laugh out of me.

Sam leans forward, lowering his voice as if sharing a state secret. "You know, speaking of the game and all, what's your take on Isabella's run with the Blades? She's pushing hard, aiming high."

I take a slow sip of my beer, considering my words. Isabella Carrington, a topic that's more complicated than it seems on the surface. "She's ambitious, driven. Knows the game inside out. Hard not to respect that," I reply, keeping my tone neutral, but inside, there's a storm of thoughts swirling.

"Yeah, she's impressive," Sam agrees, nodding. "But, man, I worry about her sometimes. She's my sister, you know? Always pushing herself to the edge, chasing after some big dream."

I glance at Sam, seeing the genuine concern etched in his features. Family ties run deep, and Sam's protective streak over Isabella is as clear as day. "She's tougher than she looks," I say, a hint of admiration slipping into my voice. "Isabella's not the type to back down from a challenge. But yeah, I get it. You want to make sure she's not burning out."

There's a brief silence as we both take a moment, lost in our thoughts. Isabella, with her sharp mind and sharper tongue, has been a constant puzzle, a challenge that I've found both infuriating and intriguing. She's more than just a colleague or a rival in the world of hockey management; she's someone who's managed to get under my skin, for better or worse.

Sam breaks the silence, his voice laced with a brother's concern. "Just... if you see her going overboard, you know, maybe give her a nudge? Tell her to take it easy?"

I chuckle, the sound a bit more forced than I intended. "What am I, her keeper?" But even as I say it, I know there's a part of me that wouldn't mind being just that. "I'll keep an eye out, Sam. She's good for the game, good for the team. Wouldn't want to lose that fire."

The game on the screen takes a dramatic turn, a crunching hit followed by a moment of tense silence before the crowd erupts. It's a scene I know too well, a mix of adrenaline and brotherhood, risk and reward. I find myself caught in a moment of raw nostalgia.

"You know," I start, my voice unexpectedly somber, "You're right. I miss it sometimes—the game, the ice, the guys. No. I don't miss it sometimes. I miss it *all the fucking time*."

Sam looks at me, his expression understanding. "I can only imagine, man. You were at the top. It's gotta be rough, watching from the sidelines."

I nod, feeling an uncharacteristic wave of melancholy wash over me. "Yeah, it's tough. But life throws you slapshots, right? Gotta learn to catch 'em or duck."

He sips his beer, thoughtful. "I sometimes wonder if I can make it as far as you did. You're a legend, Dom. Always looked up to you, you know?"

I scoff, trying to brush off the heaviness of the moment. "Legend, huh? More like a cautionary tale these days." I clap him on the back, a reassuring, firm grip. "But you, Sam, you've got talent and drive. Don't sell yourself short. You're carving your own path, and it's looking damn good."

Sam grins, a bit of pride flickering in his eyes. "Thanks, man. Means a lot, coming from you."

The game continues, the players on the screen a blur of motion and intensity. In their movements, I see echoes of my past, reminders of what once was. It isn't much longer before the final whistle blows on the screen, signaling the end of the game. Sam and I exchange looks, a mutual understanding that it's time to wrap up our night.

"One last shot for the road?" Sam suggests, a mischievous glint in his eye.

"You read my mind," I reply with a grin.

We raise our glasses, the amber liquid catching the dim light of the bar. "To the game, and to whatever the hell comes next," I toast.

"To the game," Sam echoes, and we knock back the shots, the smooth burn a fitting end to our evening.

We stand, pulling on our jackets, the buzz of the bar fading into the background. There's a sense of camaraderie, a shared love for the game that goes beyond words. We clasp hands, a firm, brotherly grip, before heading towards the door.

"Take care, man," I say, giving Sam a final nod.

"You too, D. Don't be a stranger," he replies, and then we're off, going our separate ways into the cool Seattle night.

As I walk back to my apartment, the city skyline stretches above me, a tapestry of lights and shadows. My mind, however, keeps drifting back to Isabella. Her determination, her fiery spirit, the way she challenges me without even trying—it's all etching itself deeper into my thoughts.

I can't shake the feeling that she's going to turn my life upside down. Whether it's going to be a disaster or the best damn thing to ever happen to me, I can't tell. But one thing's for sure—it's going to be a hell of a ride.

With each step, the feeling grows stronger, an undeniable pull towards something unknown, something thrilling. Isabella Carrington, with her sharp mind and even sharper tongue, has somehow become the most intriguing part of my new life here in Seattle.

7

Isabella

I'm perched at a high-top table in a cozy corner of the Metropolitan, Jenna's and my go-to place for drinks after work, a half-empty glass of red wine in front of me. Jenna's across from me, her brow furrowed in sympathy as I vent.

"Can you believe him?" I huff, swirling the wine in my glass. "Dom Steele just swaggers in like he owns the place. He's arrogant, overbearing, and thinks he can just take over the team."

Jenna sips her drink, her expression a mix of amusement and concern. "This guy really gets under your skin, huh?"

I scoff, shaking my head. "It's not about that. It's about respect. He's treating the Silver Blades like his personal playground. He has no idea the amount of work it takes to run a team."

Jenna leans in, her eyes sparkling with mischief. "Is he at least easy on the eyes? That might make up for some of it."

I roll my eyes, but I can't help the small smile that tugs at the corner of my lips. "Okay, fine. He's... well, he's not hard to look at. But that's not the point!"

She chuckles. "Sure, sure. It's all about professionalism."

I take a deep breath, trying to calm the frustration bubbling inside me. "I just don't get why he's here. The Blades were doing just fine before Mr. High-and-Mighty showed up."

Jenna reaches across the table, giving my hand a reassuring squeeze. "You're one of the best managers in the league, Isabella. Don't let this guy rattle you. You've handled bigger challenges."

Her words are a balm to my frayed nerves. "Thanks, Jenna. I just need to figure out how to work with him without wanting to throw a hockey stick at his head."

She laughs, raising her glass. "To not committing assault with a hockey stick."

Jenna pauses mid-sip, her eyes narrowing playfully. "Speaking of headstrong, where do you even get this from? You and Sam... you're both cut from the same type-A cloth. Don't get me wrong; I love it. But no wonder you're butting heads with a dude like Dom."

"Guess it makes sense. My mom and dad didn't raise me to get walked all over by any swaggering alpha male dick who waltzed his way into my life."

"Ahh," she says, as if getting it. "Mom and dad. You never talk about them, you know? They're the ones who pushed you into this kind of way of doing things, huh?"

I nod, unable to suppress a sigh. "Yeah, they were. Dad's a neurosurgeon, and Mom's a corporate lawyer. Excellence was the only option in our household."

"Sounds like a pressure cooker," Jenna observes, her tone laced with understanding.

"It was," I agree. "And still is, in a way. Emotional expression wasn't really a big thing in our house. It was more about achievements, awards, and accolades. I guess that's why I'm so driven with the StarPucks. And why Sam's excelling on the ice."

Jenna nods, understanding dawning in her eyes. "Makes sense. You two are like high achievers personified. But hey, it's brought you both pretty far. Sam's killing it in the league, and you... you're the epitome of a girlboss."

I chuckle, a mix of pride and wistfulness in my laugh. "Thanks, J. It's just... sometimes I wonder what it would have been like to grow up in a family where it was okay to just be, you know? To not always be chasing the next big thing."

Jenna reaches out, her touch warm and comforting. "You might have been raised to chase success, Isabella, but you've also got a huge heart. Don't forget that. It's one of the things that makes you such an amazing friend... and manager."

"Yeah, well, sometimes I think that same drive makes me butt heads with people like Dom," I admit, swirling my wine. "You know, strong personalities clashing."

She chuckles. "I was just thinking that. You and Dom Steele, huh? Two forces of nature. Maybe it takes someone as bullheaded as him to match up with you."

I let out a half-laugh, half-groan. "Don't remind me. The man's infuriating. But I can't deny there's... something there."

She raises an eyebrow. "Like a... *something* something?"

"No way!" I shoot the words out. "Not a chance I'd get involved with a boss. I'm thinking more like a challenge, maybe."

"A challenge, or a sexy challenge. Then again, you've already gotten him into bed once."

"And that's *it*. No mixing business and pleasure, thank you very much.:

I smile, grateful for Jenna's presence in my life. She always knows how to lift my spirits. "Thanks, Jenna. I don't know what I'd do without you."

She grins, raising her glass again. "Here's to us—the overachievers with hearts of gold."

I laugh, clinking my glass against hers. "To us."

The cool Seattle rain lightly patters around me as I make my way home, the gentle shower almost refreshing after the heat of the bar. Each drop seems to bring a clarity, washing away the buzz of wine and the weight of the evening's conversation.

Walking under the dim streetlights, I find my thoughts drifting to my parents. They were always so emotionally reserved, like affection and warmth were secondary to ambition and success. In our house, achievements were celebrated, emotions were... well, they weren't really discussed.

Growing up, I learned to mirror their stoicism, to tuck away feelings and focus on goals. It was simpler, less messy. But it left a void, a space where emotional connections should have been.

I remember seeking their approval, their recognition. It wasn't about love, not in the way other families seemed to define it. It was about being the best, about achieving what was expected and then some. My heart, my personal desires, they took a backseat to career aspirations and accolades.

As the raindrops mingle with the streetlights, casting a shimmering glow on the damp pavement, I can't help but wonder if that upbringing shaped my current struggles. Maybe that's why I clash with Dom, why his challenging demeanor unnerves me. He represents a disruption to the emotional control I've clung to for so long.

I pull my coat tighter around me, the rain growing steadier. In this quiet moment, alone with my thoughts, I realize how much I've closed off my heart. Career and success have been my armor against vulnerability, but at what cost?

8

Dom

"STEVIE, CROSS IT!"

My voice cuts through the roar of the crowd, urgent, commanding. On the ice, there's only us—the players, our breaths misting in the cold, our bodies engines of raw power and sheer determination. I'm a streak of color against the white, jersey fluttering as I punch through the opposing line, stick ready, eyes locked on the rubber disc that's about to define our fates.

"Got it, Dom!" comes the call, almost lost in the cacophony. Stevie's trusty backhand sends the puck slicing through the air, a spinning promise of victory.

Everything slows down, like I'm moving through syrup. The puck and I are in perfect sync, hurtling towards the net. The goalie's eyes are wide behind his mask, tracking the puck, tracking me. He knows what's coming. I know what's coming. But knowing isn't enough to stop it—not when I'm in the zone, not when the play is this clear, this sharp.

I let out a grunt as I slap the shot, a textbook feint to the left before snapping it to the right. The goalie bites, just as I knew he would.

It's in. The crowd goes *nuts*.

I've already started my victory turn, stick raised, ready for the cheers, for my team to pile on me—

The crash is sudden, brutal, a sledgehammer blow that derails the world off its axis. A shadow, a rival, a delayed reaction, and then I'm flying, my back colliding with the unforgiving ice. Air whooshes out of my lungs, stars explode behind my eyelids, and the pain, sharp and searing, spears through my leg.

Silence swallows the pain for a heartbeat—or maybe the pain swallows the noise. It's hard to tell when you're lying on the ice, the game forgotten, the cheers turning to a distant echo, the worried faces of teammates hovering like ghosts above.

The cold seeps in, numbing the pain, numbing my thoughts. A stretcher appears. Voices are urgent but sound muffled, as if underwater. And then there's the sensation of floating, of being untethered from the solid ice, from the solidity of my life as I knew it.

The memory fades as I come to, sprawled on my office couch, the tail end of adrenaline making my hands shake. It was a dream—no, a memory.

The silence is thick as I push off the couch, my limbs heavy from the quicksilver slide of dreams into reality. The office is dim, lit only by the moon spilling through the massive windows, casting a pale glow over the deserted rink below. I'm alone, save for the echo of my own footsteps—a solitude I've grown to appreciate, even crave, in this life where moments of peace are as rare as a clean shot from center ice.

Closing my eyes for a moment, I lean against the cool glass of my office windows, letting the quietude wash over me. My days, my nights, they merge—a relentless march of decisions, strategies, and the weighty knowledge that scores of people rely on my calls. Sleep, when it comes, is more necessity than indulgence, grabbed in snatches, often with a keyboard or phone as my pillow.

Looking out over the rink, I picture the game that's brewing, the players that will clash on this frozen battleground. The Silver Blades, my team, they're more than just a roster of names; they're an extension of a dream, a continuation of a career cut short, a testament to the fact that even when you're down, you're never out. Not if I have anything to say about it.

Isabella. Her image flickers unbidden into my mind, fierce and indomitable, a challenge that stirs both frustration and a grudging respect within me. Too hard on her? The question flits through my thoughts, an anomaly in the pattern of my usual certainty. But no, I dismiss the notion almost as quickly as it appears. It's not cruelty that guides my hand, but necessity. She's a diamond in the rough—and pressure, as they say, makes diamonds.

My mouth twists into a smirk at the thought. She's got fire, that one, and potential—more than she realizes. And if I have to stoke that fire, so be it. Because the plans I have, the vision I see when I look at this team, it's nothing short of victory. And for victory, you need warriors, not just players.

With the stadium's silence as my accomplice, I decide to seize the moment. It's a rare indulgence, but the ice is calling, a whisper from the past that I can't—and don't want to—ignore.

I make my way down to the locker room, movements sure and silent, a ghost in my own domain. The skates are right where I left them, the blades gleaming faintly in the low light. I pull them on, the familiar scrape and tug of laces snug against my fingers, grounding me, bringing back a flood of sensory memories—the cold bite of the air, the adrenaline surge of the play, the unity of team spirit.

The gate to the rink creaks slightly as I step out onto the ice. It's pristine, untouched since the Zamboni's last round. For a moment, I just stand there, letting the chill seep through my clothes, breathing in the scent of ice and possibility.

And then, I'm off, the glide of blade on ice as natural as breathing, each stroke a silent testament to years on the rink. This is where I belong. This is where everything makes sense.

As I round the net, picking up speed, I can almost hear the roar of the crowd, feel the pulse of the game, the push and pull of competition. For a moment, it's as if nothing has changed, as if I'm still that power forward with the world at my feet.

Isabella's going to be part of that legacy. She just doesn't know it yet.

I'm carving through the ice like it's nothing, the empty rink echoing back the sound of the steel blades cutting cold. It feels damn good, and I can't help the grin that stretches across my face. It's that raw, wild edge of a grin, the kind you get when you're not just running a sports empire, but leading the charge on the ice, setting the pace of the game.

I whisper to the cold, to the shadows of the stadium seats, "You still got it, Steele."

Dropping titles, forgetting for a moment about boardrooms and balance sheets. I'm that guy again, the one with the puck and the glory, not just the man behind the curtain.

The air bites at my skin, the scent of the ice sharp in my nostrils. It's heady, intoxicating. And I push harder, my thighs burning, chasing the phantom of the player I used to be.

But as I dare to fly higher, my knee screams a sharp, blinding warning. Old wounds don't like to be disturbed. I try to power through it, push it down, but my knee has a different story to tell. It snaps with pain, and suddenly, I'm no longer the master of my domain. I'm airborne, a twist of limbs and a flash of steel—and then a crash landing that has me seeing stars.

I let out a roar, a thunderous sound that's all frustration and fury. It's not just about the fall; it's the damn finality of an injury that robbed me of my place on the ice. Lying there, looking up at the dark ceiling, I take a moment, my breath ragged with more than physical exertion.

But lying here isn't my style. I push up, ignoring the ache. It's just a twinge now, a dull echo of the shout it was moments ago. It's not enough to stop me. It never is.

The skate back to the edge is slow, methodical. It's the cool down I didn't plan, a forced retreat from my temporary flight of fancy. I'm thinking about the showers, about the scalding water that's going to wash off the sweat and maybe a bit of the stubborn ache of a past life.

I shed my gear piece by piece, a routine as familiar as the ice under my skates. My shirt comes off, and I toss it aside, the fabric heavy with the honest sweat of a man who's not forgotten the grind of the game.

In the mirror, my reflection greets me with familiar lines and shades. Tattoos coil around my arm all the way up to my neck, a silent testament to the journey I've walked—or skated, rather. They're like roadmaps of ink, tracing up from my wrists, over the sinewy muscles, a living art piece that doesn't stop until it hits the edge of my jawline. Each one's got a story, a mark of victory, a memory of pain, a whisper of the thrills that've colored my life.

I let my hand drift over the puckered scars, medical precision that's left its signature on my skin. The surgeons did their job, knitting the torn ligaments of my knee back together—a technical masterpiece, a reweaving of the body's fabric. They've given me back my walk, but they couldn't give me back my game. Not at the level I crave.

My eyes move over the rest of me. Muscle clings to my frame, no ounce of fat betraying any weakness or indulgence. I've kept the machine tuned, the body of a player who refuses to hang up his skates, even if the professional rink's a thing of the past. Broad shoulders, tight abs, the sculpted form of an athlete—all maintained not out of vanity but out of respect for what I was, and for the battles still to come.

As the water hits me, hot and heavy, I let out a breath. The steam clouds around me, and I let it. The pain in my knee subsides, but the deeper ache, the one that's for the game, for the rush—that's still there, throbbing in time with my pulse.

As the hot water cascades down my back, my muscles relax under the soothing stream. My hands move automatically, soaping and working over the terrain of my body—a landscape of hard-earned muscle and scar tissue. My fingers trace the lines of ink etched into my skin, symbols of my past, of victories and losses. They skim over the roughened skin of my knee, a memento from the surgery that stitched my ACL back together—a skilled doctor's handiwork under the skin, hidden but never forgotten.

And then, unbidden, Isabella invades my thoughts. She's like a siren song, her image a flickering flame that I can't snuff out. I see her as she was in New York, the memory surfacing with startling clarity. She was all sharp wit and fiery eyes, her confidence an aphrodisiac that still lingers in my mind. I can't help but recall the curve of her smile, the arch of her eyebrow when she challenged me.

Damn sexy, not just in appearance but in her essence, the very air around her charged with a kind of electricity that's rare to find.

I shake my head, trying to dispel the image, but it's futile. The scent of her perfume, a subtle mix of something floral and citrus, seems to mix with the steam around me. It's a phantom scent, but it's as if she's here in the room, just out of sight.

The fantasy deepens, edging into dangerous territory. I see us locked in a passionate embrace, the kind of desperate, consuming kiss that you see in the movies.

It's a kiss born of all the tension that's ever crackled between us, each suppressed argument and unspoken challenge now given voice in the press of mouth against mouth. It's fierce and it's fiery, a clash of wills that finds harmony in the heat of the moment.

Her lips are soft, yielding under mine, but with a strength that matches the fervor of my own. I can almost feel the warmth of her breath, the subtle taste of wine lingering from an evening spent in close quarters, debating and parrying in our verbal sparring matches. The sensation of her mouth moving with mine is intoxicating, a heady rush that drowns out the world around us.

In this suspended reality, her hands are woven into my hair, pulling me closer, as if there's still too much space between us. My own hands are on her waist, fingers splayed over the curve of her hips, grounding her to me, to this moment that's ours and ours alone. I move my hands up over her bare stomach, then to her breasts, round and full. She gasps with surprise as I tease her nipples.

The intensity between us builds like a gathering storm, each imagined touch like a bolt of lightning, unpredictable and electric. In this world of steam and water, the boundaries between reality and fantasy blur.

"Who knew the Ice Queen could turn the heat up so high?" I tease, my voice a low rumble that's more intimate than I intend. There's a lightness to the words, a playfulness that feels foreign on my tongue.

She meets my banter with a smirk, that damn irresistible smirk that says she's always three moves ahead. "Maybe you're just not used to a woman who can handle the flames you throw, Steele."

I laugh, a sound that bounces off the tile, filling the room with its timbre. "Oh, I can handle the flames just fine," I counter, stepping closer to her in the confines of my imagined shower. "But you... you're something else. Like fire and ice, somehow both at once."

The words spill out, sweet and honest, and they surprise me—surprise us both. I'm not one to pay empty compliments, but with Isabella, they're not empty. They're truths that I've noticed time and time again, from the way she commands a room to the subtle grace of her movements.

"You're beautiful," I admit, and the sincerity in my voice is a soft thing, a side of me I don't often show. "Not just a pretty face, Isabella, but the kind of beauty that kicks you in the gut and leaves you breathless."

Her eyes soften, and for a moment, she's not the formidable manager, not the adversary I'm accustomed to sparring with. She's just Isabella, and she's never looked more stunning than she does with droplets of water clinging to her lashes like diamonds.

"And this body," I continue, my gaze tracing the contours of her through the mist, "it's not just a body. It's a map of strength and determination, every curve a testament to your power."

She watches me, the air between us thick with something that feels a lot like vulnerability. "Dom," she whispers, my name a caress that sends a shiver down my spine, "you're full of surprises."

Isabella's hands are on me, and mine on her, our bodies a tangle of need and urgency. The sensation of her pressed against me is a siren song, luring me further into the depths of this indulgence, this sweet abandon that's so unlike me.

The animal passion I've been keeping at bay is finally released. The fantasy totally consuming me, I imagine clamping my hands on those soft curves, turning her around in the shower and pushing her up against the tiles. She pulls in a gasp of surprise as I wrap an arm around her waist, pulling her ass out and against my thick, throbbing cock.

I reach around between her legs, putting my hand on her wet warmth. She moans, squirming against my fingers, her body yearning.

"You like when I touch you there, baby?" I growl into her ear.

"So... so much."

I tease her clit, feeling her heat even through the water pouring down on us. When she can't take any more, she reaches around and wraps her fingers around my manhood, guiding me to her entrance. I hold back for a moment, not letting her put me inside.

"Always a tease," she says with a smile over her shoulder.

"Just like to keep you in suspense."

I push my hips forward, the smile on her lips transforming into an *O* of pleasure. I glance down, watching my thickness move into her, Isabella's pussy clenching around my cock as I stretch her, bottom her out.

I buck into her slowly, listening to her moan as she accommodates me. Soon I'm bucking hard, the rough sound of my body colliding with hers blending with the hush of the shower. Her hands are splayed out on the tile wall, her ass shaking with each collision of my hips against her rear.

"Come for me," I growl. "Right now."

She nods, not able to get even a single word out. Then, with a long, slow moan, she comes. Her walls grip me, the tightness pulling me over the edge. I drive into her with incredible ferocity, letting out a groan like a damn caveman as I erupt inside.

I imagine that moment of release with her, the culmination of this dance of fantasy and memory, and it's a feeling so powerful, so complete, that for a second, I let myself believe it's real. That she's here with me, not just a specter from the past or a figure in a dream, but the living, breathing, undeniable Isabella Carrington.

Then it's over. I'm back in the real world—just me in that shower, alone.

As I rinse off, the images and the fantasy swirl down the drain with the soapy water. I turn the faucet off, the sudden silence in the room as jarring as the cold air that greets my skin. Wrapping a towel around my waist, I step out of the shower, my reflection in the mirror a testament to a life lived fully, if not always wisely.

Isabella's image may have faded with the steam, but the imprint of her on my thoughts seems to linger, a question mark hanging in the humid air. What is it about her that refuses to be washed away? I can't answer that—not yet. But as I dress, pulling on clothes that fit the part of the tough, alpha male I'm known to be, I acknowledge the discomforting truth that Isabella isn't just a memory.

She's a challenge—a puzzle I haven't solved, a game with moves yet to be played. And I've never been one to walk away from a challenge.

9

Isabella

"ALRIGHT, BOYS—FORM UP!"

The brisk Seattle air nips at my cheeks as I stride up to the entrance of the Rainier Medical Center, the Silver Blades in tow. These guys, decked out in team gear and lugging equipment bags filled with signed pucks and jerseys, might grumble about early mornings, but the prospect of lighting up some kid's day has a way of cutting through even the thickest fog of sleepiness.

Today's no different. We're here for a reason that's a heck of a lot bigger than hockey—a reminder that the heart of this team beats strong not just on the ice, but off it too. I've always pushed for these community events, argued for them, organized them down to the last pen for autographs. The owners may not see the direct line to ticket sales, but I see the direct line to heartstrings—and isn't that where true loyalty starts?

We navigate the sterile hospital halls, the antiseptic smell mingling oddly with the musk of athlete sweat and rubber from the soles of their sneakers. Nurses give us knowing smiles, a couple of the younger ones not-so-subtly checking out the players. I don't blame them; hockey players have a certain rugged charm that's hard to ignore.

Then we're there, the recovery wing, where life's unfairness is on full display. Kids, way too young to be here, look up as we enter, and for a split second, there's a hush—like the sharp intake of breath before a goal is scored. Then the room erupts. Smiles bright enough to light the entire Pacific Northwest break out on faces that have seen too many frowns.

I hang back, content in my role as orchestrator, watching the players bend down to talk to kids, hand out Blades' paraphernalia, and share stories. I catch the eyes of a little girl clutching a stuffed bear. Her grin is missing a couple of teeth, but it's wide and infectious, and I can't help but smile back, waving. For a moment, I wonder about kids of my own, but I mentally chuck the thought away like a hot puck. My life? It's schedules and strategies, practices and press releases. There's no room for bedtime stories and Band-Aids.

"Isabella, come take a picture!" Jack Simms, our star right winger, beckons me over. I slide in next to him, the players making room. There's a click, a flash, and it's immortalized—this moment, this team, this connection.

"Thanks for setting this up, Coach," Ryan Cutter, our goalie, says to me after the picture. His gratitude is genuine, voice hushed in reverence to the place we're in.

"It's the least we can do," I respond, and I mean it. It's easy to forget the world outside the rink when you live and breathe the game. But these visits, they're grounding, humbling.

I lean against the doorframe, my arms crossed, a contented smirk playing on my lips. The Silver Blades might be fierce on the ice, but here, in this pastel-painted recovery wing, they're teddy bears—each one of them. It's a side of the players the public rarely gets to see: their humor, their tenderness, the way they can make a room full of sick kids forget about the world outside these four walls.

One of the guys starts a goofy TikTok dance with some of the kids, and the room bursts into giggles and cheers. Another joins in, and then another. I should probably tell them to be careful about their image, but hell, this is the kind of publicity you can't buy. Plus, the sight is too pure, too joyful to interrupt.

Sam is in his element, bending down to match eye level with a boy whose eyes are bright with unshed tears of joy.

"You just focus on getting better, and I'll make sure there are tickets waiting for you," Sam promises, and I know it's not just talk. That's my brother, all heart, sometimes more than he knows what to do with.

As we step out of the room, Sam's beaming. "Good call on this, Iz," he says, giving my shoulder a squeeze. "Reminds you what's really important, doesn't it?"

"Yeah," I reply, "it's not just about what happens on the scoreboard. It's about heart. It's about community." I believe every word. You can't build a team's legacy just from wins and revenue. It's about the imprints they leave, the lives they touch.

"Where's Dom, though?" Sam frowns slightly, looking around as if he might have missed him in a corner, handing out candy or signing a cast.

I'm about to roll my eyes to the ceiling—typical Dom, always on his own schedule—when the man himself strides in. Late. Of course. But the moment he does, the room transforms. Kids straighten up, eyes wide. The murmurs rise to cheers.

Dom has that effect, the kind that ripples through a space, changes the air. It's infuriating, and... I have to admit, a bit electrifying. He's in casual gear today, but even without the suit, he carries an air of command, like a captain—no, like an owner. His presence is a natural force, the kind you can't bottle or sell, the kind you just have to witness.

He walks straight up to the boy Sam had just spoken to. "Heard you're a fan of the game," Dom says, his voice a low rumble that seems to echo even in the busy room.

The kid nods, eyes fixed on Dom like he's the sun.

"Well, you make sure you get well soon. We need fans like you cheering us on," Dom says and ruffles the kid's hair, his expression softening in a way I've rarely seen.

Dom's arrival might have been fashionably late, but as I watch him with the kids, all effortless charm and easy smiles, it's hard to stay mad at him. I lean against a wall, arms folded, a bemused expression no doubt painting my face.

"Nice of you to finally join us," I quip, the corner of my mouth lifting in a half-smile. It's half-hearted sarcasm, the sting taken out by the genuine pleasure I see in the eyes of the kids surrounding him.

"I wouldn't miss it for the world," he shoots back, that grin on his face reaching his eyes. The way he says it, you almost believe he's been here the whole time, that his heart was present even when his body wasn't.

As Dom makes his way through the room, his eyes land on a young boy sitting off to the side, his small frame curled up in a chair, separate from the bustling activity. There's a withdrawn quality to him, a quietness that seems to set him apart from the laughter and chatter of the other children. Dom's expression softens noticeably, a hint of recognition in his gaze as if seeing a part of his younger self in the boy's solitude.

He alters his path, his usual confident stride giving way to something softer, more approachable. He crouches down beside him, their eyes on a level.

"Hey there, champ," Dom starts, his voice gentle, a stark contrast to his usual commanding tone. "You know, when I was about your age, I was pretty shy too."

The boy looks up, curiosity piqued by Dom's admission.

"Yeah?" he whispers, almost inaudible.

Dom nods, a warm smile on his face. "Yeah. And you know what helped me? Hockey." He begins to gesture, his hands mimicking the movement of a player on the ice. "I was this skinny kid, not very talkative. But on the ice, I could be whoever I wanted to be. It was my escape, my way to express myself without words."

The boy's eyes widen slightly, a sense of wonder replacing the initial apprehension.

Dom continues, "I remember this one game. I was nervous, butterflies in my stomach. But then, I got the puck, and everything just clicked. I weaved through the other players like they were just cones on the ice. And when I scored that goal, it wasn't just a point on the board. It was like I found a piece of myself out there."

The boy's expression shifts, a mix of awe and understanding dawning on his face.

"You think I could do that?" he asks, a hint of hope in his voice.

Dom's smile broadens. "I know you can. Here, let me show you something." He picks up a mini stick, handling it with ease despite its size. "This move, it's simple but effective. Just like this," he demonstrates a basic stickhandling technique.

The boy watches intently, then, with a bit of encouragement from Dom, he takes the stick. His first attempt is awkward, the movements unfamiliar and hesitant.

"That's it, you're doing great," Dom encourages, his voice brimming with genuine support. "Just keep your eye on the puck, and let your hands do the work."

Gradually, the boy's movements become more fluid, confidence building with each motion. A small but triumphant smile creeps onto his face, and his eyes light up with a newfound spark.

"There you go! You're a natural," Dom praises, his own joy at the boy's success evident.

I watch from a distance, my heart warming at the scene. In this moment, Dom isn't just a former hockey star or a high-profile businessman; he's a mentor, a source of inspiration for a young boy who needed just a little push to find his own strength.

As I stand back, observing the scene unfolding before me, a moment of introspection catches me off guard. Watching the Silver Blades interact with the children, each interaction brimming with care and genuine affection, a realization slowly dawns on me. I've always been so driven, so focused on climbing the ladder of success in the male-dominated world of sports management. It's been about proving myself, about being the best. But in this relentless pursuit, have I neglected other aspects of my life?

There's a pang of something akin to regret, or perhaps it's a newfound awareness. It's as if I'm seeing a different world through a new lens—a world where personal connections, family, and maybe even motherhood, hold a place of importance. The thought is both daunting and strangely appealing.

The laughter of the children, the warm smiles of the players, the easy camaraderie—it all paints a picture of what life could be outside the confines of boardrooms and strategy meetings. Have I been so focused on professional goals that I've pushed aside the innate human longing for a deeper connection? The thought of having a family, of nurturing a life beyond my career, is something I've rarely allowed myself to consider. But here, in this room filled with joy and innocent wonder, it's a desire that bubbles to the surface, unbidden yet undeniable.

I watch as Dom gently guides the shy boy through a hockey move, his actions speaking of patience and a natural ease with children. It's a side of him I hadn't fully appreciated before, and it adds another layer to the complex man I've come to know. Could I see myself in a similar role, sharing moments like these, not just as a career woman but as a mother?

My phone buzzes in my pocket, the screen lighting up with an incoming call and snapping me out of my wandering thoughts.

The name flashes: Anthony Silverman. My heartbeat picks up a notch. The owner of the Seattle StarPucks on my line isn't a daily occurrence. I step out into the corridor for a semblance of quiet, thumb swiping the screen.

"Isabella Carrington speaking."

"Isabella, Anthony Silverman here. Do you have a moment?"

The hustle of the pediatric wing feels miles away suddenly, and I'm back in the game. "Of course, Mr. Silverman," I reply, my tone shifting, the sharp, sassy edges honing to professional sleekness. "What can I do for you?"

I don't miss the glance Dom sends my way, his eyebrows raised in question. I step further away, a clear signal that this conversation is not for public consumption. Whatever Anthony Silverman wants, it's about to change the tempo of my day. I can feel it.

***

The city lights twinkle like a field of fireflies against the night, a vibrant, pulsing backdrop to the stillness of my apartment. I'm perched on my leather couch, a glass of Merlot in hand, its rich aroma mingling with the scent of rain that always seems to linger in Seattle.

The offer letter lies open on my coffee table, a stark contrast against the dark wood, its words printed in a no-nonsense font that belies the upheaval they represent in my life. "We are pleased to extend to you the position of General Manager for the Seattle StarPucks," it begins, each word heavy with implication.

I scan the document, my eyes catching on key phrases that jump off the page: "competitive salary package," "autonomy in team decisions," "opportunities for personal and professional growth." They're offering me the big leagues, a chance to step out of the shadow of the Dom and into the spotlight that's all my own.

The last manager's departure was hush-hush, but in the sports world, whispers travel fast. Evidently, they weren't cutting it, and now, here I am, top of the replacement list. It's flattering, and terrifying, and a whole host of things I'm not sure I'm ready to unpack.

Better pay, more prestige. It's every professional's dream. And yet, it feels like a betrayal, too. The Silver Blades are more than just a job; they're family. They're Sam. They're late nights and early mornings and blood and sweat and tears. They're the taste of victory and the sting of defeat, all mixed together in a cocktail that's become my life's work.

I take another sip of wine. To accept this offer would be to walk away from all that, to turn my back on the team that's been my home since I snagged my first gig in the big time.

But then there's Dom. The thought of no longer having to jostle with him for control, of no longer being under his scrutinizing gaze, it's like a balm to my frayed nerves. Still, can I really let him drive me away? Is that the legacy I want to leave?

The city seems to hold its breath as I sit there, the weight of the decision pressing down on me. The Silver Blades, the StarPucks, Dom, Sam — they all hang in the balance, a myriad of paths and possibilities stretching out before me.

I let out a breath I didn't know I was holding and lean back against the cushions. The wine has left a warm trail down my throat, a false sense of courage that I wish could decide for me.

"What now, Isabella?" I whisper into the quiet of my apartment. The offer glows under the lamplight, an invitation and a challenge all at once. And outside, Seattle waits, indifferent to the turmoil it's witnessing, a stage for a drama yet to unfold.

10

Dom

Rick's got the schedule spread out in front of us like a general surveying the battlefield. I'm leaning back in my chair, the leather creaking under the weight of decisions to come. Our eyes trace the line of games that lead to the division finals, a route mapped out in reds and blues on the calendar.

"Back-to-back away games here could be rough," Rick muses, tapping a finger against a particularly grueling stretch. His brow is furrowed, the lines etched by years of strategizing and too many close calls.

I nod, my mind already running plays, anticipating the fatigue, the adrenaline, the push for that extra inch on ice. "We'll need the guys at peak condition. No room for slip-ups."

Rick looks up, his eyes meeting mine. "And the StarPucks are gaining momentum. They're hungry, Dom."

"They may be hungry," I reply, the edge of a challenge in my voice, "but we've got the bite."

We both know what's at stake. The StarPucks are the new kids on the block, flashy and eager to knock kings off thrones. And if my gut's right, it's going to be us facing them when the ice chips settle. I welcome it—the clash, the test. I didn't build my career on backing down from a challenge.

I stand up, pacing over to the window that overlooks the rink. Down there, Isabella's in her element, her voice ringing out clear and sharp. She's directing the players, her commands punctuated by the slap of pucks against sticks.

A smirk pulls at my lips, unbidden. She's a force, Isabella. She's got this team under her spell—my team. And I'd be lying if I said that didn't crank the dial on my respect for her up a notch every time I see her in action.

But there's tension there, too—a push and pull of wills. Isabella doesn't just bend to authority because it's authority. She questions, challenges, fights. It's why she's good. It's also why we clash. Like two lines on the ice, speeding towards the same puck. Collision is inevitable.

"Isabella's doing good work with them," Rick's voice breaks into my thoughts, a note of approval there that I can't disagree with.

"Yeah, she's got game," I admit, my gaze still on the rink. "But I need to make sure she's playing for the long haul, not just the flashy wins."

Rick gives a grunt of acknowledgment, knowing as well as I do that a season isn't just a series of games; it's a marathon. And sometimes, you need to rein in the sprinters for the distance.

I watch Isabella for a moment longer, her every move radiating confidence. And as much as it grinds my gears when she defies me, when she sparks up against my authority, I can't help but anticipate the firestorm our next confrontation will bring. Because every time we clash, something shifts—a dynamic, a perspective.

And that's the kind of friction that not only polishes steel but sharpens it.

"Can't help but notice how hard you've been riding her," Rick says. "There a long-term strategy you've got in mind?"

Rick's question hangs in the air, and for a split second, my mind betrays me, wandering down paths less professional and far more primal. Images of Isabella, fierce and unyielding, flash through my head, unbidden and unwelcome in their intensity. I push them away, a mental shove as forceful as a check into the boards.

"Isabella's good," I start, the words coming out with a grudging respect that I don't often afford. "Damn good. But good isn't the goal. I'm aiming for greatness. For her, for the team."

Rick's eyes narrow, a mix of interest and skepticism. He's seen his fair share of wannabe hotshots turn lukewarm. "And how do you plan on getting her there?"

I smirk, my mind settling on a strategy as clear in my head as our path to the finals. "Ever heard the saying 'iron sharpens iron'?"

His nod is slow, contemplative. He gets where I'm heading, the old wisdom that pressure breeds excellence.

"I plan on challenging her, pushing her. She's got the fire, Rick, I've seen it. But she needs to be forged into something stronger, something... unstoppable. And I'm just the guy to do that."

It's not just talk. I've got plans for Isabella Carrington. Plans that will test her, mold her, and, if I'm honest, will likely pit us against each other more fiercely than ever.

With that, I stand, the chair rolling back with a decisive clatter. My legs carry me to the door, my strides as certain as the plan forming in my mind. I'm not one for half-measures or gentle prods. If Isabella's going to reach the potential I see in her, she needs to be tempered by challenge, by conflict.

As I make my way down to the rink, the sounds of the stadium around me—the distant clatter of sticks, the muffled directives of coaches, the occasional burst of laughter from the team—fade into a backdrop for my thoughts.

Isabella won't like it, of course. She'll fight it—fight me—every step of the way. But that's what I'm counting on. That fight, that spirit of hers, it's what will make her great. And whether she knows it or not, I'm going to help her get there.

I pause at the top of the steps leading down to the rink, my hand on the railing, the cold metal a grounding point. Below, Isabella is a commanding figure, orchestrating the flow of drills with a conductor's grace and a general's authority.

She senses me then, her head turning, eyes locking onto mine with an intensity that sends a jolt of something through me—something that feels a lot like anticipation.

Iron sharpens iron, and I'm about to strike the flint.

I descend the steps, each one echoing in the cavernous space of the rink, my eyes never leaving Isabella. She's in her zone, a tight circle of eager players hanging on her every word, her hands moving animatedly as she outlines her latest strategic masterpiece.

This is the moment—the perfect slice of time to apply the pressure, to test her mettle. As I approach, I can see her pause, her spine straightening as she feels my presence.

Without a word, I slip into the circle beside her. The team glances between us, the air tinged with the electric charge of an impending storm.

"That's an interesting approach, Isabella," I start, my voice calm but carrying the edge of a well-honed skate blade. "But let's consider how that played out last season against the Breakers, remember?"

Her eyes flash, the storm brewing in their depths. "What worked last season doesn't work this season, Dom. The game evolves."

I nod, conceding the point with a tilt of my head. "True. Adaptation is key. But fundamentals are constants. For instance," I turn to the team, pulling their attention, "proper positioning on the ice trumps fancy footwork. It's about being where the puck is going to be, not where it's been."

I can see the tension in Isabella's posture, the clench of her jaw. I'm pushing her buttons, and I know it. But it's necessary. She needs to learn to defend her ideas, to fight for them.

"Positioning is one thing," she counters, her voice firm. "But anticipating the opponent's moves—outthinking them—that's what wins games."

I raise an eyebrow, impressed despite myself. "Anticipation is nothing without execution," I challenge back. "You know as well as I do that a game isn't won on 'what ifs.'"

The team is silent, a rapt audience to our match. Isabella steps closer, her gaze locked on mine. "And you know as well as I that you can execute flawlessly and still lose if you're not thinking one step ahead."

There's a fire in her now, a fierce determination that I respect. This is what I want from her, this passion, this strength of conviction.

"You're not wrong," I say, and the surprise on her face is almost worth the concession. Almost. "But let's make sure we're not sacrificing the basics for the sake of innovation."

She nods, a tight, controlled motion. "Agreed. Now, if you don't mind, I'd like to finish explaining the new plays."

Her voice is a blend of frost and steel, but I'm not quite finished. The team needs to see her handle the heat, needs to know she can take the punches and stay standing. That's what the game demands. That's what I demand.

"Go ahead," I say, folding my arms across my chest, my stance casual but my gaze piercing. "But how will these plays stand up under real pressure? It's easy to theorize here, but out there," I nod toward the ice, "it's a whole different beast."

I can see the flicker of annoyance in her eyes as she resumes her explanation, but I interrupt almost immediately. "And what's the contingency if the opposing team reads our setup? We've been predictable in the past. What's to stop this from being just another pattern they anticipate?"

Her explanations come rapid-fire, her strategy sound, but I keep pressing, asking for specifics, probing for weaknesses. The team's eyes flick back and forth, a silent rally unfolding before them. Isabella's starting to fray at the edges, her calm demeanor struggling to hold.

Good," I think. *She has to get used to this, has to be unshakeable.*

The back and forth continues, each question sharper, each answer more terse. I'm walking a line, pushing her, testing her. I want to draw out that brilliance I know is there. But then, I step over that line, the words out before I can rein them back.

"Perhaps you'll execute these strategies better than you handle constructive criticism. We need results, not just good intentions."

The silence that follows is sudden and complete. I've gone too far. The personal jab hangs heavy in the air.

Her eyes narrow, and I see the walls go up, her stance shifting as if she's readying herself for a face-off. "If that's how you're going to play," she says, her voice low and steady, "then fine."

She doesn't wait for a response. She spins on her heel and storms off, leaving a wake of tension and uncertainty. The team looks at me, then at the empty space where Isabella stood, and I can read the question in their eyes.

I stand there, the echo of her footsteps like a gavel judging me. Did I come at her too hard?

The rink suddenly feels colder, the distance between the players and me growing wider. I've always known where the line is, always danced on it but never crossed it. Until now.

I rub a hand over my jaw, the stubble there a reminder that I'm not infallible. I've made a misstep, let the drive to test her resolve push me into territory I should have avoided.

"Back to practice," I say, my voice lacking its usual authority.

As the team hesitantly regroups, I'm left to contemplate the cost of my strategy. Isabella is steel, yes, but even steel can bend under too much pressure. I have to ensure that when the heat is on, I'm forging her strength, not setting the stage for her to break.

11

Isabella

"HE'S UNBELIEVABLE," I say, my words sharp enough to slice through the low hum of the bar. "There he was, picking apart every line, every move, like he's the one who's been coaching day in and day out."

The clink of ice in my glass syncs with the pounding in my head, a steady reminder of the infuriating man who's the source of both. Jenna is across from me, her expression a mix of concern and the kind of righteous indignation only a best friend can muster.

Jenna takes a sip of her drink, her eyes never leaving mine. "Dom's just... what's the word? Insufferable," she says, the word hissing out like steam from a pressure valve.

I laugh, but there's no humor in it. "That's putting it mildly. He took pleasure in it, Jenna. I swear he did. Every pointed question, every skeptical look—like he wanted to see me squirm, like he was taking some kind of sick pleasure out of it."

The bartender passes by, and I signal for a refill. It's that kind of night. Jenna reaches over, giving my hand a squeeze. "You're the best thing that happened to that team. He should be on his knees thanking you, not tearing you down."

She's got a point. I've turned strategies on their heads, pulled wins out of the hat when everyone else was ready to throw in the towel. But Dom, he just sees me as another plaything in his little power games.

"He even made this snide comment," I continue, the words tumbling out as the anger boils over. "Made it personal. Right there, in front of everyone."

Jenna's eyes flash, a spark of shared fury lighting them up. "He's threatened by you, Iz. He sees you're brilliant and it scares the hell out of him."

Her words should comfort me, but they don't. They can't. Not when I have to face him again tomorrow, and the day after that, each encounter a new battle in a war I didn't sign up for.

The new glass arrives, and I take a long drink, the liquid fire doing nothing to douse the flames of my frustration. "I'm just so tired of it, you know? The constant one-upmanship. I want to coach, not play these ridiculous games."

Jenna nods, her lips pressed in a thin line. "So what are you going to do?"

It's the million-dollar question. I stare into the amber depths of my glass, searching for answers in the swirl of whiskey. What am I going to do? The offer from the StarPucks looms in my mind, a lifeboat in a stormy sea. But am I ready to jump ship?

"I don't know," I admit, feeling weary to my bones. "But something's got to give. Last thing I want is a tyrant like Dom breathing down my throat, challenging me at every damn turn."

Jenna's there, as she always is, a sympathetic ear and a shoulder to lean on. But even she can't fight this battle for me. No, this one's mine, and mine alone.

The glass chills my fingers, condensation beading like sweat on a brow — a physical echo of the turmoil brewing inside me. I've been sitting on this offer from the StarPucks like it's a grenade without a pin, and I'm not sure I'm ready to let it explode into conversation just yet. Jenna, though, she's got a sixth sense for secrets; she always has.

"You're squirming, Iz," she notes, her keen eyes fixed on me over the rim of her own glass. "Spill it."

I hesitate, the words teetering on the tip of my tongue. "It's nothing," I try, knowing even as I say it that Jenna will see right through the lie.

"Isabella Carrington," she says, my name a gentle reprimand, "you've never 'nothing' a day in your life. What's going on?"

Her directness is a force of nature, and under its weight, my resistance crumbles. "I got an offer," I confess, the words tumbling out in a rush.

Jenna's eyes go wide, and I can almost hear the gears turning in her head. "An offer? Like, a job offer?"

I nod, my fingers tracing the lip of my glass, round and round. "General Manager. For the StarPucks."

"For real?" She's practically bouncing in her seat now, the excitement written all over her face.

Before I can even form my own thoughts into a coherent question, she's already there, her response a sharp exclamation: "Do it!!"

I blink, taken aback by her vehemence. "Just like that?"

"Yes, just like that," she insists, her enthusiasm undimmed. "Isabella, this is huge. It's what you've been working towards. Plus, it's the StarPucks — they're independent, which means you won't be under Dom's... what did you call it earlier? 'Patriarchal thumb'?"

Her words are a mirror, reflecting my own unspoken desires and fears back at me. It's true, the StarPucks offer autonomy, a chance to build something from the ground up, without the looming presence of a man who manages to get under my skin like no one else.

But then, Jenna's phone buzzes, the sound slicing through our bubble of conversation. "Sorry, duty calls," she says, shooting me an apologetic look as she stands to take the call, her voice shifting into her professional doctor mode.

Left alone with my swirling thoughts, I mull over Jenna's words. Is she right? Is this the natural next step? The offer is great — better pay, more responsibility, and a chance to prove myself without Dom overshadowing every decision.

Yet, doubt nibbles at the corners of my mind. The Silver Blades are my team; I've poured my heart and soul into them for three damn seasons. Can I just walk away? And then there's Dom. Complicated, infuriating Dom. Would leaving be letting him win, or would it be claiming a victory of my own?

Jenna's unwavering "do it" echoes in my head, a mantra of encouragement or perhaps a siren call to a new chapter. The decision looms large, an Everest I've yet to climb. But one thing's for sure: whatever I choose, it'll be on my terms. Because that's how Isabella Carrington plays the game.

***

The waiting room of Anthony Silverman's office is an eclectic gallery, each piece a bold statement. There's a sculpture that looks like a stack of chrome pancakes in one corner and a painting that I'm pretty sure is just a series of splattered fruit across the canvas. Eccentric doesn't even begin to cover it.

I'm perched on the edge of a couch that feels more like modern art than furniture, my posture as composed as I can muster in the face of... whatever this decor is supposed to be. Then the man himself bursts through the door, a whirlwind of energy dressed in a suit that probably costs more than my car.

Anthony Silverman is a walking, talking shockwave in the most electric sense. There's something about him that screams 'self-made,' from the youthful energy that radiates off him like heat from sun-soaked pavement, to the undeniable charisma that clings to his tailored suit. He's the embodiment of success with a twist, his reputation for eccentricity as well-known as the innovative path he took to his billions.

He made his fortune by flipping the tech industry on its head, starting with an app that somehow turned people's idle doodles into viral sensations, then riding the wave into more serious ventures. It was a blend of art and technology, of genius and sheer audacity. Now, he invests in ideas that seem to come from science fiction, from space tourism to AI that composes symphonies.

And now, evidently, hockey teams.

"Isabella! Fantastic to see you!" Anthony's handshake is firm, his smile wide. He's the epitome of confidence, his demeanor as quirky as the art on his walls, but there's a sharpness in his eyes that tells you he's not just some rich eccentric. The guy's got gears turning in his head that most people can't even fathom.

"Thanks for having me, Mr. Silverman," I reply, standing to meet his energy with my own steady force.

He waves off the formality with a flick of his hand as we walk into his office, a space that's no less bizarre than the waiting room. There's a desk that looks like it was carved from a single giant tree, and the view of Seattle through the floor-to-ceiling windows is breathtaking.

"Believe me, the pleasure is all mine. So, Isabella," he starts, leaning against his desk with a casualness that somehow doesn't clash with the setting, "what made you decide to come talk to me about the offer? Truth be told, I was starting to feel like I was getting left on read." He flashes me a knowing smile.

I draw in a breath, ready with my reasons. "The opportunity, Mr. Silverman. It's not every day you get the chance to shape a team from the ground up. To really make your mark." I carefully skirt around the subject of Dom. No need to bring personal drama into this.

Anthony nods, his expression eager. "Exactly! That's what the StarPucks are all about. We're not just another team; we're a statement." He walks over to a strange, abstract sculpture that somehow perfectly encapsulates his vision. "I created the StarPucks here, in a city already bleeding blue and green for the Blades, because I believe in shaking things up, in challenging the status quo."

He turns, his gaze piercing. "We're independent because we don't follow the well-trodden path. We blaze our own trail, Isabella. We're about innovation, about passion, about the raw spirit of the game. And that's what I see in you. You're not afraid to take the ice by storm."

I find myself nodding, caught up in his vision. It's infectious, his belief in what the StarPucks could be, what I could be as part of it. And for the first time since this whole thing started, the thought of leaving the Silver Blades doesn't feel like a betrayal; it feels like a beginning.

Anthony's demeanor shifts, the playful light in his eyes hardening into the sharp glint of cut diamond. This is the man who turned whimsical ideas into a technology empire, who sees through the clutter and grasps the core of what makes or breaks success.

"I want you for the job, Isabella," he says, each word deliberate, hitting the table between us like a gavel. "I've looked at the other candidates, but no one else measures up. You've turned mediocre plays into wins, you've brought the Silver Blades from the brink more than once, and your knowledge of the game is... it's unparalleled."

He's serious, and the intensity in his gaze is something I've learned to recognize—it's the look of a person who doesn't just hope for success; he expects it.

He starts laying out the offer—numbers, benefits, the kind of figures that most would jump at. But then he leans in, his voice dropping to a conspiratorial whisper that somehow fills the room.

"But I suspect what will really seal the deal for you isn't the salary. It's the chance to be the architect, to be in charge without having to look over your shoulder. To be at the foundation of something that's set to be huge."

"You're right about that," I reply without hesitation. The idea of steering my own ship, of being the one calling all the shots—it's intoxicating.

His grin is back, spreading across his face like he's just won his own private championship. He slides a contract across the table, the paper crisp, the ink seemingly still drying, as if it's fresh from the future he's so eager to dive into.

"I'll give you all the time you need to talk to your GM and owner," he says, but the eagerness in his voice tells a different story. "But between you and me, I want you on board yesterday."

The pros and cons start a frenzied dance in my head. It's a tango of opportunity and risk, a choreography I've been practicing all my career. But as my eyes scan the contract, as I see the numbers and the title waiting to be mine, the music swells to a crescendo.

My heart races, a sprinter at the blocks, and I find myself reaching for the pen with a hand that doesn't shake. I'm ready for this. I was born for this.

With an eager smile that feels like it's lighting up the entire city of Seattle, I sign my name. Isabella Carrington, General Manager of the Seattle StarPucks. The ink on the page isn't just a signature; it's a declaration.

I slide the contract back to him, our hands brushing in the process, a transfer of energy, of destiny. I've just turned the page, and a new chapter is waiting to be written.

12

Dom

THE LOCKER ROOM IS charged with the kind of tension that precedes battle, each player suited up, eyes fixed on me as I stand before them. This is my terrain, where I mold individual talent into a single, unstoppable force. I relish it—the power, the control, the unity.

"Listen up," I start, my voice the commanding rumble of thunder before a storm. "The Wolverines are coming into our house for the next game." I let the name hang in the air, a target painted in their minds. "They're fast, they're dirty, and they think they've got our number. But here's the thing—" I pause, a predator's smile tugging at my lips, "—they don't have a damn clue what's waiting for them."

The team nods, a sea of helmets bobbing in agreement, the growl of 'yeah' rolling through them like a wave. I pace before them, locking eyes with each player, ensuring the gravity of my words sinks in deep.

"We're more than just a team; we're a brotherhood. We watch each other's backs. We move as one. And when one of us scores," I punch a fist into my palm, the impact a punctuation, "we all score."

It's a speech I've given a hundred times, but today, it feels different. Because as I look out at the sea of faces, there's a gap where there shouldn't be one. Isabella's spot is empty, her usual punctual presence conspicuously absent.

I wrap up, "We're going to outskate them, outplay them, and if it comes down to it, we will outlast them. This is our ice, our game, our victory to take. Let's show the Wolverines what it means to mess with the Blades."

A chorus of agreement follows, the room a cacophony of claps and cheers, but my focus has already shifted. Where the hell is Isabella?

The team disperses, clattering out towards the rink, and I catch sight of Sam, his gear half-on, his expression unreadable. He's her brother; if anyone knows why Isabella's MIA, it's him.

I stride over, my approach direct, the question unasked but already burning in my gaze. Sam looks up, and there's a flicker of something there, a hesitation that has me bracing for news I'm not sure I want to hear.

I catch Sam just as he's about to head for the ice, his gear half-strapped and his mind clearly somewhere else. "Sam," I call out, my voice cutting through the residual noise of the locker room.

He turns, his expression tight. "Yeah?"

"Where's Isabella?" I ask, the question blunt, a hammer looking for a nail. "She's never late."

Sam's brow creases, and he looks at me like I'm speaking a foreign language. "You didn't hear?" he finally says, a note of disbelief in his tone.

"Hear what?" I press, feeling an unfamiliar tug of concern in my chest. Last practice got heated, sure, but Isabella's got skin thicker than most.

Sam's silent for a beat, his eyes shifting to the floor before meeting mine again. "Izzy's gone," he says, the words hitting me like a blindside check. "Greener pastures, I guess."

Gone? The word doesn't make sense. Not Isabella. Not in the middle of the season.

"Greener pastures?" I echo, the confusion must be written all over my face.

"Yeah," Sam nods toward Rick's office, a silent signal that the GM would have the answers I'm after. "Talk to Rick. He'll fill you in."

I'm moving before I even decide to, my strides long and purposeful as I head to Rick's office. Isabella, leaving? It doesn't add up. She's as much a part of this team as anyone, more than some. I push the door open without knocking, urgency rendering me tactless.

Rick looks up, startled by the intrusion. "Dom," he starts, standing up, "what—"

But I don't let him finish. "Isabella," I demand, "she's gone? To where?"

Rick's eyes hold mine, a silent conversation before he even speaks. "You better sit down, Dom. We've got things to discuss."

***

From the high-rise vantage point of my penthouse, Seattle sprawls out like a kingdom. Here in my office, surrounded by glass walls and steel ambition, I'm a king in waiting, poised for the next conquest. But tonight, the city lights feel like distant stars—close enough to see, too far to touch.

I'm at my desk, an expansive slab of dark wood and chrome, the skyline reflecting in its polished surface. My laptop's open, a silent sentinel as I wait for the investors' call to begin. Normally, I'd be reviewing stats, but tonight, my mind is on a different game entirely.

Isabella's gone.

Rick's words play on repeat. She gave her notice quietly, slipping away without fanfare. He respected her decision, said she needed to fly. But me? I was left in the dark. And I can't shake the feeling that she wanted it that way.

Did I drive her to it? Was it that last practice, that final jab that pushed her over the edge? I've always prided myself on knowing how far to push, but with Isabella... with her, it was different.

The room's ambient lights dim, a reminder that the call for my investor meeting is imminent. The screens flicker to life, windows to the faces that control the purse strings of empires. It's showtime.

But as I prepare to don the mask of the indomitable Dom Steele, a sliver of doubt worms its way into my fortress of solitude. Isabella was a pillar, as much a part of this team's spirit as I am. Her absence is a shadow, a cold spot where the fire used to be.

The first investor pops onto the screen, his smile as polished as the pitch I know he's expecting from me. I click into business mode.

The screen before me lights up, a mosaic of expectant faces framed in sleek digital squares. It's a gathering of power, wealth, and influence, and I'm center stage. My fingers are steepled, a calculated gesture of composure and confidence as I greet each investor by name. They nod, their responses a chorus of pleasantries, but my mind is elsewhere, haunted by a ghost with sharp eyes and a sharper tongue.

"Good evening," I begin, the timbre of my voice filling the room, commanding attention. "As you all know, we're here to discuss not just the future of the Silver Blades, but the future of hockey in Seattle."

The words flow from me with the practiced ease of many such meetings, but Isabella's face intrudes, uninvited, into my thoughts. I push it away, focusing on the task at hand.

"We stand on the cusp of something monumental," I continue, gesturing to the mockup of my baby, Apex Arena, that materializes on the screen behind me. It's a vision of steel and light, an architectural marvel designed to be the heart of hockey in the Pacific Northwest.

"The most modern, high-tech stadium ever conceived," I say, letting the image speak for itself. The design is futuristic, with sweeping curves and a retractable roof that promises to bring the stars into every night game.

"As you know, we're looking at a state-of-the-art stadium that will redefine the fan experience," I begin, my voice carrying the excitement of the vision. "The Apex Arena will have a seating capacity of over twenty thousand, ensuring not a single fan misses out on the action."

I gesture to the mockup behind me, where images of the stadium cycle through on the screen. "Every seat will have unparalleled views, with personal touch-screen interfaces for live stats and ordering concessions. The exterior will boast dynamic lighting that'll become a beacon in Seattle's skyline, and the retractable roof will allow for open-air games under the stars. It's more than a stadium; it's the future of sports entertainment."

I've pitched this dream before, woven this narrative to skeptical ears and seen them turn into believers. But tonight, I sense a current of hesitation, a ripple of doubt that wasn't there before.

As I outline the latest advancements, the sustainable materials, the state-of-the-art facilities, I watch their faces closely. There's a flicker of uncertainty in some of their eyes, a tightening around the mouths of others.

I lean forward, elbows on the table, the picture of assertive leadership. "I want this to be a dialogue, not a monologue," I say. "If there's any hesitation, any concern, I encourage you to voice it now. We're in this together, and it's only through candid collaboration that we'll succeed."

Silence hangs for a moment, pregnant with unspoken objections and the weight of millions of dollars hanging in the balance.

"Speak your minds," I urge, locking eyes with each of them through the screen. "This is the foundation of our future. Let's ensure it's built on solid ground."

The pause stretches, a high-wire moment of tension in a room full of decision-makers. I'm not one to shy away from confrontation, from challenge.

The investors' faces are a tableau of diplomacy and concern, but it's Elizabeth Marston, CEO of Marston Enterprises and one of our heaviest hitters, who leans into her camera, her presence commanding even through the screen.

"Dom," she starts, her voice carrying the weight of her billions, "I'll cut straight to the chase."

I brace myself, the mental image of Isabella an unwelcome prelude to whatever bomb Elizabeth is about to drop.

"We're worried," she admits, and the straightforwardness of her concern pierces the armor I've built around this meeting. "You came to Seattle to tour your holdings, to ensure everything was in order. Yet, it seems things are quite the opposite."

I can feel my control slipping, a wince betraying my façade of unshakeability. But I recover quickly, schooling my features back into a mask of attentive neutrality.

"Isabella Carrington's departure to a competitor," Elizabeth continues, "just as you arrive? It raises questions, Dom. It doesn't inspire confidence in how you'll manage other, more costly endeavors here in Seattle."

I nod, acknowledging the blow. "Elizabeth, your concerns are valid, and I take full responsibility for the turnover. Isabella's decision was unexpected, but it's a testament to the caliber of talent we nurture within the Blades," I say, my voice smooth as the aged whiskey in my cabinet.

Her eyes narrow slightly, not quite sold, and I press on. "It's my job to ensure that our team — and our investments—thrive, regardless of individual changes. And that's exactly what will happen."

My words fade into a tense silence as I conclude the presentation on the Apex Arena. There's a moment where I can almost hear the investors digesting the grandeur of the project—its sleek design promising to be the pulsing heart of Seattle's sports scene.

Then, Robert Hastings, a silver-haired lion of the investment world, leans forward. His gaze, sharp and calculating, pins me like a butterfly in a case.

"Dom," he starts, his voice a gravelly baritone that's commanded boardrooms for decades, "this shakeup with the Silver Blades... it's concerning."

I keep my expression neutral, giving away nothing. "Change is part of the game, Robert. It's about adapting and overcoming."

"Yes, but Isabella Carrington leaving for the StarPucks... That's not just change. That's a potential shift in power," he says, steepling his fingers with a gravity that sends a murmur through the room.

Another investor, Eleanor Chu, known for her sharp instincts and sharper investments, chimes in, "She's a force, Dom. We've seen what she can do. What if she turns the StarPucks into the new darlings of Seattle?"

I fight to keep the concern off my face, to maintain the alpha composure that's been my armor in boardrooms and locker rooms alike.

"Isabella is talented, but the Blades are more than one person. We're a team, a legacy," I assert with confidence I'm not entirely feeling.

Eleanor leans back, her eyes still holding mine—a silent challenge. "A legacy can be a fragile thing," she says softly, almost a whisper but loud enough to echo against the walls of my certainty.

The investors share looks among themselves, a silent conversation at a frequency I can't quite tune into. It's clear they're reassessing, recalculating, considering the weight of my words against the potential of Isabella's next moves.

I know I need to regain control, to steer this back in my favor.

"Let me assure you, the Silver Blades have a strategy in place. And as for Isabella, I'm confident her departure won't disrupt our trajectory. In fact," I pause, gauging their reaction as I prepare to play my ace, "we're exploring a... collaborative approach with the StarPucks that will ensure both teams, and the Apex Arena, thrive."

Their interest is piqued, I can tell. It's an unexpected play, but then, I've made a career out of those.

"A collaboration...," Robert starts, a slow smile creeping across his face, "that could be a game-changer."

"Yes," I agree, a matching smile tugging at my lips, "a game-changer indeed."

I hold the investors' collective gaze, letting the term "game-changer" linger between us, a tantalizing taste of potential profit and success. I can almost hear the cogs turning in their heads, each one of them recalculating their stakes, reassessing the risk. Good.

"We'll be in touch with the details," I say, wrapping up the call with an air of finality that suggests I've got all my pieces in place—even if the board is still in flux. "Thank you, everyone, for your time."

The screens blink out one by one, and I'm left in the quiet afterglow of the call. The investors are intrigued, their appetite for risk whetted by the hint of something big, something unifying. But what exactly?

I lean back in my chair, steepling my fingers, my eyes fixed on the cityscape stretching out before me. Collaboration with Isabella. The idea had been a spur-of-the-moment feint, a way to regain control of the narrative. But now, as I consider the possibilities, it starts to take on a life of its own.

I need something solid, something public to show that Isabella and I—no, the Silver Blades and the StarPucks—are aligned. A partnership that will smooth over any investor concerns and solidify my position.

And then it hits me, the perfect ruse.

A fake engagement.

It's just crazy enough to work, just bold enough to catch everyone off-guard and spin the story in our favor. It would tie Isabella's success to my own, and the StarPucks' rise to the Blades'.

A smirk finds its way onto my lips as I think about the plan, about pulling Isabella into this dance of deception. It's a gamble, but I've never been one to shy away from those. After all, the biggest risks often bring the greatest rewards.

I rise from the chair, my reflection in the glass showing a man ready to take on the world. A partnership with Isabella Carrington—imagine that. The very thought is electric, a current running hot and fast through my veins.

This could be the move that defines my career, that elevates the Blades and the StarPucks to new heights. It's a power play, one that will have the whole city watching, waiting, talking.

And as the details begin to coalesce in my mind, I can't help but feel that rush of anticipation, the thrill of the chase. This "collaboration" could be my masterstroke, a stroke of genius that will change the game.

I just might've come up with the perfect plan indeed.

13

Isabella

ONE WEEK INTO MY new life and I'm standing for the first time in front of what is, let's say, the "charming" home of the StarPucks—Polar Arena. It's a far cry from my last place of work, but ambition wasn't built on looks alone. I push through the doors, my heels clicking on the concrete with the rhythm of new beginnings.

The interior is a kaleidoscope of chaos and potential. Wires dangle from open panels, and the scent of fresh paint battles the mustier notes of sweat and determination. It's not the gleaming spaceship I imagined, but it's ours, and that's what counts.

As I stride through the corridors, I can feel the weight of history yet to be written pressing against the walls. This is where the magic will happen, where dreams will be made or broken. It's a fixer-upper's dream, and I've always been good with my hands.

Anthony emerges from the guts of the stadium, his usual flamboyant self somehow subdued by the stark reality around us.

"Isabella, welcome to the frontier," he says with a flourish that feels a bit forced in the stark lighting.

I take in his apologetic stance, the way his eyes skirt around, avoiding direct contact with the less glamorous details of our surroundings.

"Building a stadium is a whole other beast," he admits, scratching the back of his neck. "But acquiring the team? That was the easy part."

I offer him a grin, unphased. "I've never shied away from a challenge, Anthony. And I'm not about to start now."

His relief is palpable, and he matches my smile with one of his own. "That's what I wanted to hear. Shall we meet the team?"

Eagerness, like a live wire, sparks within me. "Lead the way," I say, my voice steady. There's work to be done, a team to mold, a legacy to build from the ground up. And I'm just the woman for the job.

As we walk, I catalog everything—the peeling stickers on lockers, the scuff marks on the floor, the hum of a place that's seen better days. This is a place waiting for a spark, for someone to breathe life back into its lungs.

"Less than impressive now," I concede, my mind already painting the future over the present, "but not for long."

Anthony chuckles, a sound that bounces off the concrete and steel. "Exactly. This is just the cocoon, Isabella. Wait until you see the butterfly we're going to become."

And as we approach the locker room, the muffled sounds of conversation and laughter leaking through the door, I square my shoulders. This is it. Time to meet the team, to start this journey. Time to take these underdogs and turn them into contenders.

Stepping into the cavernous belly of the locker room, I can feel dozens of eyes on me, sizing me up, wondering if I'm the real deal or just another suit with a title. There's a flutter in my stomach, a hint of nerves — it's not every day you get to reinvent a wheel or, in my case, a puck. But as I stand there, their gazes heavy upon me, something clicks into place. This is exactly where I'm meant to be.

"Morning, StarPucks," I announce, stepping into the circle of expectant faces, my voice steady and infused with the confidence that's carried me through the toughest of negotiations. "I'm Isabella Carrington, your new general manager."

I let the title hang in the air, a mantle of responsibility that I wear with pride. My heels punctuate the silence, a sharp staccato in the hush of the locker room, as I start to weave my way through the sea of jerseys and hopeful eyes.

"I come here with a record," I continue, my tone even but forceful, "A record with the Blades that speaks of hard-fought victories, strategic triumphs, and games that we clawed back from the edge of defeat." I pause, locking eyes with a few of the players, letting them see the determination that's fueled my rise, the fire that's going to ignite theirs.

"But I'm not here to boast about past glories. I'm here to talk about the future—our future." I gesture to the room, to each of them, to the emblem on their chests. "I'm here to talk about the legacy we're going to build, together."

I take a step closer into the center, my presence commanding their full attention. "I don't do second place," I assert, my gaze sweeping across the room, challenging, inviting them to meet my level of ambition. "I do banners. I do championships. That's what I've done, and that's what I'm here to do."

I let those words sink in, watching as nods begin to ripple through the group, as the spark of belief starts to light their faces.

"With me at the helm, we're not just going to compete; we're going to dominate. We're going to be the team that no one wants to face because they know it will be the toughest game they'll ever play."

I pause, allowing a smile to play on my lips, one that speaks of secrets and shared conspiracies of greatness. "We're going to be the team that when we step on the ice, our opponents feel it in their bones, the inevitability of our victory."

I let my gaze settle on each player, ensuring they feel seen, feel important. "You were chosen to be a StarPuck because you have the talent, the drive, and the heart. Now, with me, you'll have the direction and the strategy to unleash it."

I straighten, my final words a vow, a promise. "Get ready, gentlemen. Prepare to work harder than you've ever worked, to play smarter, to be fiercer. Because we're going to raise banners. We're going to hoist trophies. And we're going to do it together."

Silence follows, thick with the weight of potential, of futures unwritten. Then, as if on cue, a single clap cuts through, followed by another, and another, until the room is a thunder of applause. And I know, without a doubt, they're with me.

"Let's get to work," I say, and the StarPucks roar their readiness.

There's a shift in the room, almost imperceptible, like the tide pulling back before a wave. Heads nod, respect replacing skepticism, and by the time I'm done, I can feel the change in the air — the first sparks of belief.

"Let's hit the rink. I want to see what I'm working with," I command, and like a well-oiled machine, they move.

Anthony leans in as the players file out, a grin splitting his face. "I'm impressed," he says, and I can tell he means it.

"You haven't seen anything yet," I reply, the edge of my smile sharp enough to cut through the ice.

He guides me to my new office, a glass-fronted space that looks out over the rink. It's not as nice as my old pad, but it's mine, and that's what counts. The view is less than picturesque — old banners hang like tired soldiers, the seats empty and waiting. But it's filled with potential, with the echoes of future victories and the cheers of crowds yet to come.

I step up to the window, my hands resting on the cool glass, watching as the StarPucks take the ice. This is where it begins, where we build something from nothing. Where we show the world that the underdog can have its day, its season, its era.

Anthony leaves me to it, the quiet of the office wrapping around me like a challenge. I watch the players, their movements raw and unrefined, but hungry. Hungry for direction, for success, for someone to believe in.

And believe I do. With every fiber of my being, I believe in this team, in this city, in this moment. Because this is my team now, my city, my moment.

The ring of my phone cuts through the quiet of the new office, a tether to the life I've just left. Sam's name flashes on the screen, and for a second, I hesitate, but old habits die hard. I swipe to answer.

"Hey, big brother," I greet, a smile in my voice that I hope sounds more genuine than it feels.

"Izzy! How's the first day in the big chair?" Sam's voice is a balm, familiar and welcome.

"It's great," I reply, my eyes wandering over the empty seats in the rink below. "But, you know, can't shake the feeling that I've turned traitor on you guys."

There's a pause, and then a chuckle, warm and reassuring. "Traitor? Come on, we're thrilled for you. You've earned this, sis. And besides," his tone turns playful, conspiratorial, "just watch out, because we're not going to go easy on you. You're the competition now."

I laugh, the sound more relieved than I'd like to admit. "They'd better not. I expect nothing less than your worst."

"So... how's Dom taking it?" I venture, curiosity getting the better of me.

Sam goes quiet for a beat. "Honestly? He gets weird when you're brought up. Clams up like a kid who lost his favorite toy. But otherwise, he hasn't said much. He's Dom. You know how he is."

I nod, even though Sam can't see it. Dom Steele, the enigma. A part of me wonders if he's seething, plotting, or if, just maybe, he's indifferent.

As if on cue, my computer pings with a new email. I glance at the screen, and there it is, bold against the stark white background: an email from Dom, the subject simply reading, "Chat?"

I let out a breath I didn't realize I was holding. So, the man of steel wants to talk. The timing couldn't be more Dom — just as I'm settling into my new kingdom, he reaches out.

"I've gotta go, Sam," I say, my gaze still locked on the email. "Looks like I've got some business to attend to."

Sam's voice takes on a teasing edge. "Go get 'em, GM."

We say our goodbyes, and I'm left alone with the blinking cursor, a decision hovering in the space between click and ignore. Finally, with a mixture of trepidation and a dose of that Carrington sass, I click the email open.

"Free for a talk?" is all it says. Classic Dom. Short, sweet, and to the point. His words are followed by the name of a restaurant and a reservation time.

What the *hell* could he possibly want?

Part of me wants to reply with my own short, sweet, and to the point response—"screw off."

But the greater part of me wants to know why he's reaching out.

I sigh, sitting down and typing a response.

One way to find out.

14

Dom

THE CLINK OF FINE dining cutlery forms a high-class soundtrack as I sit at a table with a view of downtown Seattle's lunch hour pulse. I've chosen a place discreet yet impressive—mirroring the nature of the conversation I'm about to have. I'm rehearsing lines in my head, each one sounding more ridiculous than the last. A fake engagement? It's a Hail Mary slapshot from down-rink, but I'm down by two goals and there's a minute left on the clock.

I glance at my watch, the seconds ticking down like the final moments before a game-winning shot. That's when Isabella walks in, and I swear the room tilts slightly on its axis.

She's in a suit that means business, tailored to perfection, making her look like she's stepped right out of a high-powered board meeting. There's a confidence in her stride, a certainty that's always been her signature. It's damn hot, I admit reluctantly. The subtle wave of her hair, the cut of her jacket, the way her skirt outlines her stride—she owns it, owns the room, owns the moment.

She sits, her guard up, eyes already asking the questions her lips haven't yet formed. I don't blame her; our last few encounters have been less than friendly.

"You're looking... sharp," I start, the understatement hanging between us. It's true, though. She's sharp in every sense of the word—her style, her wit, her hockey sense.

She arches an eyebrow, unimpressed by the small talk. "Dom, let's cut to the chase. What's this all about?"

Straight to the point, just like Isabella.

I take a deep breath, laying the foundation first. "I hear you're doing good work with the StarPucks," I say, and it's not flattery—it's a fact. "You've got them rallying, and that's no small feat."

She nods, accepting the compliment with a grace that suggests she's well aware of her accomplishments. But her eyes remain fixed on me, expectant.

I lean forward, forearms on the table, locking onto Isabella's scrutinizing gaze. "The thing is, Isabella, your move... it rattled some cages. My investors are nervous, and when they're nervous, I've got to fix it."

She tilts her head slightly, the gesture loaded with skepticism. "Which investors?"

I take a breath, laying it all out. "The ones backing the Apex Stadium," I say, watching her closely.

Her eyes sharpen, a flicker of understanding crossing her features. "I've heard rumors about that. Some grandiose project to transform the skyline and the sports scene here in town."

"That's the one," I confirm.

"But what I need to know is, what the hell does that have to do with me?"

I can't help but grin at the directness of her question. If there's one thing I admire about Isabella, it's her ability to cut through the BS.

"Well, here's the thing," I start, my grin widening because I know what I'm about to propose is borderline insane. "I'm suggesting a partnership. The personal kind."

The color doesn't drain from her face, which is something. But the mix of disbelief and mirth that flickers across her features tells me she thinks I'm joking.

"You're screwing with me," she says, but there's a question in her voice, a hint that she's not entirely sure.

"Far from it," I reply. The smile falls away, and I lean in, deadly serious now. "I'm talking about a fake engagement, Isabella."

She blinks, once, slowly, like she's rebooting her brain to make sure she's processing the words correctly.

"Explain. Now," she demands, and I can tell by the steel in her voice that I'm on thin ice.

So I lay it all out—the benefits, how it would ease my investors' minds, showing them there's stability and unity at the core of this supposed rivalry between our teams.

"And the StarPucks," I continue, playing what I know is my ace card, "would gain access to the Apex Arena for practices and games. It's an unparalleled facility, Isabella. It would be a game-changer for your team."

She's silent for a long moment, her brain ticking over, weighing my words. I can practically hear the cogs turning as she considers the angles, the risks, and the rewards.

I lay it out for her, clear as the ice after a fresh Zamboni run. "We make a few public appearances together, get snapped by the press looking cozy. Share some laughs, maybe touch on some cute social media posts — nothing over the top. A little PDA, but all above board. And once the deal with the investors is secure, we can quietly call it off."

Her eyes are sharp, dissecting every word I say, every implication. "And when we call it off?" she asks, her tone suggesting she's both intrigued and skeptical.

I shrug, an easy lift of my shoulders that I hope conveys confidence. "We'll have a slew of believable reasons. Scheduling conflicts, career demands, the classic 'mutual decision' bit. The public eats up that sort of drama. And even better, we'll be nice and diplomatic about it, show the world that we're adults who can work together."

She listens, absorbing, the gears turning behind those calculating eyes. Is she considering the pros and cons, tallying them up like points in a game? Or is she plotting ten steps ahead, figuring out how to play this to her advantage? With Isabella, it's probably both.

I watch her, trying to get a read, but she's as inscrutable as ever. I've seen her call bluffs with less at stake than this, but now, as the silence stretches between us, I'm left to wonder at the poker face that's giving nothing away.

"Think about it, Isabella," I press on. "This could be what we both need to get ahead. It's a partnership, of sorts. Business, purely strategic."

She's still for a moment, and then she takes a sip of her wine, as if we're discussing something as mundane as the weather, not fabricating an engagement. "And you think this charade will work?" she finally says, her voice even, but I catch a trace of something else there—curiosity, maybe.

I lean in, my confidence unwavering. "I know it will. We're convincing enough. We've got history. People love a story, and we'll give them one."

She sets down her glass, a soft clink that feels like a timer counting down. "A story," she repeats, and there's a flicker of amusement in her tone now, a slight warmth that wasn't there before.

"Exactly," I affirm. "A story that ends with the Apex Stadium deal locked down and the StarPucks stepping up their game."

She nods, once, slowly, and I'm left to wonder what's behind that nod. Agreement? Understanding? The first step in a dance neither of us knows the steps to?

Finally, she leans back, her expression inscrutable. "This is absurd, Dom. You know that, right?"

"Absurd, but effective," I counter. "It's a win-win. You get the facilities and the clout, and I get my investors off my back."

Her eyes haven't left mine, and there's a new calculation in them now, a new consideration. She's thinking about it, really thinking about it.

I wait, the tension between us thick enough to skate on. She's a strategist, my Isabella. She'll see the potential here. She has to.

The silence stretches out, taut as a power play in overtime. I've pitched wild strategies in boardrooms and locker rooms, but this? Proposing a fake engagement to Isabella Carrington takes the cake. I can see the cogs turning in her head, the slow realization that I'm dead serious.

"Are you effing serious?" she finally bursts out, her incredulity written all over her face.

I can't help but grin, amused by the bombshell I've just dropped into her lap. "Dead serious," I confirm with a nod.

She stares at me for a moment, the gears clearly turning in her head, and then it starts—a torrent of reasons why my proposal is the worst idea she's ever heard.

"Dom, are you hearing yourself? This is crazy," she begins, her hands gesturing with every point she ticks off. "It's completely unconventional. Do you know how things like this can spin out of control? And the risks—what if this backfires? Our reputations, the team's integrity, the media circus it could become…"

She pauses for a breath, and I'm bracing for the knockout punch.

"And let's not ignore the elephant in the room—you're a jerk, Dom. A charming jerk on your best day, but still a jerk. You're asking me to pretend to be in love with a man who's made half my professional life a battlefield."

Her words are like slapshots, fast and hard, each one hitting its mark. I can't deny she's got valid points; it's a wild idea, a gamble that could very well end up in the penalty box.

But as she lays out all the reasons why we shouldn't, I'm already thinking of all the ways we could make it work. Because that's what I do—I turn the impossible into the possible.

I lean back, my grin never fading. "I can be nice when I want to be," I say, a subtle reminder of that one night when 'nice' was a gross understatement. "You, of all people, should know that."

She scoffs, her eyes rolling in a way that would have been comical if we were discussing anything less than a fake engagement. "Please," she retorts, but there's a hint of pink on her cheeks that wasn't there before.

I observe her, noting the lack of immediate rejection. "You're considering it," I point out. "Otherwise, you would've stormed out by now."

She doesn't answer, but her silence is as telling as a shout.

Rising from my chair, I straighten the lines of my jacket, an outward echo of the internal attempt to straighten my thoughts.

"Take your time," I say, my tone serious, stripped of its earlier amusement, all traces of jest gone. "Mull it over. Weigh the prospects for the StarPucks, the opportunities that Apex Stadium access could open up. It's a temporary play, Isabella, but the rewards could be significant."

Isabella remains still, her posture a study in contemplation, her fingertips lightly circling the rim of her wine glass. The intensity of her silence speaks volumes; the wheels are turning, the strategist in her mapping out the vast, uncharted territories this arrangement could navigate.

As I watch her for a moment longer, I acknowledge the weight of the situation I've placed on her shoulders. It's a bold move, a deviation from the playbook, but then, that's always been my style.

With a nod, firm and decisive, I turn and walk away, leaving her with the space to deliberate a decision that could very well change the game for both of us.

15

Isabella

THE CITY'S RHYTHM FILTERS through the windows of my apartment, a steady thrum that matches the racing of my thoughts. I'm pacing the length of my living room, the cool hardwood beneath my feet grounding me as I replay the meeting with Dom. His proposal hangs in my mind, audacious and cunning.

A fake engagement. The words taste like a risky play, but I can't ignore the allure of what he's offering—the exposure, the resources, the undeniable leap forward it would mean for the StarPucks.

With access to the Apex Arena, we'd be stepping into a whole new realm of possibilities. The Apex is designed to be more than just a state-of-the-art facility; it'll a symbol of prestige and progress in the hockey world.

Firstly, the arena boasts cutting-edge training facilities. We're talking high-tech gym equipment tailored for hockey players, advanced rehabilitation centers with the latest in sports medicine technology, and ice rinks equipped with elite performance tracking systems. For a team like the StarPucks, this means access to resources usually reserved for the top-tier teams.

Secondly, the location of Apex itself is a strategic advantage. Nestled in a high-traffic area downtown, it guarantees larger audience attendance and greater media coverage. This exposure would be invaluable, offering the StarPucks an opportunity to build a stronger fan base and attract significant sponsorships, both of which are crucial for a growing team.

Moreover, the player amenities are slated to be second to none. Luxurious locker rooms, state-of-the-art video analysis rooms, and spaces designed for optimal rest and recovery. These are factors that not only boost player morale but also contribute to better on-field performance.

Additionally, hosting games at Apex would mean a significant increase in revenue. The arena is a magnet for vendors and high-paying advertisers, which translates to more funds for the team—funds that can be reinvested in player development, scouting, and other critical areas.

As I consider all these factors, it's clear that gaining access to Dom's new arena would propel the StarPucks into the upper echelons of the league. It's an opportunity to accelerate our growth, to challenge the bigger teams on a more equal footing.

But it's a deal with the devil. And not just any devil—Dom Steele, the man who's as infuriating as he is... no, I won't go there.

I stop at the window, watching the city lights dance like fireflies caught in an urban jar. This is more than a business decision; it's a moral conundrum. Can I really entangle myself in this web of pretense? Is the potential success worth the charade?

My mind is a warzone, strategy and instinct locked in a fierce duel. I've always played by the rules, climbed the ladder rung by painstaking rung. But this? This is uncharted territory, a shortcut that's as tempting as it is treacherous.

I sink into the couch, elbows on knees, head in hands. The silence of the room is a stark contrast to the noise in my head. I've always been a straight shooter, calling the shots as I see them, leading my team with unwavering honesty.

And yet, as I map out the potential paths before me, I can't help but see the sense in Dom's proposal. With one bold stroke, we could change the game, elevate the team to heights that would otherwise take years to reach.

It's time to choose—play the game or change the rules. And as the night deepens around me, I know that no matter what I decide, there's no turning back. The die is cast, and the future of the StarPucks rests in the balance of this next move.

Settling into the deep cushions of my couch, I open my laptop with a sigh, ready to immerse myself in spreadsheets and strategy. But the glow of the screen does nothing to wash away the after-image of Dom's last look—part challenge, part plea. It's annoying how he's etched into the back of my eyelids.

I try to focus on the numbers, the schedules, the roster moves, but my traitorous mind keeps veering off course. It drifts to Dom—the way his voice drops when he's serious, the rare moments when the mask of the confident bad boy slips, and he's just... Dom.

I abandon the fruitless attempt at focusing on work and reach for the novel tucked away in my drawer. It's a historical fiction romance, a genre I find both indulgent and irresistibly entertaining, this book called 'The Duke's Hidden Heart.' The book's cover shows a dashing duke in a brocade coat and a woman in a corseted gown, her expression one of both defiance and desire.

Set in the regency era, the story unfolds in an opulent world of balls, intrigue, and whispered scandals. I immerse myself in the narrative, where our headstrong heroine, a lady of high society, meets a notorious duke, known for his charm and rakish ways.

As I delve deeper, my imagination begins to intertwine the characters with Dom and myself. In this lush fantasy, I am the spirited lady, navigating the complexities of high society while harboring a fiercely independent spirit. Dom transforms into the duke, a man of power and mystery, with an allure that's hard to ignore.

Our first encounter is at a grand ball. The room swirls with gowns and uniforms, but it's Dom, or rather the duke, who captures my attention. He approaches with a confident stride, his gaze locking onto mine with an intensity that sends a thrill down my spine.

Our conversation is a dance of words, each sentence dripping with double meanings and subtle challenges. His reputation as a scoundrel precedes him, but there's a depth in his eyes that suggests there's more to him than mere rumors. Our banter is sharp and playful, a battle of wits that leaves me both frustrated and intrigued.

As the night progresses, we find ourselves in a secluded garden, the moon casting shadows over the manicured hedges. The air between us is charged with a tension that's both exhilarating and dangerous. He speaks of his travels, of art and poetry, revealing a side seldom seen by others. It's in this moment, under the starlit sky, that our façade cracks, giving way to genuine connection.

The duke's hand finds mine, his touch sending a jolt of electricity through me. He leans in, his lips hovering just inches from mine, his breath mingling with my own.

We find ourselves in a quiet corner, and that's when he drops the act, when fantasy becomes reality—kind of. "You know, Isabella," he'd say, his voice a low rumble, "all this... it could be real if you wanted it."

And I'd laugh because it's absurd, right? But then his hand would find mine, and the laughter would die in my throat. Because his touch is warm, and it feels like coming home.

In this little movie in my mind, I'm not a manager, and he's not the owner.

The kiss is impulsive, born out of all the fights, the frustration, the fiery banter that's always bordered on flirtation. It's not soft; it's a clash, a war of wills that ends in a truce sealed with lips and breath and yearning.

In the cinema of my thoughts, where reality is suspended, Dom and I are stripped of our titles, our conflicts. We are distilled to our essence, a man and a woman entangled in an electric narrative of our own making.

He leans in, the archetypal bad boy with a heart hidden beneath layers of bravado. His eyes, dark and intent, lock onto mine, a silent conversation we've had a thousand times in boardrooms but never like this, never so close that I can count the flecks of gold circling his pupils.

"Isabella," he whispers, the sound of my name on his lips a caress that ignites tiny flames on my skin. "Are we really going to do this?"

The question is rhetorical, a tease laced with the promise of a moment we both know is inevitable. I tilt my chin up, defiance mixed with desire. "Afraid of getting burned, Steele?"

The corners of his mouth twitch, a near-smile that beckons me closer. "With you? Always. But who says I don't enjoy playing with fire?"

And then his lips are on mine, a collision of everything we are to each other. The kiss is not soft—it's a declaration, a battle of wills that finds its resolution not in surrender, but in a mutual claiming. His mouth moves over mine with an intensity that speaks of every heated debate, every lingering glance that we've ever shared.

My hands, rather than pushing him away as they have so many times in anger, now pull him closer, fingers grasping at the fabric of his shirt as if I could anchor myself in the storm he always seems to stir within me. His hands are just as insistent, tracing the curve of my waist, leaving trails of heat through the fabric of my dress.

The world narrows down to the space where our bodies meet, the soft sound of a sigh lost between us, the taste of him—something like whiskey and recklessness—that has always tempted me beyond reason. I feel the press of his body, solid and unyielding, yet molding to mine with a perfection that shouldn't be possible, not with all the space our battles should require.

We break apart, breathless, the air between us shimmering with the remnants of the storm we've just weathered together. His forehead rests against mine, and for a heartbeat, we're just two people caught in the aftermath of something seismic.

"You see? Explosive," he says, his voice a low rumble that seems to vibrate through me.

I let out a laugh that's half-choked with the residual intensity. "You might be right. But remember, in explosions, it's not just the fire that's dangerous—it's the fallout."

He pulls back, a wicked gleam in his eye. "Then let's enjoy the blaze while we can, and worry about the ashes later."

As I stand there, the space between us charged with the aftermath of our kiss, I can't help but let my gaze wander over him. It's as if I'm seeing Dom for the first time—not the brash owner of the Blades, not my adversary, but the man. And the sight is... arresting.

His build is like a player's—broad-shouldered and muscular, each curve and angle of his physique speaking of strength and power. It's the kind of body that's been honed not in a gym, but in the rink, with purpose and determination. His shirt, which clings to him in all the right places, suggests the solid heft of his chest, the beefy expanse of his arms.

My eyes trace the ink that winds its way up his left arm, a tapestry of tattoos that tells a story I've never read but find myself wanting to. The designs ebb and flow over his muscles, drawing my focus and stirring a curiosity about their meanings—about the moments in his life significant enough to be etched into his skin.

And then there's his knee—the scar from the surgery that ended his career. It's a stark reminder of his vulnerability, a blemish on the otherwise imposing canvas of his body. It's proof of his mortality, a battle wound.

I can't quite believe it, this pull I feel towards him. It's like gravity, inevitable and undeniable. It's not just his looks, not the raw physicality of his presence—it's everything. The way he carries his past, the confidence with which he navigates the present, the undeniable intensity he brings to the future.

Caught in my unabashed scrutiny, I barely register the shift in his stance until his voice breaks through my reverie, laced with that characteristic blend of arrogance and charm. "What's the matter, Isabella? You going to stare all day, or is there something on your mind?"

His cheeky quip snaps me back to the present, and an impish impulse seizes me. With a laugh that bubbles up from some place free of our tangled history, I reach out, my hand boldly finding the firmness of his backside—a testament to years on the ice. It's as if his body was sculpted for power and agility, each muscle defined to perfection, a solid testament to his discipline and athleticism.

In a move that's both playful and charged with an undercurrent of our unresolved tension, I pull him towards me. Our bodies collide with a familiarity that's both thrilling and terrifying. The memory of his hands on me, the anticipation of his touch—it all converges into a moment of heady abandon.

He pushes himself into me, his impossibly thick manhood splitting me open in the best way imaginable. I reach around and clamp my hand down onto the solid muscles of his ass once again, gripping them tightly, savoring their power. I push him down, guiding him where I want him. He moves deeply inside, bottoming me out completely.

As we find ourselves wrapped up in each other once again, there's a sense of inevitability. Our breaths mingle, our heartbeats synchronize, and the world narrows down to the space we occupy. It's a rapid ascent, a whirlwind that captures us in its intensity, bringing us to a precipice we're all too willing to leap off together.

"Isabella," Dom murmurs, his voice rough, barely more than a breath against the shell of my ear. "If I'd known you'd react like this, I would've suggested a fake engagement a long time ago."

I let out a breathy chuckle, my fingers tracing the hard lines of his muscles. "Keep talking, Steele, and I might just believe the lie," I tease back, the words tinged with a desire that's all too real.

He tightens his grip around me, pulling me even closer, if such a thing is possible. "No lies between us now," he says, his lips tracing a path along my jawline, sending shivers down my spine. "Just this—just us."

The sincerity woven through the huskiness of his voice sends a jolt straight to my core. "Dom," I whisper back, my hands venturing beneath his shirt, feeling the heat of his skin. "This is madness."

"Mmm," he hums in agreement, his hands mirroring mine, exploring with a boldness that speaks of the fire we've stoked. "The best kind."

The release when it comes is swift, a shared shudder that echoes the passion of our connection. It's a moment of unguarded truth, an acknowledgment of the fire that burns between us—a fire that, for all its dangers, we're both drawn to like moths to a flame.

Lying back against the pillows, I'm awash with a tangle of emotions, the echo of my fantasy still resonating through my body. I can't believe I let myself go there, even if it was only in the secluded theatre of my mind. It was a moment of weakness, a slip into a world where caution and professionalism come second to raw, unchecked desire.

I shake my head, as if the motion could dislodge the lingering thoughts, the remnants of a scenario that should have never played out, even in the deepest corners of my imagination. It's okay, I reassure myself, it's not like any of that would happen in real life. It was just a fantasy, nothing more—a brief lapse that I can tuck away into the shadows of my mind.

But the seed that Dom planted has taken root, and despite the tumultuous journey my mind just embarked on, I can't deny the potential benefits his ludicrous proposal might hold. The exposure, the resources, the leg up in the hockey world—it's all too significant to ignore.

Sitting up, I pull my laptop toward me, the keys cool under my fingertips—a stark contrast to the heat of my recent reverie. I start typing, each click a step toward a future that's suddenly within reach.

"Dom," I begin, the familiarity of his name a strange comfort in the professional tone of the email. "After careful consideration, I've decided to entertain your proposal. However, let's get one thing straight—this is strictly business. If we're going to do this, it'll be on my terms. Public appearances, yes. Social media, fine. But no blurring lines, no personal entanglements. We keep it professional, we make it believable, and when the time comes, we end it cleanly."

I pause, reading over the words, ensuring there's no room for misinterpretation. "We'll need a contract," I continue, "detailing the specifics of our arrangement. Boundaries, expectations, duration. And let's not forget the most important part—the StarPucks' access to the Apex Arena. That's non-negotiable."

After a final review, I sign off with a formal, "Regards, Isabella Carrington," and send the email into the void.

Leaning back, I feel a strange cocktail of apprehension and excitement bubble up inside me. I've just agreed to partner up with Dom Steele, of all people, in one of the most unorthodox moves of my career.

I stand, walking over to the window that frames the cityscape. The skyline is a chessboard, and I've just made a bold play. This could be the game-changer I've been looking for, the chance to put the StarPucks—and myself—on the map in a way I never thought possible.

And as I look out over the city, my resolve crystallizes. This is it. The next move. The next challenge. And if there's one thing I know about Isabella Carrington, it's that she plays to win, no matter how unconventional the game.

16

Dom

MORNING LIGHT CUTS ACROSS my home office, casting sharp lines across the hardwood. It's another day, but not just any day. Today, I find out if Isabella buys into the crazy scheme I pitched her. I'm not usually one to second-guess myself—I make a play, and I commit. But today, there's a thread of tension knotted tight in my gut.

I've always played the game on my terms, controlled the board, but with Isabella, the rules are different. She's a wildcard, brilliant and unpredictable. I've pushed her, tested her—hell, I've been a real dick, and I know it. So, there's a very real chance she might turn me down. Even worse, she could blow the whistle on this whole charade, and where would that leave me? The thought is like a blade, sharp and cold against my skin.

I'm staring at the blinking cursor on my screen, trying to distill my thoughts into the semblance of work, when the notification pops up. An email from Isabella. My pulse kicks up a notch, and I click on it with a mix of apprehension and something like hope.

Her words are there in black and white, setting terms, drawing lines, but underneath it all, there's an agreement. She's in. Relief washes over me, a wave that cleanses away the doubts and solidifies my resolve. This is happening. We're doing this.

I don't waste a second. My fingers fly over the keys, crafting a response. I tell her we should meet here, at my place, to hash out the details. Neutral ground, no office politics, no prying eyes—just the two of us, architecting our little plot.

"Isabella," I write, opting for a setting that ensures both neutrality and discretion, "Let's set the stage for our performance. How about dinner at the Azure Room, downtown? It's a quiet place, perfect for conversation away from the hustle of our usual circles. We can iron out the fine print and strategize our next move in a setting that's neutral for both of us."

I hit send before I can second-guess the decision. It's done. The invitation is out there, hanging in the digital void between us.

I push back from the desk, standing to stretch my legs, my body too wired to sit still. I wander over to the window, hands tucked into my pockets, and look out over the city that's become the playing field for my most audacious game yet.

Tonight, Isabella Carrington steps into my world, and we begin this dance in earnest. I have to be ready, be on point, because there's more riding on this than just appeasing skittish investors or securing a stadium deal.

I've always been good at keeping my feelings in check, at keeping the game and the players at a comfortable distance. But as I think of Isabella—her fire, her intelligence, the way she's always managed to get under my skin—I wonder if this time, I might be playing with fire.

The stakes are high, the risks even higher. But that's the way I like it.

***

A flicker of something like nerves tickles my stomach as I glance around my penthouse. It's not like me to fuss over details, but then, Isabella Carrington isn't just anyone. She's—hopefully—about to become my faux fiancée in the most high-stakes performance of my life. I straighten a cushion on the leather couch, my movements precise, a silent acknowledgment of the tension I can't quite name.

As I stand in front of the mirror, I take a moment to assess my attire, ensuring it strikes the perfect balance between sharp businessman and charm. I've chosen tailored black trousers, the fabric high-quality, fitting snugly in all the right places to accentuate my athletic build. The trousers are paired with a crisp white shirt, the top button casually undone, giving a glimpse of my tattoos, the contrasting persona beneath the polished exterior.

I forgo a tie, opting instead for a sleek, silver tie clip—a subtle nod to my less conventional side. My shoes are classic leather, impeccably polished, reflecting my attention to detail.

I give myself a final once-over, my reflection in the mirror satisfying my critical eye. This outfit says I mean business, but on my terms.

Arriving early at the Azure Room, I find myself momentarily captivated by the restaurant's interior. The ambiance is a blend of modern sophistication and understated elegance—dimmed lights casting a warm glow over rich, dark wood furnishings and plush seating. The subtle hum of conversation and the soft clinking of glasses create an atmosphere that's both intimate and lively.

I'm seated at a table with a clear view of the entrance, my back to the wall—a habit from my days on the ice, always wanting to see the play before it unfolds. The rare flutter of anxiety in my chest is an unfamiliar sensation, one I quickly quash with a sip of my drink.

When Isabella enters, there's an unmistakable shift in the atmosphere, as if the entire space has taken notice of her presence. She's absolutely striking—a vision of poise and power that commands the room's attention effortlessly.

Her suit is impeccably tailored, hugging her figure in a way that's both professional and alluring. The fabric contours to her form, highlighting the curve of her hip and the elegant line of her shoulders. The cut is sharp, exuding a sense of authority, yet it's undeniably feminine, emphasizing her strengths while showcasing her natural allure.

The color of her suit is a deep, rich hue that complements her complexion beautifully. It's paired with a blouse that adds just the right touch of softness to the ensemble. The subtle details—a hint of lace at the collar, the gentle drape of the fabric—only add to her elegant appearance.

Her hair is styled to perfection, framing her face in a way that accentuates her features. There's a certain glow about her, a radiance that comes not just from her physical beauty but from the confidence and intelligence she exudes.

As she moves through the room, every step she takes is measured and deliberate, a testament to her self-assuredness. Her eyes, sharp and observant, scan the room before landing on me, and in that moment, I'm struck by their intensity—a deep, captivating gaze that speaks of strength and determination.

"Isabella," I greet as she approaches the table, my voice a controlled baritone. The underlying tension of our situation is palpable, but I keep my expression carefully neutral.

"Dom," she replies, her tone cool yet courteous. Our eyes lock briefly, an acknowledgment of the complex dynamic we're navigating.

As she takes her seat, there's a dance of formality, a careful balance between the professional and the personal. I can't help but admire how she carries herself—the confidence, the poise. It's compelling, even more so given our current predicament.

The waiter approaches, and we order our meals, the exchange with him a brief respite from the undercurrents between us. Once he departs, I lean in slightly, my elbows on the table.

"So, let's discuss the details of our arrangement," I say, keen to get down to business. The sooner we iron out the particulars, the sooner we can present a united front to the world.

Isabella nods, her expression turning more business-like. "Agreed. We need to set some ground rules for this... engagement."

And so, we delve into the specifics, our conversation a careful negotiation of boundaries and expectations. Throughout it all, I'm acutely aware of her, of the subtle shifts in her expression, the nuances in her voice. Despite the professional veneer, there's an undercurrent of something more, something neither of us is ready to acknowledge.

But rules have always been a starting point for me, a baseline to deviate from when the play calls for it.

Isabella, with her notes and files, is all efficiency and sharp edges. I'm all leaned-back nonchalance, or at least, that's the image I project as we hash out the logistics of this farce we're about to embark on.

"So, public appearances at key events, strategically timed social media posts..." Isabella ticks off the points on her fingers, her eyes never leaving the page. "And this..." she flicks a look up at me, "engagement party we're supposed to have?"

"Ah, yes, the party," I drawl, savoring the way her mouth tightens just slightly at the mention. "It'll be the talk of the town, nothing too extravagant, of course."

Her snort is delicate, but it's there. "Since when is anything associated with Dom Steele not over-the-top?"

I grin, unrepentant. "Fair point."

We continue, the tension a living thing as our hands occasionally brush while exchanging papers. Each accidental touch sends a frisson of awareness down my spine, a silent, electric conversation that we're both determined to ignore.

In an effort to maintain a semblance of normalcy, we delve into our meal, which seems almost like an afterthought amidst the charged atmosphere. The food is exquisite—a testament to The Azure Room's reputation. We're served a perfectly cooked filet mignon, its flavors rich and satisfying, accompanied by a side of delicately seasoned vegetables. The presentation is impeccable, each plate a small work of art, but it's hard to focus on the culinary delight in front of us when there's so much left unsaid between us.

To complement the meal, we've chosen a bottle of wine—a robust, velvety red that adds another layer to the evening's sensory experiences. The wine is smooth, its subtle complexities unfolding with each sip. It's an excellent vintage, one that would usually command my full appreciation, but tonight it plays a mere supporting role to the unfolding drama across the table.

The moment arrives to take the photo that will publicly define our narrative. As I position myself beside Isabella, I'm acutely aware of the significance of this act. It's not just a picture; it's a statement, a declaration to the world that will irreversibly change how we're both perceived.

I sense Isabella's hesitation, a slight stiffness in her posture as I reach out. My hand settles lightly on her shoulder, a gesture meant to convey intimacy without crossing boundaries. Despite the professional nature of our touch, I'm hyper-aware of her presence—the softness of her skin beneath my fingers, the subtle fragrance of her hair, and the elegant curve of her neck just inches away.

As the camera captures the moment, I know this image will soon take on a life of its own. "I'll upload this to my Instagram," I inform her, my voice low. "Once it's out there, word will spread quickly. We're officially in a relationship in the public eye. There's no going back from here."

Isabella nods, a flicker of resolve crossing her features. She understands the weight of this step as much as I do. The posting of this photo isn't just a formality; it's a commitment to our ruse, a plunge into a narrative we'll have to live out in the glare of public scrutiny.

I pull out my phone, opening the Instagram app. With a few taps, the photo is ready to be shared with the world. I pause for a moment, considering the gravity of this simple digital action. Once I hit 'Post,' our fake relationship becomes a public spectacle, open to interpretation, speculation, and scrutiny.

"Here goes," I say, more to myself than to Isabella, and press 'Post.'

The deed is done. The photo, a carefully crafted display of our supposed affection, is now floating in the digital ether, soon to be consumed by followers, fans, and the media. It marks the beginning of a new chapter for both of us, one where the lines between reality and pretense will inevitably blur.

"Was that so hard?" I tease, withdrawing my hand reluctantly, folding it back with my other arm.

She stands, smoothing her skirt, all poised composure. "No harder than any other business arrangement."

But we both know it's a lie. This is unlike any deal I've ever struck, unlike any game I've ever played. There's a danger here, a thrill that has nothing to do with the boardroom or the rink.

"Then it's settled," I say, standing to match her, our gazes locked. "We're engaged."

The word hangs heavy, fraught with implications and unsaid promises.

"Engaged," she repeats, and the word crackles between us, laced with a challenge, her eyes sparking with that familiar fire.

The silence that follows is palpable, charged with a tension that's almost alive. I can almost hear the cogs turning in Isabella's head, the weight of the word 'engaged' settling over her like a cloak. Her posture is as composed as ever, but there's a tightness around her eyes, a subtle clench of her jaw. The fire in her gaze flickers with something else now—uncertainty, perhaps, or the gravity of the pretense we're about to commit to.

"Well, *almost*. We're going to need a ring," I find myself saying, the idea sparking suddenly. It's a detail that hadn't occurred to me until now, but as soon as it's voiced, it feels essential, another piece to solidify our ruse.

"A ring," she echoes, the word almost a whisper, as if the reality of this charade is crystallizing before her.

I nod, a slow, deliberate motion. "Leave it with me. I'll find something... suitable."

She looks as if she wants to argue, to say that it's unnecessary, but then she closes her mouth, swallows, and nods. "Fine. But nothing too... extravagant."

I can't help the grin that spreads across my face. "Trust me. It'll be perfect."

The air between us shifts, becomes something to wade through as I stand, signaling the end of the evening. "Tomorrow, then," I say, my voice steady. "At the Space Needle. It's public, iconic—the perfect place for a proposal."

She doesn't respond at first, just nods, her eyes locked on mine, searching for something I can't quite read. But she agrees, and that's enough for now.

As the evening draws to a close, the waiter brings over the check. Without hesitation, I slip my card into the folder and hand it back before Isabella gets a chance to react. I notice a fleeting look of irritation cross her face, a subtle but clear indication that she's the kind of woman who likes to pay her way. Recognizing this, I lean in with a slight grin.

"You know, considering our... unique partnership, I think I can handle dinner," I say, trying to infuse a bit of charm into the moment. "Consider it the least I can do. Not to mention, this *is* our first public date as a couple. What kind of boyfriend would I be if I didn't treat now and then?"

Isabella looks at me, the edge of her lips curling into a reluctant smile. "Well, in that case, thank you," she concedes, her tone suggesting she's not entirely miffed.

With the bill settled, we stand to leave. I open the door for her, stepping back to let her pass. "Goodnight, Isabella," I say, my voice softer now. "Sleep well. Tomorrow's a big day."

As she walks by, our proximity allows me to catch a hint of her scent—something floral and crisp, the kind of fragrance that lingers in your senses, inviting you to breathe deeper. It's a small, intimate detail that feels oddly significant in the context of our arrangement.

"You coming with?" she asks, gesturing to the elevator.

"Nah. Gonna have a nightcap at the bar. Take care."

In that moment, all I want is to kiss her *hard*, to take her by the hips and pull her against me. I push the thought away as she steps into the elevator, the enigmatic smile on her face the last thing I see before the doors shut.

Moments later I'm at the bar with a drink, thinking about tomorrow, about the Space Needle and the ring and the woman who's just walked out of my penthouse. It's all a game, a play, a strategy—but as I look out at the lights of the city, I can't shake the feeling that with Isabella, it's always been something more.

17

Isabella

STANDING IN FRONT OF the full-length mirror in my apartment, I take a deep breath, still somewhat in disbelief at the scene about to unfold. Today, I'm stepping into a role I never scripted for myself—the soon-to-be-fiancée of Dom Steele, in a performance that will fool the city, the media, and hopefully, his investors.

It's for the StarPucks, I remind myself. The Apex Arena is the game-changer we need, the key to elevating my team to heights previously just dreamt of.

I adjust my outfit, a choice that's both strategic and symbolic. I've opted for a chic, form-fitting navy blue dress that falls just above the knee, professional yet elegant, its simplicity a counterbalance to the complexity of today's charade. The neckline is modest, the sleeves three-quarter. It's paired with nude heels that add just the right amount of sophistication without trying too hard. My hair is styled in a sleek, no-nonsense bun, a few strands artfully framing my face—professional, yet with a hint of softness.

Jewelry is minimal, just a pair of understated diamond earrings and a thin silver bracelet. Makeup is classic, enhancing my features without being overpowering. I need to look like myself, the Isabella Carrington the public knows, yet ready for a moment that will be splashed across the front pages.

I take one last look in the mirror, my reflection steady. The woman staring back at me is poised, composed, ready for battle. Yet, there's a tremor of something else beneath the surface—a flicker of excitement, a dash of apprehension, a pinch of something that feels dangerously like anticipation.

I grab my clutch, a small, elegant affair that contains just the essentials. As I step out of my apartment, I feel the weight of the moment settle on my shoulders. The cool corridor of my building is a stark contrast to the warmth of the day outside, a symbolic transition from my personal haven into the unpredictable world that awaits.

The drive to the Space Needle is a blur, the city passing by in a whirl of colors and sounds. My mind races with thoughts of the proposal, the reactions, the repercussions. But through it all, there's a singular focus—the StarPucks, my team, our future. This faux engagement is a small price to pay for the success that access to Apex Stadium will bring.

As the car pulls up to the bustling vicinity of the Space Needle, my phone buzzes with an incoming message. It's from Dom.

Change of plans. Meet me at Chihuly Garden and Glass, the text reads. I frown, confusion knitting my brows together. We had meticulously planned this out—a simple proposal at the Space Needle, enough to be seen but not enough to cause a spectacle.

Reluctantly, I steer my car towards the new location Dom has specified. As I approach the Chihuly Garden and Glass, I'm immediately struck by its unique and visually striking setting. This place is a world away from the straightforward, low-key spot we had initially discussed for our fake proposal.

The Chihuly Garden is nestled in the heart of the city, a renowned art exhibit known for its vibrant and whimsical glass sculptures. The garden itself is a vivid tapestry of color and light, with large, organic forms of glass rising amidst the lush greenery. Each sculpture is an intricate dance of color and form, catching the sunlight and transforming it into a kaleidoscope of hues that paint the surroundings with a dreamlike quality.

"Oh, you've *got* to be freaking kidding me." The words tumble out of my mouth as I take in the sight at the garden.

Stepping out of the car, the scene before me is nothing short of overwhelming. The area is swarming with people, and my heart sinks as I spot the throng of reporters and photographers. Cameras flash like lightning in a summer storm, and the murmur of the crowd rolls over me like thunder.

This is no intimate proposal.

As I weave through the crowd, the reality of what Dom has planned begins to set in. I had expected some onlookers, perhaps a few discreetly taken photos, but this... this is a media circus. I spot banners with the Silver Blades and StarPucks logos fluttering in the breeze, and a stage set up with two chairs and a microphone.

My steps falter as the full implication of Dom's change of plan hits me. This isn't just a proposal; it's a press conference, a public spectacle designed to capture headlines and create buzz. A sinking feeling settles in my stomach. Dom has taken control of the narrative in a way I hadn't anticipated, turning our faux engagement into a grand declaration.

As I approach the designated spot for our publicized 'proposal,' I immediately spot Dom. He's standing there, his posture relaxed, exuding an air of casual authority, but his eyes are alert, scanning the crowd. He's dressed in business casual, but it's the kind of outfit that on him looks effortlessly sophisticated.

He's wearing a pair of well-fitted dark jeans, the kind that subtly accentuate his athletic build without being too informal. Paired with the jeans is a crisp, white button-down shirt, its sleeves rolled up to his elbows, revealing his forearms and the intricate tattoo work that snakes its way up his skin. The shirt is tailored perfectly to his form, highlighting the breadth of his shoulders and the lean strength of his torso.

His footwear completes the ensemble—a pair of sleek, dark leather shoes, stylish yet understated.

As I take him in, I can't help but be struck by how hot he looks. The outfit is a perfect blend of casual and professional, showcasing his sense of style without trying too hard. It suits him incredibly well, complementing his confident demeanor.

But it's not just the clothes. As his gaze finds mine across the distance, there's an intensity in his eyes that adds another layer to his appeal. Despite the public spectacle he's orchestrated, there's a flicker of something genuine in his expression—perhaps an apology for the surprise or an acknowledgment of the intricate game we're playing.

I square my shoulders, drawing upon every ounce of my professional poise. This might not be the scenario I prepared for, but I'm not about to let it throw me off.

The cameras turn towards me, the crowd hushes, and all eyes are on us as we prepare to step into our roles. This is it—the moment of truth, played out on a stage far grander than I ever imagined.

The urge to lash out at Dom for this over-the-top charade is almost overwhelming. I want to pull him aside, demand an explanation for turning our controlled, discreet proposal into this... this carnival. But with every step I take toward him, under the scrutinizing eyes of the media, I'm acutely aware of the role I have to play. Getting angry now would only serve to throw fuel on the fire of speculation that's about to engulf us.

As I take it all in, a realization dawns on me. This over-the-top proposal, set against such a vibrant and public backdrop, is going to make waves—fast. News like this spreads like wildfire, especially in today's digital age. It hits me that my parents, always keen on following my life closely, will find out through some social media feed or a news article before I have the chance to explain.

Sam, who's always been my confidant, will hear about my 'engagement' in a way I never intended. And Jenna, my best friend who's been with me through thick and thin, will learn about this significant moment in my life from a source other than myself. The thought makes me uneasy. This isn't how I wanted my loved ones to find out about something so important, even if it is a ruse.

As I approach Dom, my mind races to align my expression with the narrative we need to present. I plaster on a look of surprised delight, a mask that feels as heavy as lead but necessary under the circumstances. He's all smiles, the epitome of the dashing fiancé, and as he spots me, his grin widens.

"Isabella, my love!" he exclaims, loud enough for the microphones to catch his words.

Before I can react, he sweeps me into his arms, and I'm caught in his embrace. His arm wraps firmly around my waist, and he pulls me in for a kiss that the crowd responds to with a collective cheer. For a moment, I'm too stunned to react, my brain still processing this unexpected turn of events. But then, almost against my will, I find myself melting into the kiss.

It's infuriating how natural it feels, how easily my body responds to his. Our lips move in sync, and for a fleeting second, I forget the cameras, the reporters, the prying eyes of the public. It's just Dom and me, in a bubble of our own making.

Dom whispers in my ear, "You're a natural at this," his breath warm against my skin.

I manage a tight smile, still reeling from the kiss. "You're not too bad yourself," I reply, aware of the cameras still on us, capturing every exchange, every glance.

But as quickly as the moment envelops us, reality crashes back in. We break the kiss, and I'm left reeling, my heart pounding in my chest. It's a mix of anger, shock, and an unsettling flutter of something that dangerously resembles genuine affection.

Dom turns to the crowd, his arm still possessively around me. "Ladies and gentlemen, we are so excited to share this moment with you," he announces, his voice booming with practiced charisma.

I force myself to smile, to nod, to play the part of the overjoyed fiancée. My mind is a whirl of emotions—anger at Dom for his unilateral decision to turn our engagement into a spectacle.

As Dom strides confidently onto the stage, his presence magnifies, drawing the crowd into his orbit. He's in his element, basking in the attention, his charisma palpable even from several feet away. Standing there, watching him command the audience, I'm struck by the stark contrast between us.

I've always preferred the strategy rooms, the quiet corners where decisions are made and plans are laid out. Not Dom. He thrives under the spotlight, fueled by the energy of the crowd.

Dom stands confidently at the podium, a smile playing at the corners of his lips as he surveys the crowd before locking his eyes with mine. There's a sparkle in them, a hint of the showman ready to captivate his audience.

"Ladies and gentlemen," he begins, his voice smooth and engaging, "today I'm not just the owner of the Silver Blades. Today, I'm the luckiest man in Seattle, because I get to talk about the love of my life, Isabella Carrington."

He pauses, letting the words hang in the air, and the crowd shifts with murmurs of anticipation.

"Isabella is a force to be reckoned with. As a manager, she's unparalleled," he continues, his gaze still fixed on me. "Her intellect, her dedication to the sport, her innovative strategies on and off the ice... these are just a few of the qualities that make her one of the most respected professionals in the league."

A blush creeps up my cheeks, and I have to remind myself to keep up the act, to look bashfully pleased rather than embarrassingly exposed.

"And let's not forget her remarkable ability to keep me on my toes," he adds, a playful note creeping into his voice. "It's no small feat, keeping up with Dom Steele, but Isabella does it with grace and, might I add, an incredible sense of style."

The crowd chuckles, and I roll my eyes, though I can't help but smile at his charm.

"But beyond her professional prowess," Dom continues, his tone softening, "Isabella is a woman of extraordinary character. She's passionate, fierce, and deeply loyal. She brings out the best in those around her, myself included."

He steps away from the podium, his movements fluid and assured as he approaches me. There's a sincerity in his approach that gives weight to his words.

"Isabella," he says, looking into my eyes, "you are not only stunningly beautiful, but you've also captured my heart with your wit, your strength, and your unwavering commitment to excellence. You inspire me every day, and I'm honored to stand beside you, not just as a partner in business, but as a partner in life."

I feel a warmth spread through me at his words, a response that's as unexpected as it is unsettling. He's playing the part flawlessly, but there's an undercurrent of truth that tugs at something deep within me.

"And now that Isabella is making her mark with the StarPucks, we don't need to hide our love any longer," he declares, his voice swelling with a mix of pride and affection.

The crowd is hanging onto his every word, and I can sense the story we're crafting taking root in their minds. It's a perfect narrative, one that's sure to dominate the headlines.

Before I can react, he pulls out a ring box, opening it to reveal a diamond ring that's nothing short of ostentatious. The stone is massive, almost comically so, and I can't help but think it's over-the-top, even for a staged proposal.

He drops to one knee, and suddenly all eyes are on me. The moment feels surreal, as if I'm an actor in a play I never auditioned for. Dom looks up at me, his expression a blend of showmanship and something softer, something more genuine.

"Isabella Carrington," Dom begins, his voice echoing clearly across the hushed crowd. "Will you marry me?"

The question hangs heavily in the air, a pivotal moment in our carefully choreographed dance. I'm acutely aware of every eye on us, of the cameras capturing this staged spectacle.

Standing here, in the midst of this elaborate fake proposal, I find myself thinking back to the simple, enchanting engagements I used to dream about while watching Disney movies as a kid. This grand display is a far cry from those fairy tale moments, where true love, not strategy, was the name of the game.

As I pause, the seconds stretching out, I'm suddenly gripped by an uncertainty that feels as vast as the open sky above us. Am I really just playing a part, or is there more to this than I'm willing to admit?

The line between our ruse and reality blurs, leaving me to wonder one question above all others: Am I having second thoughts?

18

Dom

STANDING THERE, ON ONE knee, with the extravagant ring extended towards Isabella, a flicker of doubt crosses my mind. For a split second, I entertain the possibility that she might back out, might reject this grand gesture in front of the entire crowd. She wouldn't... would she?

But then, her hesitation gives way. She steps forward, a graceful nod that seals our fate in the eyes of the public.

"Yes," she says, her voice barely audible over the roar of the crowd that erupts around us. Relief washes over me, quickly replaced by a surge of triumph.

We've pulled it off.

I slip the ring onto her finger, a little snug but perfectly dramatic for the spectacle we've created. Standing up, I pull her into an embrace, and the crowd's excitement crescendos. Cameras flash, capturing the moment from every angle, immortalizing our staged love story.

The next hour is a whirlwind. We're swept into a sea of adoring fans and flashing cameras. Selfies, congratulations, and questions are thrown at us from every direction. I keep a protective arm around

Isabella, leading her through the crowd, playing the part of the doting fiancé to perfection.

I can sense her discomfort, though. Isabella is a powerhouse in the boardroom, but being the center of such public attention is clearly out of her comfort zone. She smiles and nods, her grace under pressure evident, but her eyes occasionally dart to the exit, longing for an escape.

Finally, when I feel we've given enough, I signal to my security team. It's time to make our exit. "Let's get out of here," I whisper to her, a promise of respite from the chaos.

We make our way to the waiting car, the noise and fervor of the crowd fading behind us. As the door closes, sealing us inside the quiet luxury of the vehicle, Isabella lets out a long breath, her shoulders dropping as the tension leaves her body.

"That was intense," she says, a touch of understatement in her voice. I can't help but chuckle.

"Understatement of the year," I reply, glancing over at her. "You did great, though. Had me convinced you were actually happy to marry me."

She gives me a wry smile, the kind that's always been uniquely Isabella. "Oh, the things we do for our teams," she says, her gaze drifting to the ring on her finger. It's a symbolic chain, linking us in this charade.

"Yeah, the things we do," I echo, my mind already racing ahead to the next steps, to how we'll navigate this fake engagement in the public eye. But a part of me, a part I don't often acknowledge, lingers on the feel of her hand in mine, on the brush of her lips against my cheek as we posed for a photo.

The car pulls away, taking us from the spectacle we've created into the privacy of the evening. We're both lost in our thoughts, the line between pretense and reality blurred by the adrenaline of the moment.

As the car glides through the city streets, I can't resist the urge to pull out my phone and dive into the sea of social media reactions.

Scrolling through the feeds, I see our proposal everywhere—it's the hot topic, trending across multiple platforms.

Photos of us, the ring, the kiss, it's all there, painted in the vibrant, unstoppable colors of viral content. I can feel a surge of satisfaction welling up inside me. We've made the splash I wanted, turned every eye in our direction.

I glance over at Isabella, her face lit by the soft glow of the city lights passing by. She's scrolling through her own phone, but her expression is less enthused, her brow slightly furrowed in what I interpret as concern or perhaps irritation.

"You okay?" I ask, pushing a bit to get beneath that composed exterior she's so good at maintaining.

She looks up, locking her phone before meeting my gaze. "It's a lot," she admits, her voice betraying a hint of weariness. "More of a spectacle than I was prepared for."

I nod, understanding where she's coming from. Isabella's always been more about the game than the fame, more at home in strategy sessions than in the spotlight.

"But you know why we needed to do it this way," I say, trying to reassure her. "The bigger the story, the more attention it draws away from the real play. It's about creating a diversion, keeping the focus on us and off the business moves we're making."

She sighs, the tension in her shoulders suggesting she's still grappling with the reality of our situation. "I get it, Dom. It's just not how I'm used to operating."

I reach over, placing a hand reassuringly on her arm. "People will get bored, they always do. They'll move onto the next big story soon enough. We just need to ride the wave until then."

There's a pause, a moment where she seems to weigh my words, to balance her discomfort against the strategy we've committed to. Finally, she nods, a reluctant agreement to the path we've chosen.

"I know," she says, a trace of her usual fire returning to her voice. "I just don't like being the center of a media circus."

Before we can dive any deeper into our conversation, Isabella's phone chimes with an incoming email. She flicks it open, and as her eyes scan the screen, a small, almost incredulous smile forms on her lips. It's a rare sight—Isabella smiling at her phone—and it piques my curiosity instantly.

"That was fast," she murmurs, her eyes still glued to the screen.

"What's up?" I ask, leaning in slightly, trying to catch a glimpse of her screen.

She locks her phone and turns to me, the smile still playing on her lips. "That was Anthony Silverman, the owner of the StarPucks—not to mention, my boss. He's already caught wind of our engagement and is absolutely thrilled."

"Thrilled, huh?" I reply, my interest now fully piqued. "What does he have in mind?"

She chuckles, shaking her head in what seems like disbelief. "He wants to arrange a joint training camp next week between the Pucks and the Blades. His idea of celebrating our engagement and showing the world that our teams aren't destined to be rivals."

I can't help but let out a low whistle. "A joint training camp, that's ambitious. And a smart PR move." The wheels in my head start turning, considering the implications, the potential benefits.

Isabella nods, her professional demeanor slipping back into place. "It's a great opportunity for both teams. Publicity, team morale, a chance to build a narrative around unity and sportsmanship."

I lean back in my seat, mulling over the idea. "Silverman's playing his cards right. But he's not just doing this for the teams. He's banking on our 'engagement' drawing more attention."

"Yeah, he is," Isabella agrees, a hint of resignation in her voice. "But it could work in our favor. If we're going to do this, we might as well go all in."

I grin at her, admiring her pragmatic approach. "That's the spirit, Carrington. Let's turn this circus into a parade."

***

I'm now in my apartment, settled in front of a screen for a remote conference with my investors. The mood is tangibly different from the last time we spoke—there's an air of excitement, an undercurrent of anticipation that wasn't there before.

As their faces pop up on the screen, one after another, the congratulations start rolling in.

"Dom, this is fantastic news!" Robert Hastings exclaims, his smile beaming through the digital divide. "Your engagement to Isabella Carrington is the talk of the town."

I lean back in my chair, a smirk playing at the corners of my mouth. "Thanks, I thought it might catch a few headlines," I say, playing it cool but feeling the adrenaline rush of success.

Eleanor Chu jumps in. "It's not just the headlines, Dom. This gives us much more confidence moving forward with the Apex Arena. We thought that your relationship with her problem... but now we see why you did what you did."

"Sorry to keep you all in the dark," I say with a smile. "Couldn't let the news slip before we were both ready."

"Understandable," Robert said.

Their words are music to my ears. Everything is falling into place, just as I planned.

"I appreciate your patience with my, ah, tumultuous personal life," I respond, keeping my tone even but my satisfaction undeniable. "We're all in this together, and the Apex Arena is going to be a game-changer for us."

The conversation moves to logistics and future plans, but I can sense the shift in their attitude. The doubt has been replaced with enthusiasm, the hesitation with eagerness. As the call wraps up, with promises of further discussions and expedited plans, I can't help but feel a surge of triumph.

But as I end the call and the screen goes dark, a sobering thought intrudes upon my victory. If our ruse is ever exposed, if the truth behind our "engagement" comes to light, all of this could crumble like a house of cards. The investors' newfound confidence, the momentum for the Apex Arena, the public's perception—everything hinges on this delicate facade we've constructed.

I stand up, pacing the length of my living room, my mind racing through scenarios. I have to stay ahead, have to keep control of the narrative. Isabella and I have set the stage, but the performance is far from over. We're walking a tightrope, and there's no safety net below.

Determined, I grab my phone to send a message to Isabella. We need to be in sync, now more than ever. Our fake engagement isn't just a charade anymore; it's the linchpin of my future plans. And I'll be damned if I let it slip through my fingers.

19

Isabella

THE SHARP SOUND OF my whistle pierces the cold air of the rink as I oversee the StarPucks' practice. This is where I belong—in the thick of it, strategizing, commanding, leading. With each passing day, my rapport with the team strengthens, and their respect for me solidifies. I can sense the change, feel their trust in my decisions growing.

"Alright, let's tighten up those formations!" I call out, my voice echoing off the walls. The players respond instantly, their skates carving precise patterns on the ice.

During a brief water break, Tyler "Blaze" Morgan, one of our young forwards known for his quick moves and quicker wit, skates up to me, a mischievous grin plastered on his face. "So, coach, how's the fiancé life treating you?" he teases, wiggling his eyebrows playfully.

I can't help but laugh, rolling my eyes. "Oh, you know, it's a whirlwind of romance and paparazzi," I retort, my tone dripping with sarcasm. "Just another day in paradise."

The team chuckles, and I'm glad to see them relaxed. It's important to maintain a balance of authority and approachability.

I gather them around to discuss the upcoming training camp with the Blades.

"This is more than just practice. It's a chance to build camaraderie, to learn from each other," I say, meeting each player's gaze. "Let's show them what the StarPucks are made of, both on and off the ice."

The team nods, their faces a mixture of determination and excitement. They're ready for the challenge, eager to prove themselves against the Blades. They're hungry, and I love it.

As we resume drills, my phone buzzes in my pocket. Glancing at the screen, I see it's Anthony, the owner. Excusing myself, I turn things over to one of my assistant managers and make my way to the office.

The cool corridor of the stadium offers a stark contrast to the rink's chilly environment. As I walk, my mind races with possibilities. Anthony's calls are rarely without reason, and I wonder what's on the agenda this time.

Reaching his office, I knock and enter. Anthony is seated behind his desk, his expression serious but not unkind.

"Isabella, thanks for coming up," he starts, gesturing for me to take a seat.

I nod, settling into the chair across from him. "What's up, Anthony? Something on your mind?"

He leans back, interlocking his fingers. "It's about the training camp," he says, his tone measured. "There's a bit of a situation I need to discuss with you."

I sit up straighter, my instincts kicking in. A 'situation' in Anthony's terms could mean anything from a minor hiccup to a major crisis.

I take a seat and lean forward, my focus sharp as he outlines his plans. "Isabella, I'm not looking to be the StarPucks' only financial pillar. We need to broaden our base, get some investors and sponsorships on board," he states, his tone a mix of business-like and hopeful.

"That's music to my ears, Anthony," I reply, my voice laced with approval. "Relying on one person's wallet, no matter how deep, is never a good game plan."

He grins, obviously pleased. "Exactly my thoughts. And with your recent engagement, we've got the perfect spotlight for attracting some big names."

I raise an eyebrow, a sly smile on my lips. "Is that right?" I ask, thinking of the media circus Dom and I have unleashed.

"It's more than paying off," Anthony says, leaning in with an air of conspiracy. "I've already lined up an investor for the training camp. Someone you evidently know."

His words pique my curiosity, and I'm about to demand names when he beats me to it, signaling the door.

"Let me introduce him."

As the investor steps in, my heart doesn't just skip a beat; it does a full gymnastics routine.

"J...Jason?"

It's him.

"Good to see you, Bella."

Only Jason called me "Bella." I *hated* it.

Jason Sinclair, my blast-from-the-past college ex, saunters into the room, looking every bit the poster boy for a high-end men's magazine. He's aged like a fine wine—still pretty easy on the eyes, and he clearly knows it. His hair is styled just so, adding to his clean-cut, I-spend-more-time-in-the-barber's-chair-than-you-do vibe. The suit he's wearing screams 'more money than sense,' tailored to a T, clinging to his gym-honed physique like it's been sewn on him.

But along with the sharp suit and the GQ look comes that unmistakable air of Jason-ness—that blend of snootiness and entitlement that he wore like a badge of honor in college. It's all there in the way he holds himself, like he's expecting a red carpet to roll out any second.

That familiar arrogance twinkles in his eyes, the kind that says, 'I'm here, aren't you impressed?'

He's the kind of guy who's never known a life without platinum credit cards and VIP status. It hangs around him, this aura of privilege, almost tangible. It's a reminder of why, despite his good looks and charm, we were always more fire and ice than fairytale romance.

As he stands there, a figure from a past I thought I had neatly filed away, my initial shock gives way to a simmering discomfort. There's an unease that settles in the pit of my stomach, an unwelcome reminder of a chapter I had closed long ago.

All the same, I need to be professional.

"Jason Sinclair, as I live and breathe," I say, keeping my voice steady despite the turmoil churning inside. My words are laced with a forced casualness, a defense mechanism against the unexpected intrusion of my college ex into my professional world.

He greets me with that familiar smile, but now it feels like a veneer, masking intentions I can't quite decipher. "Bella, Bella - you're a hard woman to forget. I've been following your career. You're doing impressive work," he says, his tone smooth, practiced.

I resist the urge to roll my eyes. "Following my career or just following me?" I retort, a hint of sharpness cutting through my playful facade. His presence, his interest in my life, it's disconcerting.

His laughter does little to ease the tension I feel. It's rich with history, a reminder of a time when things between us were more complicated than I care to remember.

Anthony, oblivious to the undercurrents of our exchange, enthusiastically chimes in about the training camp. "With Jason on board, this is going to be a major event. A fantastic opportunity for everyone."

I nod, my professional mask firmly in place, but internally I'm reeling. Jason's sudden appearance, his involvement with the StarPucks—it's a curveball I hadn't anticipated.

"Well, then. Let's make this a camp to remember," I say, injecting a note of enthusiasm into my voice. It feels hollow, even to my own ears.

As we delve into the details, part of me remains guarded, wary of Jason's intentions. The past is a tricky thing, and with Jason back in the frame, old wounds threaten to reopen.

I can't help but wonder what his game is, why he's chosen to re-enter my life at this precise moment. One thing is clear—Jason Sinclair's presence complicates an already intricate web of professional and personal challenges. And I need to be on my guard, now more than ever.

***

Later that day, I slide into a cozy booth at one of our favorite bars, the familiar hum of conversation and clinking glasses enveloping me like a comforting blanket. Across from me sits Jenna, her animated face lit up with the excitement of sharing her latest work escapade.

"So, there I was," Jenna begins, her hands gesticulating wildly to emphasize the drama of her story, "in the ER, right in the thick of a super intense operation. The team's all there, and I'm leading the charge."

I lean forward, a smile tugging at my lips despite the heaviness of my own thoughts. Jenna has this uncanny ability to turn even the most intense moments of her job into riveting tales.

"And you know Dr. Thompson, right? The one who always looks like he's about to explode?" she continues, her eyebrows dancing for emphasis.

I chuckle, nodding. Dr. Thompson's notorious temper is a legend in Jenna's hospital tales.

"He's right there, observing, and I swear, Isabella, his face is all scrunched up like he's about to freaking self-immolate!"

I shake my head in disbelief, thoroughly entertained, yet a part of me remains preoccupied. Jenna's story, as engaging as it is, can't fully distract me from the morning's developments—Jason's unexpected entry into my professional life, the upcoming training camp, and the tangled web surrounding my fake engagement with Dom.

"You OK?" she asks, putting her story on pause.

"Yeah. I mean... I don't even know."

"Something's up," Jenna states, her tone a mix of concern and a hint of irritation. "You just got engaged, and yet, here you are looking like you lost your best friend. Plus, I'm a bit miffed you didn't even tell me about you and Dom!"

She leans back, her brows knitting in confusion. "I mean, it's weird, right? You and Dom Steele in a secret romance? It's like something out of a soap opera. When did this even start? How did you keep it under wraps?"

I cut in before she can spiral further with her theories. "Jen, that's exactly why I brought you here. To tell you the truth." I pause, taking a deep breath. "The engagement... it's fake. It's all a strategic plan."

Jenna's eyes widen, a look of shock quickly replaced by understanding. "Fake? You mean, this whole thing is just an act?"

I nod, quickly spilling out the details of the arrangement with Dom, the reasons behind it, and how it's all just a carefully crafted ruse for the benefit of our careers and the teams. As the story unfolds, Jenna listens intently, her initial shock giving way to a slow nod of comprehension.

"So, this whole engagement is just a power play?" she asks, her voice a mixture of disbelief and admiration. "That's... kind of brilliant, but also insanely complicated."

I let out a sigh of relief, grateful to finally share the burden of this secret. "Yeah, it's definitely not your typical fairy tale engagement."

She cocks her head to the side, sensing something.

"There's more—I can tell. What's going on?"

I let out a resigned sigh, knowing there's no evading Jenna's inquisition. "It's... It's actually about someone from the past who's just reappeared in my life."

Her interest piques immediately. "Who? Someone I know?"

"Jason," I said. "He's investing in the StarPucks."

"Jason? Jason Sinclair?" she exclaims, her voice rising in disbelief. "Your ex-boyfriend? That controlling, possessive asshole?"

Her eyes narrow at the thought of him. We all went to college together, so Jenna knew all about my history with this particular prick.

Jenna starts, her voice taking on a serious tone. "Jason was so... *awful* back then. Even though you two were just casually dating, he acted like he owned you."

I nod, a sour taste in my mouth at the memory. "Yeah, he didn't like me making my own decisions. Hated it, in fact."

"And after you finally broke up with him," Jenna continues, her voice laced with concern, "he wouldn't leave you alone. He started showing up everywhere you went. It was like he couldn't stand losing control over you. Remember how he would just 'coincidentally' appear at all those places you liked to hang out or study?"

I nod, the memories vivid and unsettling. "Yeah, I remember," I say, a shiver running down my spine. "It was more than just coincidence. It felt like he was stalking me." The recollection of that time brings back a flood of unease. "There were moments when it genuinely scared me. I never knew when or where he'd turn up next."

Jenna's expression turns dark, her eyes hardening. "That's beyond creepy, Isabella. It's terrifying. He was trying to intimidate you, to keep you under his thumb even after you'd ended things."

Her words hit home, echoing the fear and anxiety I had felt back then. "Exactly," I agree, feeling a renewed sense of apprehension at Jason's sudden re-emergence in my life.

Jenna's expression hardens. "And then at the formal, when you went with that guy Mark from econ, Jason showed up out of the blue. He made such a scene that you had to leave early. He always had to have things his way, didn't he?"

"Yeah, he did," I say, the unpleasant memories bubbling to the surface. "It was like he couldn't stand the thought of me being happy without him."

The memory, long buried under years of other college memories, resurfaces with a clarity that stings. Jenna's right. Jason had always been possessive, his charming facade barely concealing a need for control.

Jenna reaches across the table, her hand covering mine, her expression serious. "Be careful, Isabella. People like him don't change easily. What does he want with the StarPucks, anyway? It's not like him to just randomly invest in something without a motive."

I shrug, the weight of uncertainty pressing down on me. "He's an investor now. Wants to be involved in the training camp with the Blades. It seems like a great opportunity for the team, but with Jason... I can't help but be wary."

Jenna's grip on my hand tightens. "You think he's trying to get back into your life? To regain some sort of control?"

The thought had crossed my mind more times than I cared to admit. "Maybe," I admit reluctantly. "He always had a way of making everything about him, about his control. This sudden interest in hockey, in something I'm so invested in... it feels like more than a coincidence."

Jenna nods, her brows furrowed in thought. "It does seem suspicious. And with this whole fake engagement with Dom, he might be trying to stir up trouble, make things difficult for you."

A pang of anxiety hits me at the thought. "I wouldn't put it past him. He always did have a knack for showing up and turning my life upside down."

Jenna's eyes are filled with determination. "Well, we won't let him this time. You're not alone in this, Isabella. You've got Dom, and you've got me. We're your team, and we'll handle whatever Jason throws your way."

Her words bolster my spirits, and I manage a small smile, grateful for her support. "Thanks, Jen. Knowing I have you and the team... it means a lot. I'll be careful. I promise."

Jenna squeezes my hand reassuringly. "Just keep an eye out, okay? And don't hesitate to lean on us. Whatever his angle is, we'll figure it out. And we'll make sure he doesn't get the chance to play any of his old games."

As I nod, a sense of resolve settles within me. Jenna's right. With her, Dom, and my team behind me, I can face whatever Jason might be planning. We'll be ready for him.

Our conversation, deep in the dissecting of my complicated past with Jason, is abruptly interrupted by the familiar chime of my phone. Glancing down, I see a message from Dom flashing across the screen.

Reminder: Tonight's the big move-in night. Don't forget to bring an overnight bag, it reads, punctuated with that infuriatingly charming wink emoji.

Jenna, ever the inquisitive one, leans in with raised eyebrows. "So, how's the cohabitation going to work with Mr. Hockey Hotshot?"

I let out a sigh, tucking a strand of hair behind my ear. "Dom's Dom," I say, a touch of resignation in my voice. "He can be a bit pig-headed, but he has his moments. It's all part of the show."

Jenna's gaze drops to the ostentatious ring on my finger. "I'll say," she comments, a playful edge to her voice. "That rock is quite the moment."

I glance down at the ring, its size and sparkle completely opposite to my taste. "Yeah, well, it's not exactly what I would have picked for myself," I admit with a shrug.

As we wrap up our evening, Jenna stands, throwing in a cheeky comment as we part ways. "Just remember, Izzy, keep it strictly professional. No 'method acting' with your fake fiancé," she winks, her tone teasing but with an undercurrent of genuine advice.

I laugh, the sound light and genuine. "Trust me, Jenna, the last thing I need is to complicate this charade any further."

We exchange goodbyes, and as I step out into the cool evening air, my mind is a whirlwind of thoughts—about Jason, the upcoming training camp, and the impending 'cohabitation' with Dom. It's going to be an interesting night, to say the least. But as I walk away, I can't help but feel a thrill of anticipation. This fake engagement might be a ruse, but it's certainly not lacking in excitement.

20

Dom

Waiting for Isabella to show up at my place feels like I'm back on the ice, seconds before a game-changing play. The anticipation is a familiar thrill, a mixture of adrenaline and eagerness. I've prepped my apartment, not that it needs much. It's a stylish space downtown, a blend of modern luxury and masculine comfort.

I've made sure my apartment is ready for her—not that it needed much preparation. It's a stylish space in downtown, a perfect blend of modern luxury and masculine comfort. The high ceilings and expansive windows offer a panoramic view of the city, while the sleek, contemporary furniture adds to its upscale vibe.

As part of our fake engagement arrangement, we agreed that for the sake of plausibility, Isabella would stay at my place for the duration. It makes sense—a newly engaged couple often lives together, and it would look odd to the public if we didn't. Plus, it lends an air of authenticity to the whole setup, a crucial element if we're going to convince everyone of our 'love story.'

I can't deny there's a part of me that's curious about how this living arrangement will play out. Sharing my space with Isabella, having her here in my personal haven—it's going to be an interesting experience. I've always been a lone wolf, but the thought of Isabella in my space, in my world, adds a new layer to our already complex relationship.

I glance around, ensuring everything is in place. The bar is stocked, the living area is inviting, and I've even cleared the guest room's closet and drawers for her things—a small gesture, but one that shows I'm taking this seriously.

I hear her footsteps approaching the door, and my heart kicks up a notch. When she steps inside, it's like a live wire jolts through me. There she stands, Isabella Carrington in all her glory. She's dressed casually, but damn, even in a simple pair of jeans and a fitted top, she's a knockout. Her hair falls perfectly around her shoulders, framing her face in a way that makes it impossible not to stare.

God*damn* do I want her. My cock twitches to life at the sight of her, my heart skipping a beat, my eyes tracing over her curves, lingering on her perfect, round ass. I snap my gaze back to her eyes before she suspects a thing.

"Welcome to my humble abode," I say, my voice a smooth drawl, as I step aside to let her in. Her scent wafts by me as she enters, and I close my eyes for a moment to focus on it. Everything about the woman is a turn-on.

She arches an eyebrow, a small smile playing on her lips. "Humble isn't the word I'd use," she replies, her gaze sweeping across the open-plan living area.

I take the leather duffel she's carried in with her.

"We can send for whatever else you need," I say. "You're going to be living here, after all."

She purses her lips. "Still can't get over that."

"Don't worry about it—we're both going to be so busy with work that the time's going to fly by. Not to mention the place is so big that we can both be here at the same time and not even know the other's here. You'll have all the space you need."

I sweep my hand towards the interior.

"Let's do the grand tour, huh?"

"Lets."

I lead her through the apartment, pointing out the various features—the state-of-the-art kitchen, the expansive living room with its panoramic city views, and my personal favorite, the entertainment area with a top-of-the-line sound system and a collection of signed sports memorabilia.

With each room, I watch her reactions closely, her interest piqued by certain elements—a nod of appreciation at my book collection, a quirk of her lips at the neatly arranged row of hockey sticks.

The air between us crackles with an unspoken energy, each comment and observation loaded with an undercurrent of something more. Our eyes meet frequently, lingering just a moment too long, charged glances that speak volumes.

"So, this is where the magic happens?" she quips as we enter the bedroom, her tone teasing but her eyes betraying a flicker of curiosity.

I can't help but chuckle, leaning against the doorframe. "Only the best kind of magic," I reply, my voice low and suggestive. The look she gives me is a mix of amusement and challenge, and it sends a clear message—she's not as immune to this tension as she'd like to appear.

Leading Isabella to the spare bedroom that will be hers, I can't help but feel a pang of something... anticipation, maybe? The room is smaller than the rest of the apartment but no less comfortable. The walls are adorned with tasteful art, and a plush queen-sized bed sits invitingly in the center. But the real showstopper is the view. Large windows offer a breathtaking panorama of Seattle, the city lights twinkling like a carpet of stars against the night sky.

As she steps into the room, her eyes immediately drawn to the view, there's a moment of awed silence. She walks over to the window, gazing out at the cityscape, and I watch her, taking in her silhouette against the backdrop of the illuminated city.

"It's beautiful, Dom," she says, her voice tinged with genuine appreciation.

"I'm glad you like it," I reply, leaning casually against the doorframe.

She turns from the window and sits on the edge of the bed, testing the softness of the mattress. In that moment, an unbidden thought flashes through my mind—Isabella, on this very bed, her lips, my cock... I shake my head, pushing the thought away. This is my fake fiancée, not some one-night stand.

"Yeah, it's cozy," she comments, looking around the room. I set her bag down on the bed and nod back towards the hallway.

As we circle back to the living room, the tour complete, there's a moment where our hands brush against each other, a spark of contact that sends a jolt through me. I catch her eye, and there's a silent acknowledgment of the electricity that's building, a shared recognition of the line we're toeing.

She clears her throat, breaking the moment. "Nice place, Dom. It definitely has your... signature style."

I flash her a grin, the kind that's gotten me into and out of trouble more times than I can count. "Glad you approve. Make yourself at home, Isabella. Tonight, we're just two people enjoying each other's company."

But as I say it, I know it's more than that. There's something brewing between us, a storm of attraction and tension that's ready to break.

As Isabella settles into the living room, I head to the kitchen to put the final touches on dinner. It's nothing too extravagant—I'm a decent cook, but I'm no chef. Still, I've learned that a well-cooked meal can say a lot about a man.

I serve up the dishes—a simple, hearty carbonara with a side of garlic bread and a salad.

To pair with the meal, I've selected a wine that I'm particularly fond of—a 2015 Brunello di Montalcino.

As we sit down to eat, I pour us each a glass of the Brunello, its rich aroma filling the air. Isabella seems pleasantly surprised by the effort put into the meal, and I can't help but feel a sense of satisfaction at her reaction. It's moments like these—sharing good food and fine wine—that can turn a simple dinner into something more, an experience to remember.

As Isabella settles into her seat at the table, I head over to my stereo system—one of my prized possessions for its killer sound quality.

I flick through my collection, looking for something that strikes the perfect balance between background music and something with a bit of an edge, something that reflects a bit of my personality. My fingers stop on a classic—*Sticky Fingers* by The Rolling Stones. Perfect.

I hit play and let the opening chords of *Wild Horses* fill the room as I head over to the table and ease into my seat.

Across from me, Isabella seems a bit off. There's a distracted look in her eyes, a faraway gaze that suggests her mind is elsewhere.

"You okay?" I ask, trying to catch her eye.

She blinks, refocusing on the present. "Yeah, it's nothing," she says, but there's a hesitation in her voice that tells me it's definitely something.

I lean forward, concern edging my tone. "You sure? You look like something's on your mind."

She pauses, then lets out a small sigh. "It's probably silly, but on my way over here, I had this weird feeling that I was being watched. It's nothing, probably just my imagination running wild."

I feel a sudden jolt of protectiveness, my instincts kicking in. The idea of someone lurking around, watching her, doesn't sit well with me at all. "Listen, Isabella, if you ever feel like someone's messing with you, I want to be the first to know, okay?"

I see a flicker of surprise in her eyes, followed by a softening. "Thanks, Dom," she says, and there's a warmth in her voice that tells me her thanks are genuine. "I appreciate that. And I'm sure it was nothing. Besides, your place is like Fort Knox. I doubt anyone could get past your security."

Her attempt to brush off the concern doesn't completely ease my mind, but I nod, respecting her wish to move on from the topic. Still, as we continue with our meal, part of me can't help but wonder who might be watching her, and why. My gaze drifts to the windows, the city lights twinkling beyond. Whoever it is, if they're out there, I won't let them get anywhere near Isabella. That much I'm sure of.

I decide it's time to change the subject.

"So, how's the fake fiancée life treating you?" I start, a playful edge to my voice as I pour us both a glass of wine.

She laughs, a light, melodic sound that does strange things to my stomach. "It's a rollercoaster. Never thought I'd be part of a media circus."

I grin, pouring us wine. "Think of it as an alternate reality. It's not every day you get to play a role like this."

As we delve into our pasta, the conversation naturally shifts away from the superficial layers of our fake engagement and toward the upcoming training camp.

"So, the training camp with the Blades," I start, twirling a forkful of spaghetti. "You think the teams will get along?"

Isabella takes a bite, considering. "It'll be interesting, for sure. There's always been a bit of a rivalry, but I think it's a great opportunity for some camaraderie. Might even help dispel some of the tension our 'engagement' has caused. This is *really* good, by the way."

I nod, taking a sip of wine. "Yeah, it's a good chance for both teams to see we're not just pawns in some PR game. And glad you like it."

As we're halfway through our pasta, I decide to lighten the mood with a bit of humor.

"You know, I've always wondered if you strategize your relationships like you do your hockey plays," I joke, a playful smirk on my face.

Isabella pauses, her fork midway to her mouth, and I notice a slight stiffening in her posture. Her smile seems to falter, replaced by a more serious expression.

"What's wrong?" I ask, sensing I may have hit a nerve.

She puts her fork down, her gaze meeting mine directly. "You know, being a part of the sports world as a woman..." she starts, her voice trailing off, a mix of determination and exasperation coloring her tone. "It's not always easy."

I lean back, realizing the gravity of what she's about to share. "How so?" I ask, my own tone shifting to match hers.

She takes a deep breath, collecting her thoughts. "It's like I'm constantly having to prove myself, over and over. My strategies, my decisions—they're questioned far more than they would be if I were a man. It's exhausting, always having to justify my position and my expertise."

I nod, the levity of my earlier joke completely forgotten. "That sounds incredibly frustrating."

"It is," she says, a flash of vulnerability in her eyes. "But I love the game too much to let it beat me."

I can't help but admire her determination, the fire in her eyes. "You shouldn't have to prove a damn thing," I tell her firmly. "Anyone who questions your place in the sports world is an idiot. You're one of the best, Isabella."

She looks at me, a trace of surprise flickering in her eyes. "I didn't expect you to understand."

I lean back, a half-smirk playing on my lips, feeling an unexpected connection in our shared experiences. "You'd be surprised."

Isabella smiles. "Try me."

"After my ACL injury, when I was trying to transition into a managerial role in the NHL, I wasn't just seen as a former player. I was the wounded athlete, the guy whose glory days were behind him. It felt like I was constantly fighting against this perception that I was just this... broken warrior."

I shake my head, almost surprised at my own candor. "I had to work twice as hard, prove myself over and over, just to get people to see past the injury, to see that I had a mind for the game, not just skills on the ice."

As I speak, a sense of vulnerability washes over me, a rarity in my usually guarded demeanor. I'm not one to open up about my struggles, but with Isabella, it feels different, almost natural.

Her expression softens, and I can tell my words have resonated with her. "I guess we both know what it's like to fight against stereotypes, to be seen for more than just the surface assumptions people make."

I nod, a newfound respect for her tenacity and drive building within me. "Exactly. It's not just about what you can do, but also about breaking down those barriers, those preconceived notions."

It's a strange feeling, this openness, but it's not unwelcome. It seems that this fake engagement might be revealing more truths than I had anticipated.

"That's not all," I say, feeling more just pouring out of me.

"That's not all?" Isabella's clearly intrigued.

"Started at a young age, I guess. Growing up it was just me, my mom, my sisters, and my grandma. Dad passed when I was just a kid. It was rough, but it showed me real quick how tough women are. My mom and grandma, they were like these unstoppable forces, you know? They handled everything, no matter how tough it got. It made a big impression on me, seeing their strength. Guess that's why I've always had a thing for strong women."

She smiles, clearly liking my answer. In those moments, however, all I can think about is how *weird* it is that I'm sharing so much about my past. This is the kind of stuff that never came out on other dates.

Who is this woman?

After dinner, I stand up, offering Isabella a slight grin. "Now, for the best part of the apartment," I say.

"The best part?" There's no missing the curiosity sparking in her eyes. I lead her towards the large glass doors at the far end of the living room.

As we step out onto the terrace, the ambiance shifts dramatically. It's my favorite spot in the apartment, a stunning terrace with a sweeping view of the city and the bay. The lights of the skyline twinkle like distant stars, painting a breathtaking urban nightscape.

I flick a switch, and soft music from the outdoor speakers begins to mingle with the night air, a perfect backdrop to the stunning view. To ward off the evening chill, I turn on the terrace heater, ensuring we're enveloped in a comfortable warmth.

Isabella's eyes light up as she takes in the view. "This is incredible," she says, her gaze sweeping across the city lights.

I nod, feeling a sense of pride. This terrace, high above the hustle of the city, has always been my sanctuary, a place to think, to dream, to escape. Sharing it with someone else, especially Isabella, adds a new dimension to the experience.

We find a spot to sit, the comfortable outdoor furniture allowing us to relax while still taking in the impressive panorama. The music, the city lights, and the cozy warmth from the heater blend together.

We clink glasses, and I can't help but notice how the light catches her eyes, giving them an extra sparkle. "To our very convincing engagement," I toast, my voice laced with a hint of irony.

Isabella smirks, raising her glass. "To the best performance of our lives."

As we sip our drinks, the conversation naturally veers towards our public facade. "We need to make sure we're on the same page with this whole affection thing," I say, setting my glass down. "We don't want to overdo it, but we can't look too distant either."

She nods, her expression thoughtful. "Right. Maybe start with something simple, like hand holding, or... me resting my head on your shoulder?"

"Sounds like a plan," I reply, aware of how such gestures will mean constant contact in public. The thought sends an unexpected thrill through me.

As we talk, Isabella shifts slightly closer to demonstrate, her hand finding mine. Her touch is light, but it sends a jolt of electricity through me. I can feel the heat from her body as she leans in, her head coming to rest gently against my shoulder. The scent of her perfume is subtle but intoxicating, filling my senses.

I try to focus on the conversation, but her closeness is increasingly distracting. Every small movement she makes sends my heart racing, and I find myself hyper-aware of every point where our bodies almost touch.

"So, something like this?" she asks, her voice soft, her breath warm against my neck.

"Yeah, exactly like this," I manage, my voice a little rougher than I intend. I can feel my arousal building, a testament to the physical effect she's having on me.

I can't help but let my eyes wander over her, taking in the curve of her neck, the way her hair falls just so. The more we talk, the more I find myself wanting to close the distance between us, to see if her lips feel as soft as they look.

But I hold back, reminding myself that this is all just a ruse, a game we're playing for the public. Yet, as I sit there with Isabella, her head on my shoulder, her hand in mine, it's getting harder and harder to separate the fake from the real, the act from the actual desire.

The charged atmosphere in the living room seems to thicken with every passing moment. With Isabella so close, the air between us feels electric, every shared laugh and glance laden with unspoken implications. Emboldened by the setting and the undeniable chemistry, I decide to push the envelope.

"You know, for the sake of authenticity, we should probably practice kissing too," I suggest, my voice tinged with a mix of humor and challenge.

Isabella raises an eyebrow, her lips curving into a smile that's both amused and cautious. "That might be a bad idea," she counters, but there's a hint of intrigue in her eyes that tells me she's not entirely opposed to the idea.

"Just a quick peck," she finally concedes with a playful chide, as if laying down ground rules.

"Of course, nothing more than that," I agree, trying to sound nonchalant while my pulse races.

We lean in, and our lips meet in what's meant to be a simple, quick kiss. But the moment our lips touch, it's like a dam bursts. The kiss is intense, far more than I had anticipated. Every fiber of my being screams to deepen it, to really feel her, but I muster all the restraint I possess not to pounce on her.

Then, unexpectedly, her tongue finds mine, turning the 'quick peck' into something far more passionate, far more dangerous. I pull back slightly, a cocky expression on my face. "I thought we agreed on a quick peck," I tease, trying to mask just how affected I am by her.

She looks slightly flustered but then laughs, a sound that's equal parts embarrassment and desire. "Sorry, I guess I got a bit carried away," she admits, her cheeks flushed with a rosy hue that makes her look even more enticing.

I lean in closer, our faces just inches apart. I can smell her perfume again, mixed with the faint scent of wine from our dinner. It's intoxicating, drawing me in like a moth to a flame.

"How about we get really carried away?" I suggest, my voice a low whisper, barely containing the intensity of my desire.

Without waiting for her response, our lips crash together again, this time with a fervor that leaves no room for pretense. It's raw, passionate, a whirlwind of emotion and desire that consumes us both.

As our lips meet, it's more than just the electric surge of lust that courses through me. Sure, there's an undeniable physical attraction, a raw desire that's hard to ignore. But as I kiss Isabella, it's her spirit, her drive, that resonates with me on a deeper level.

I've watched her, seen how she maneuvers in this high-stakes world of hockey management, carving out her place, standing her ground with a kind of grace and strength that's rare.

And there's admiration there, a deep-seated respect for what she's accomplished and what she's sacrificing. I know she's got dreams, ambitions that probably go beyond the strategies and plays on the ice. Yet, here she is, putting a part of herself on hold, playing this complex game for the sake of her team, for something bigger than herself.

So, as I pull her closer, feeling her respond to the kiss, I'm acutely aware that this isn't just about physical attraction. It's about recognizing her resilience, her dedication. It's about seeing someone who's not just a partner in this crazy ruse we've concocted but a fellow warrior in the trenches, fighting battles that go beyond what most see.

Our hands explore, our breaths mingle, and the world around us fades into a blur. The kiss deepens, each moment more intense than the last.

The passion between us escalates quickly, each touch and kiss more fervent than the last. In a haze of desire, we help each other shed our clothes, the barriers between us falling away.

Standing there, with Isabella almost bare before me, something akin to reverence washes over me. This isn't just lust; it's something deeper, more profound. She stands there, confident yet vulnerable, and I'm struck by her beauty, her strength.

"You're incredible," I find myself saying, the words spilling out from a place of genuine admiration. It's not the kind of thing I usually let slip, but with Isabella, everything feels different.

As the words hang in the air, I can't help but reflect on what it is about her that sets her apart. Maybe it's the way she carries herself—that blend of strength and grace, a kind of resilience that's both alluring and inspiring. She's not just a pretty face; she's sharp, witty, and has this way of cutting through the BS that I find refreshing.

There's a depth to her, a complexity that goes beyond the surface. She's battled her way through a world that's not always kind to people like her, and yet, she's come out on top, not just surviving but thriving. She's a fighter, but there's a kindness in her too, an empathy that she doesn't let the world see too often.

And then there's the way she challenges me—not just in our fake engagement charade, but on a personal level. She doesn't let me get away with the usual Dom Steele bravado and bullshit. She sees through the facade, and in a weird way, it feels good to be seen.

Sitting here with her, sharing this moment, I realize that she's not just playing a role in our little engagement scheme—she's making me reevaluate my own walls, my own defenses.

Yeah, she's different alright—different in a way that's got me feeling things I didn't expect, things that are both exciting and a little unnerving. But as I look at her, taking in her reaction to my unexpected compliment, I can't help but think that maybe, just maybe, different is exactly what I needed.

She smiles, that radiant, captivating smile that's become my weakness. Leaning in, she kisses me again, a soft, lingering kiss that promises so much more. "And you, Dom," she whispers against my lips, "you're not so bad yourself. In fact, some parts of you are quite impressive."

She pulls back slightly, her eyes sparkling with a playful mischief that sends a shiver down my spine. Her fingers trace a path down my chest, each touch sending waves of anticipation through me. "You know, for a tough guy, you sure do have some... tender spots," she teases, her voice a sultry murmur.

I chuckle, the sound a mix of desire and admiration. "Is that right? Care to explore those spots a bit more?" I reply, the challenge clear in my tone.

Her answer is a mischievous grin as she leans in closer, her breath warm against my skin. She plants soft, teasing kisses along my jawline, each one a tantalizing promise of what's to come. I can feel the heat rising between us, an electric current that pulses with every brush of her lips.

As she moves closer to my cock, her kisses become more purposeful, her hands exploring with a gentle yet confident touch. The sensation is intoxicating, a dance of desire that has me completely captivated. With every kiss, every caress, she takes me further into a realm of pure pleasure, a place where only her touch matters.

I watch as she licks me slowly, her tongue dragging up and down the length of my manhood. When she's at the top she kisses my head a few times, her eyes smiling up at me before she opens her mouth and takes me inside.

Soft sounds fill the air as she moves her lips up and down, her hand gripping my length as she sucks me. I can't set it, but I can sure as hell feel her tongue teasing me, licking me. The woman's a damn pro, and I know that if I'm not careful, I'll come right into that pretty little mouth of hers.

"Isabella," I breathe out, my voice husky with need. The way she's teasing me, it's both agony and ecstasy, a perfect balance that leaves me wanting more.

Her response is a soft laugh, a sound that vibrates against my skin and sends my senses into overdrive. She continues her exploration, her kisses growing bolder, her touches more insistent. It's a slow, deliberate seduction, one that has me completely under her spell.

She rises, her eyes locked with mine, a playful yet intense look in them. "As much as I'd love to make you come, drink down every last drop," she whispers, her voice thick with desire, "I want more. I want all of you."

I grin, my own desire mirrored in her gaze. "Game on," I reply, my tone laced with challenge and anticipation. There's a spark between us, a fiery dance of mutual want and need.

In a swift motion, I pull her close, my arms encircling her waist, drawing her against me. Our bodies meld together, the heat of our skin igniting a flame that's been simmering just beneath the surface. I lower my lips to hers, the kiss deep and consuming, a perfect blend of tenderness and passion.

Her hands roam my back, her touch both gentle and demanding. I respond in kind, my hands exploring the curves of her body, each discovery sending a jolt of excitement through me. The way she moves against me, the soft sighs escaping her lips—it's all the encouragement I need.

"We might need a bigger rink for this game," I murmur against her lips, my voice a low growl of desire.

She laughs, a sound that's both seductive and joyous, and nods. "Lead the way, captain."

21

Isabella

Rising up from my position, I can still taste Dom on my lips, a reminder of the passion that's crackling between us like a live wire. His eyes are dark with desire, a look that sends a shiver down my spine. He reaches for me, his hands strong and sure, and in one swift movement, he flips me onto my back.

"Got you," he whispers, a sexy-as-hell grin playing on his lips.

I meet his gaze, my own eyes flashing with challenge and desire. "You think you can handle me, Steele?" I retort, my tone teasing yet laced with promise.

He leans in close, his breath hot against my skin. "I'm more than up for the challenge, Carrington."

There's a tension that's ready to snap at any moment. It's a dance we've been doing since we met, a push and pull that's as infuriating as it is intoxicating.

Then, without warning, he makes his move. It's bold, confident, exactly what I'd expect from Dom. He knows what he wants, and right now he wants *me*. Every touch is a spark, every kiss igniting a fire that threatens to consume us both.

I lose myself in the moment, in the sensation of Dom's body against mine, the way he moves with a mix of power and care. It's overwhelming, intense, and for a few heartbeats, I forget everything except the here and now.

From behind, his powerful form moves with a primal rhythm that is both exhilarating and grounding. I feel every defined muscle of his back and arms as he holds me close, his strength a protective and passionate embrace. There's a sense of security and wildness combined in his embrace, a testament to his athletic prowess and his deep, unspoken affection for me.

His thickness stretches me out in the best way imaginable, his hips colliding with my ass, the sound cracking through the room. He grips my hips, holds me in place as he bucks like a wild animal, pure power and lust in every deep drive into my cunt. I lose myself in him, lose myself in a slow trance of passion, focusing on the way he feels inside, the way he reaches around and holds my breasts as they sway underneath me.

He leans in, his lips brushing the shell of my ear, and whispers, 'You are everything I ever wanted, Isabella. Every move, every breath, it's all for you.' His voice is a low rumble that vibrates through me, turning the rising tension into a fiery crescendo, heightening the intensity of the moment.

As he brings me closer to the edge, my body responds to his every touch, every thrust. It's a dance of desire, perfectly in sync, as if we are two parts of the same whole. The sight of his strong, sculpted body moving with such purpose and passion is a vision that will forever be etched in my mind.

And then, as we reach the crescendo, I feel a wave of ecstasy crash over me, a release so powerful and all-consuming that I can't help but cry out his name. He joins me, a hard grunt sounding from the depths of him as he explodes inside. I feel his warmth spread throughout, inside of me, then trickle down my shaking thigh.

Post our passion, we find ourselves sprawled on the plush rug in front of the fireplace, the flickering flames casting a warm glow over us. The city sprawls out beyond the windows, a tapestry of lights against the night sky. We're sipping wine, the taste bittersweet on my tongue, as reality slowly seeps back in.

My mind races, trying to piece together the shift from my strictly-business demeanor to this unexpected craving for intimacy with Dom. His disclosure about his family, the way he spoke about growing up surrounded by strong women, it resonated with me on a deeper level. For the first time, I felt like he truly understood the battles I face, not just in the boardroom but as a woman striving to make her mark.

And then, there was the way he reacted when I mentioned feeling watched. The genuine concern in his eyes, his instinct to protect me—it stirred something in me, a sense of safety and care that I hadn't realized I was seeking. The combination of feeling understood and protected has unexpectedly bridged the gap between us, turning what was meant to be a mere arrangement into something more, something that feels a lot like a real connection.

I'm lost in a whirl of thoughts when I feel a gentle nudge. I turn to find him smirking playfully.

"Hey," he teases, "you seem miles away. Did I lose my charm already?"

His words pull me back to the present, and I can't help but smile at his mock concern.

Leaning closer, his voice drops to a mischievously suggestive tone. "Or do I need to find a more... persuasive way to keep your attention?"

I let out a laugh, the sound light and genuine. "Trust me, Dom," I respond, playfully rolling my eyes, "you've had all my attention, and quite effectively so."

The lightness and ease of this intimate moment surprises me. There's a growing connection between us, one that's evolving beyond the pretense of our arrangement. It's an unexpected development, but not an unwelcome one.

In the quiet comfort of the moment, my gaze drifts to his knee, where a scar—a stark reminder of his past as an NHL player—marks his skin. Without thinking, I reach out and gently trace the line with my finger, a silent question hanging in the air.

He tenses immediately, pulling his leg away with a sharpness that takes me by surprise. "Don't," he says tersely, a shadow crossing his face.

I retract my hand, taken aback. "Sorry, I didn't mean to—"

He shakes his head, sighing heavily. "No, I'm sorry. It's just... a sensitive subject." His voice is laced with a mix of regret and pain, emotions that he usually keeps hidden.

I nod, understanding. His injury wasn't just a physical setback; it was a turning point in his life, a dream derailed.

Lying there, the weight of what we've just done begins to press down on me. "This was a mistake," I say, the words tasting like ash in my mouth. "A fun mistake, but a mistake nonetheless."

He looks at me, his expression unreadable in the firelight.

"We need to keep things professional. We can't... do this. We can't be pawing at each other like horny teenagers."

He nods slowly, a resigned look in his eyes. "Yeah, you're right. Professional. That's what this should be."

But as he agrees, I catch a flicker of something else in his gaze, a reluctance, maybe even a hint of regret. And I can't help but wonder if keeping things strictly professional is going to be as easy as we're making it out to be.

"I should get to bed." I rise, glancing over my shoulder at Dom.

For a moment, he looks like he has something to say. But it fades, his expression going flat.

"Yeah. Good night."

I leave without another word.

Retreating to the sanctuary of my temporary bedroom, I can't shake off the tangled web of emotions and memories that tonight has unraveled. As I stand by the window, gazing out over the city's glittering expanse, a stark realization hits me—the way Dom used to treat me when he was my boss.

He was often rude, sometimes downright tyrannical. He wielded his authority with a heavy hand, leaving me to navigate his temper and demands. And yet, in the most intimate way possible, I had given myself to that same man. The irony of the situation isn't lost on me, and it stings.

I have a flashback to my time with Jason. He was so overbearing, always needing to be in control, and it kind of snuffed out my spark. I lost a part of myself with him, and I've sworn not to let that happen again.

And then there's Dom. Sure, he's got charm and an undeniable presence. But he's also got that alpha thing going on, and it's hitting too close to home. Despite the genuine connection we've shared, I can't help but be wary. What if his strong personality starts to eclipse mine, like Jason's did?

So, here's the plan: keep my heart under lock and key. It's my go-to move, my safety net. Falling for Dom? That's a risk I'm not ready to take. I've worked too hard to rebuild myself after Jason to let someone else come in and shake things up.

Standing there, staring at the city, I know it might sound a bit over-cautious, but hey, better safe than sorry, right? For now, it's all about keeping things professional with Dom. My heart? It's staying off-limits.

This fake engagement is a means to an end, a strategic play in the game of professional sports management. I'll get what I need from this arrangement—exposure for the StarPucks, a boost in my career—and then I'll walk away. That's the plan. No more getting lost in what might be or what could have been.

I'll harden my heart against Dom. I'll focus on my goals, on the future I'm building for myself. This engagement, this brief lapse in judgment, it's just a blip in my journey, nothing more.

With that thought anchoring me, I slip into bed and close my eyes, determined to keep my promise. Tomorrow, I'll face Dom and the world with a new resolve. I swear it.

***

The next morning, back in the familiar confines of the rink, I feel more like myself—focused, determined, ready to take on the world. The buzz of the previous night with Dom is pushed to the back of my mind as I gather the StarPucks team around me.

"Alright, guys, listen up," I begin, my voice echoing slightly in the vast space of the rink. "We've got the joint training camp with the Silver Blades coming up. It's going to be held at the Cascade Mountain Lodge, a top-notch ski resort with excellent facilities. This is a fantastic opportunity for us to learn and grow as a team."

The guys exchange excited glances, the mention of the luxury lodge sparking their interest. I can see the anticipation building in their eyes, the prospect of training in such a high-end location clearly appealing to them.

"But remember," I continue, my tone turning more serious, "this isn't a vacation. We're there to work, to hone our skills. And just because we're practicing with the Blades doesn't mean we're going to take it easy on them."

A murmur of agreement ripples through the team. I can feel their energy, their eagerness to prove themselves.

"When it comes down to it, on the rink, it's game on. We're going to show them exactly what the StarPucks are made of," I declare, my voice firm and confident.

A chorus of enthusiastic responses fills the air. "Yeah, let's show them!" one of the players shouts, and the others quickly join in, their enthusiasm infectious.

Satisfied with their reaction, I watch them disperse to start their drills, a sense of pride swelling in my chest. This team has come so far, and I know we're only going to get better.

With my spirits lifted, I head to my office to plan the logistics of the camp. But as I open the door, I'm stopped in my tracks. There, sitting casually in one of my chairs, is Jason Sinclair. His sudden, unannounced presence sends a jolt of surprise—and an unwelcome flutter of unease—through me.

"Jason," I say, my voice cool, masking the turmoil inside. "What the hell are you doing here?"

He stands up, a confident smile playing on his lips. "I thought I'd drop by, see where the magic happens. We've got a lot to discuss about the training camp, after all."

As Jason Sinclair lounges in my office chair, he exudes an air of smug self-assuredness, a trait I remember all too well from college. But now, it's amplified by his success, a story he's all too eager to share.

Jason leans back in the chair across from my desk, the picture of self-satisfaction. "You know, Isabella, after we went our separate ways, I dove headfirst into the tech world. Turned out to be a goldmine."

"Up."

He pauses for a moment, as if letting me know that he's moving on his own time. Finally, he rises out of the chair and makes his way over towards me. I put a good bit of distance between us.

I cross my arms, already bracing for the onslaught of self-aggrandizing details.

"I got in early on some startups. Maybe you've heard of them?" He lists off several companies, now giants in the tech industry, his tone casual but loaded with the intent to impress. "Those investments paid off big time. I'm talking seven, no, eight-figure returns."

He pauses, as if to ensure each word sinks in, his smile growing with every moment of my silence.

"And the perks, well, they've been nice," he continues. "I've been on more exotic vacations in the past few years than most people see in a lifetime. Bali, Maldives, you name it. And the cars..." He chuckles, a sound devoid of genuine warmth. "Let's just say I've got a collection that would make any enthusiast green with envy."

I resist the urge to roll my eyes. Typical Jason, always needing to brag.

"And the penthouse," he adds with a flourish, "it's in one of the most coveted buildings in the city. The view, Isabella, it's spectacular. Rivals Dom's, I'd bet."

I freeze for a moment, a flurry of questions racing through my mind. How does he know about Dom's penthouse? The realization hits me like a ton of bricks—he must have been following me, keeping tabs not just on my career but on my personal life too. It's a disturbing thought, one that dredges up old fears and insecurities.

Trying to mask my growing unease, I fix him with a steady gaze. "How do you know where Dom lives?" I ask, my voice steady but my heart pounding.

Jason leans back, an all-too-innocent expression on his face. "Oh, come on, Isabella. Steele and his infamous penthouse—it's hardly a secret. How many tabloid photos have been taken of him leading his girl-of-the-month up there?"

But his casual dismissal doesn't sit right with me. It's too convenient, too rehearsed. I can't shake off the suspicion that Jason is more involved than he's letting on, that his presence here is part of something bigger, something more calculated.

I maintain my composure. "Sounds like you've been busy," I say, keeping my voice neutral, trying to turn the subject away from Dom.

Jason leans forward, his intense gaze trying to unnerve me. "Very busy, I see. But you know, Isabella, I've been keeping an eye on your career too, even before the StarPucks. What you've achieved is nothing short of impressive."

He lists off my accomplishments with a tone that's a bit too familiar for comfort. "Your time with the Silver Blades, for instance. You were the youngest person to ever be appointed as their Strategy Manager. And then there's the record-breaking sponsorship deal you negotiated with PowerAde. It was the talk of the league."

He pauses, a sly smirk forming. "Not to mention, you were the first woman to lead a major team to the national playoffs. Quite the trailblazer, Isabella. It's impressive, your knack for making history."

His words, intended as compliments, feel more like an invasion, a reminder of his tendency to keep tabs on me. His close watch on my career, especially my milestones and breakthroughs, leaves me feeling exposed, a bit too seen. I shift uncomfortably, reminded once again of Jason's need to always be in the know, to hold some kind of edge.

His sudden shift to acknowledging my accomplishments does little to soften the blow of his earlier bragging. It feels more like a calculated move than genuine praise.

I nod, not giving away much. "Thanks, Jason. We all find our paths."

"It's been quite the ride since our college days, Bella," he says, leaning back with a self-satisfied smile. "You must feel a bit silly for not sticking with me, considering where I've ended up."

His arrogance irks me, and I can't help but scoff. "Silly? Hardly," I reply, my tone laced with disdain. "I've never wanted to be a 'kept woman,' Jason, a concept you could never wrap your head around. I've always been about my independence, my career."

As Jason's prying eyes continue to unsettle me, I casually hold up my hand, displaying the engagement ring Dom gave me. "Besides, I'm taken now," I say, tilting my hand so the diamond catches the light.

Jason's reaction is immediate, a mix of feigned surprise and a knowing smirk. "Ah, the engagement," he says, his tone dripping with something akin to amusement. "How could I forget? Dom Steele's grand proposal has been the talk of the town. Quite the spectacle he put on for you."

That creeping unease intensifies within me. It's clear that Jason is more than just passingly aware of my life's recent developments. The realization that he's been keeping such close tabs on me, following not just my career moves but my personal life as well, sends a shiver down my spine.

"You're starting to sound like my biographer."

Or *stalker*. But I keep that comment to myself.

"It's hard to miss such news, especially when it's splashed all over the media. You and Dom are quite the hot topic these days," he adds with a nonchalant shrug.

He snorts at this, offering a wry congratulation. "Dom Steele, huh? He's quite a step away from your usual type. I've heard he's trying to play the big business tycoon to make up for his crashed NHL dreams."

I feel my patience starting to fray at his provocations. "Jason, if you're here just to insult me and Dom, you can show yourself out," I say, my voice firm, masking the irritation boiling inside me.

"Easy, Bella." Unfazed, he stands, his smirk unwavering. "Just wanted you to know I'm looking forward to the training camp this weekend."

His words catch me off guard. "You're going to be there?" I ask, a mix of surprise and dismay coloring my tone.

"Of course," he replies with a nonchalant shrug. "It's my money, after all. I like to keep an eye on my investments, make sure they're paying off."

The implication hangs in the air—the training camp, a venture I'm deeply involved in, is now under his scrutiny. It's unsettling, to say the least.

As he turns to leave, the smugness in his step is palpable. "See you at the camp, Isabella. It's going to be an interesting weekend."

The door closes behind him, and I'm left alone in my office, the weight of his visit settling over me like a dark cloud. The upcoming weekend, meant to be a step forward for the StarPucks, now feels like a minefield I'll have to navigate. Dom, our fake engagement, and now Jason - each element adding complexity and tension to an already challenging situation.

I lean back in my chair, a heavy sigh escaping me. The training camp was supposed to be a highlight, a chance for professional growth and team building. Now, with Jason's involvement and his unsettling presence, it feels more like a chess game, one where I need to be careful with every move I make.

22

Dom

THREE DAYS LATER

THE MORNING LIGHT FILTERS through the blinds of our shared apartment, casting a warm glow over the kitchen. I'm already up, coffee in hand, as Isabella strolls in, her hair pulled back in a casual ponytail. She still looks amazing, even in her pajamas and with sleep in her eyes.

"Morning," I greet her, my voice carrying a hint of the night before—a whirlwind evening of dodging paparazzi and smiling for the cameras.

She grumbles something that sounds like a greeting, reaching for her mug. "I can't believe how much attention we're getting," she says, scrolling through her phone. Her tone is a mix of awe and annoyance.

I lean against the counter, watching her. "Comes with the territory," I reply with a shrug, trying to keep the conversation light. "Besides, I thought you'd be used to it by now, what with all your successes."

Isabella looks up, a skeptical eyebrow raised. "There's a difference between being recognized for your work and being hounded for... whatever this is." She gestures vaguely between the two of us.

I can't help but chuckle. "You mean our whirlwind romance?" I tease, but I can see it's not really a laughing matter for her. The truth is, I don't mind the attention. It's been a while since I've been in the limelight, and a part of me missed it. But I can tell Isabella's not on the same page.

She sips her coffee, her eyes scanning the headlines. "Just look at this," she mutters, showing me a photo of us from last night, splashed across some gossip site. "They're analyzing everything—from the way we look at each other to how we hold hands."

I take a look at the photo, and even I have to admit, we make a convincing couple. There's a chemistry there, something that goes beyond our fake engagement. It's unnerving, but also... exciting.

"Maybe we're just really good actors," I say, trying to keep the mood light. But Isabella doesn't seem amused.

She sighs, placing her phone down. "I just want to focus on the team, on the arena. This," she waves her hand again, "is just a distraction."

I understand where she's coming from. Isabella's all about her career, her team. But part of this fake engagement is keeping up appearances, and that means dealing with the media circus.

"Look, I get it," I say, my tone turning serious. "But let's just ride this out. Once the arena deal is sealed, we can go back to normal."

Isabella nods, though there's a hint of uncertainty in her eyes. I wonder if she's thinking about what 'normal' will be for us once this is all over.

As we finish our coffee in silence, I find myself oddly aware of her presence. Living with Isabella, even under these peculiar circumstances, has been an unexpected journey. And as much as I hate to admit it, a part of me doesn't want it to end.

I clear the cups, trying to shake off the feeling. "I've got a meeting with the investors today," I tell her, changing the subject. "What's on your agenda?"

She's back in her professional mode, listing off meetings and team strategies. I listen, nodding, but part of my mind is still stuck on that photo—on us.

Isabella's voice trails off into the background as I watch her, her fingers scrolling through her phone with that focused intensity she always has. She's all business, and yet, in this quiet morning light, there's a softness to her that's hard to ignore. My mind, traitorous as ever, starts to wander, painting vivid images of just how that softness might feel under my hands, of peeling away those pajamas to reveal the curves beneath.

I start imagining what it'd be like to step over to her, to put my hands on her hips and bend her over the kitchen counter, to pull those panties down and run my hand over the head of her cunt. She'd tell me it wasn't a good idea, but the way she'd buck into my hand, the way she'd moan at my touch, would tell me all I needed to know.

I'd pull out my cock and drag it over her lips, her pussy wet and hot for me. She'd muttered one more perfunctory line about how it was a bad, bad idea, all the while reaching back and taking hold of my length, guiding it where she'd want it.

My hands on her waist, I'd push inside, stretching her out and—

A sudden shift in her posture snaps me out of my reverie. She's looking at me now, her gaze sharp, penetrating. "Dom, are you even listening?" she asks, one hand on her hip, the other still clutching her phone.

I can't help the smirk that curls my lips. "Guilty as charged," I admit. "I was just thinking about how... focused you are."

She rolls her eyes, but there's a hint of a smile there, too. "Yeah, I bet you were," she retorts, her tone teasing yet wary. "We can't afford to get distracted, Dom. Not now."

The air between us crackles with unspoken words, with the tension that's been building since the day we started this charade. For a fleeting moment, the space between us feels charged, like we're both on the edge of something neither of us is ready to admit.

But then her phone buzzes, breaking the spell. She glances at the screen, her expression shifting back to business. The air shifts as Isabella's expression tightens, her usually unreadable face giving away a hint of concern. I watch her closely, curious about the sudden change.

"Who was that?" I ask, my tone light but probing.

She exhales slowly, her gaze meeting mine with a mix of reluctance and resolution. "That was my Mom," she says. "Apparently, my parents caught wind of our engagement. They're... less than thrilled about being the last to know."

I raise my eyebrows, a mix of amusement and intrigue coloring my reaction. "Oh? And what does that mean for us?"

Isabella's eyes lock with mine, a certain gravity in her gaze. "It means," she starts, her voice steady, "that they want to meet you. Tonight. They're not the type to be kept in the dark, and apparently, they're eager to meet the man who's 'swept their daughter off her feet.'"

I can't help but grin at the thought. Meeting the parents—a milestone in any relationship, even a fabricated one. "Sounds like a party," I quip, leaning back against the counter. "And let me guess, they're expecting the full Dom Steele charm offensive?"

Her lips twitch in an almost-smile. "Something like that," she replies. "Just be prepared. They're... intense. Think high-powered, high-expectation types."

I nod, my mind already turning over how to handle the situation. Isabella's parents, huh? This could be interesting. "Well, then," I say, pushing off from the counter, "I guess I better brush up on my 'meeting the in-laws' etiquette. Don't worry, Isabella, I'll be on my best behavior."

I have to be—the future of this fake thing of ours is on the line. Time to meet the parents, Dom Steele style.

23

Isabella

Stepping into La Terrazza, an upscale Italian restaurant bathed in soft golden light and the hum of subdued conversations, I feel a familiar knot of tension in my stomach. It's the kind of place my parents, Richard and Evelyn Carrington, choose for dinners—elegant, prestigious, and a little stiff. Just like them.

Richard, a distinguished neurosurgeon with silver hair that hints at his years of experience, sits with perfect posture, scanning a wine list with an analytical eye. Beside him, Evelyn, a corporate lawyer whose sharp features mirror her mind, surveys the room with an air of authority. Both exude a sense of controlled elegance.

I approach the table, smoothing down my dress, a subconscious attempt to present myself as the put-together daughter they expect. "Mom, Dad," I greet, leaning in for a brief, formal hug.

"Isabella, dear," Mom says, her smile more polite than warm. "You look well."

Dad sets down the wine list, his gaze piercing. "Good to see you, kiddo. We were surprised to hear about your engagement from the press. You usually keep us in the loop with such significant life events."

The reproach in his tone stings, even if I had anticipated it. "It was a bit sudden," I admit, trying to keep my voice even. "Dom and I wanted to share the news personally, but things got ahead of us."

"Dom?" Dad raises an eyebrow. "This is the owner of the Silver Blades, correct?"

I nod, suddenly very aware of Dom's absence. He's on his way, caught in traffic, but part of me wishes he were here already, a buffer against their scrutinizing eyes.

Mom tilts her head, assessing. "We've read about him. A former player, wasn't he? Quite the shift from the ice to the boardroom. We're curious to meet him."

Her tone is laced with skepticism, a reminder of the high standards they've always held for anyone entering our lives. I fight the urge to defend Dom, to explain how he's more than just a former athlete, how he's made a name for himself beyond hockey.

As the waiter approaches, poised to take our order, my mother assumes command of the table with an air that brooks no argument. "We'll start with the bruschetta and the carpaccio," she states, her voice firm, each word enunciated with precision. "For the main course, the sea bass for me. Grilled, not pan-seared. And make sure it's deboned. My husband will have the filet mignon, medium-rare. Isabella?"

"Uh, the filet. Same as Dad."

The thought that this dinner is more than a casual family catch-up; it's an evaluation, a test of my life choices irks me, but it's not un-expected. Growing up with Richard and Evelyn Carrington meant constantly proving your worth, your decisions, your path in life. And now, with Dom about to walk into this, I can't help but feel a mix of apprehension and a defiant desire to show them that I've made the right choice, for me.

The sound of the door opening catches my attention, and I see Dom, his presence commanding yet easy, as he scans the room. Our eyes meet, and he offers a reassuring smile, unaware of the gauntlet he's about to walk into. As he approaches, I brace myself, ready to introduce Dom Steele, my fiancé, to the two most challenging critics I've ever known.

Dom arrives with his characteristic confidence, striding into the restaurant with an ease that belies the tension at the table. He greets my parents with a polite firmness, extending a hand to my father and offering a warm smile to my mother. Their reception is cool, guarded, a mix of apprehensiveness and curiosity in their eyes.

"Mr. and Mrs. Carrington, it's a pleasure to finally meet you," Dom says as he takes his seat, his voice smooth and assured.

My father, a man not easily impressed, scrutinizes Dom with a calculating gaze. "Mr. Steele, we've heard a lot about you. Owner of several hockey teams, including the Silver Blades," he remarks, his tone threading the line between acknowledgment and challenge.

"That's correct," Dom replies, unphased by the undercurrent of my father's words. "It's been a rewarding journey. Building teams, nurturing talent. It's not just business; it's about creating a legacy in the sport."

My mother, sharp as ever, interjects, "A legacy that apparently now includes our daughter. We were quite surprised to hear about your... marriage."

Her emphasis on 'marriage' is loaded, a clear indicator of their displeasure at being left out of the loop. I tense, but Dom remains composed, his response measured yet sincere.

"I understand your surprise," he acknowledges, locking eyes with each of them in turn. "And I apologize for not informing you sooner. Our relationship evolved in unexpected ways, and before we knew it, we were caught up in something truly special."

He reaches across the table, taking my hand in his, a show of solidarity that sends a small, reassuring current through me.

"We both value family," Dom continues. "And I assure you, the respect and admiration I have for Isabella extend to you as well. We didn't intend any disrespect."

There's a moment of silence, my parents weighing his words. Dom's poise under their scrutiny, his ability to handle their interrogations with such aplomb, impresses even me. I can see a flicker of reconsideration in my parents' eyes—perhaps the first crack in their initial apprehension.

The dinner progresses with a cautious warmth, but there's an underlying tension that refuses to dissipate. My parents, though somewhat softened by Dom's charm and intelligence, are still clearly uncomfortable with the path I've chosen.

"So, Isabella," my father begins, his tone more pointed now, "we've always hoped you'd pursue a career that's... well, more substantial. Something befitting your potential."

Dom's eyebrows arch slightly, but he remains composed. "May I ask why it matters? Isabella's career in sports management is both substantial and impressive."

My mother purses her lips, her disapproval palpable. "Sports are... frivolous. We had higher aspirations for you, Isabella. A doctor, a lawyer, an engineer—careers that truly make a difference."

I feel a flare of frustration, but before I can speak, Dom interjects. "With all due respect, Mr. and Mrs. Carrington, I think you're underestimating the impact of Isabella's work. She's not just managing teams; she's shaping lives, building communities, inspiring countless young people."

His voice is firm, his conviction clear. I'm taken aback by the intensity of his defense, a warmth spreading through me at his unwavering support.

"Her strategic acumen, her leadership—they're unparalleled. Isabella's contributions to the sports world are significant, and they extend far beyond the rink. She's a trailblazer, breaking barriers in a male-dominated field."

My parents exchange glances, a mix of surprise and reconsideration in their eyes. It's clear they've never seen my career through this lens before.

My mother, seemingly caught off guard by Dom's passionate advocacy, softens her tone. "We simply want what's best for you, Isabella. We've always believed in your brilliance, your capability to achieve great things."

I nod, appreciative of their concern, even if misguided. "I understand, Mom, Dad. But this is my passion, my choice. I love what I do, and I'm good at it."

Dom squeezes my hand under the table, a silent show of solidarity. "Isabella's already achieved greatness," he says. "And she's only just begun. Her impact on the sports world will be remembered for generations."

The appetizers arrive, breaking the tension that had subtly woven itself into our conversation. My parents, though still holding on to their traditional views, seem to be contemplating Dom's words. It's a small victory, but a significant one considering their usual unwavering stances.

My father, ever the pragmatist, makes a half-joking remark, "Well, Isabella, there's always law school if you change your mind." He gives me a small, teasing smile, a rare glimpse of his softer side.

I chuckle, shaking my head. "I think I'll stick to sports, Dad. But I'll keep it in mind."

As we delve into the starters, I find myself stealing glances at Dom. His defense of me and my career choice, his passionate advocacy in the face of my parents' skepticism, has sparked a new kind of admiration in me. It's a warmth that goes beyond professional respect, touching something deeper, more personal.

I observe him as he interacts with my parents, effortlessly charming yet forthright, a combination that seems to gradually wear down their defenses. There's a genuineness to his demeanor that's hard to resist, even for my usually stoic parents.

The conversation shifts to lighter topics, and the atmosphere at the table becomes more relaxed. My parents share stories from their careers, and Dom reciprocates with anecdotes from his days on the ice and his transition into management. I find myself laughing more freely, the earlier tension dissipating like morning fog.

Who is this Dom? And why the hell is he making me feel ways I *never* thought I'd feel about a man?

24

Dom

As we walk through the cool Seattle streets, I notice Isabella's uncharacteristic silence. The usually sharp and spirited woman beside me seems lost in thought, a stark contrast to her usual demeanor.

I can't resist the opportunity to tease her. "What's the matter, Isabella? Embarrassed I made best buds with your old man at dinner?" I ask with a chuckle, throwing her a cocky grin.

She glances at me, her lips curving into a small smile. "No, Dom, that's not it," she says, her voice softer than usual. "Actually, it's the opposite. I wanted to thank you... for standing up for me tonight."

Her words catch me off guard. It's rare for Isabella to show this kind of vulnerability. "Thank me?" I ask, raising an eyebrow. "I was just speaking the truth."

She stops walking and turns to face me, her gaze steady. "I know, but... it's not easy with my parents. I believe in what I do, in my career. But with them, it's always been a challenge to feel that my path is valid. To have someone like you, who not only understands but also believes in me... it means a lot. Even if this whole thing between us is just for show."

I look at her, really look at her. There's an earnestness in her eyes that's hard to ignore. "Isabella, you don't need anyone to validate your choices. You're brilliant at what you do. Anyone with half a brain can see that."

She lets out a soft laugh. "Yeah, but it's different coming from you. You've been there, you know the game, the industry. You get it in a way they never will."

I nod, understanding what she means. "Well, I've got your back, Carrington. Fake engagement or not, I respect the hell out of you. And for what it's worth, I think you're doing an incredible job."

Her smile grows, and there's a spark in her eyes that tells me my words have hit home. "Thanks, Dom. That means a lot, really."

We resume walking, the city lights casting a warm glow around us. The air between us feels different now, charged with an unspoken acknowledgment of the mutual respect and perhaps something more, a connection that's been growing despite our best efforts to keep things strictly professional.

As we approach our apartment building, I stop and turn to face her. "Isabella, just remember one thing. This whole arrangement... it doesn't define you. You're more than capable of standing on your own two feet. And if you ever need someone to remind you of that, you know where to find me."

She looks up at me, and there's a hint of something like appreciation in her gaze. "Thanks, Dom."

The elevator ride up to our shared apartment is a quiet one, the soft hum of the machinery the only sound breaking the silence. Standing beside Isabella, I can't help but steal glances at her from the corner of my eye. There's something about her tonight, maybe it's the way the soft light of the elevator accentuates the contours of her face or the thoughtful look in her eyes, but she looks stunningly beautiful.

I find my thoughts wandering, replaying our earlier conversation and the heartfelt words I shared at dinner. As the floors tick by, I reflect on the fact that what I said wasn't just a front for her parents—it really was the truth. Isabella is unlike any woman I've ever known, her strength and determination captivating me in ways I hadn't anticipated.

The elevator dings, signaling our arrival at our floor, and we step out into the quiet hallway. We walk side by side to our apartment door, the tension between us palpable. It's a strange and unfamiliar feeling, this mix of professional respect and personal attraction.

As Isabella unlocks the door and steps inside, she pauses, turning to face me. Her eyes meet mine, and for a moment, there's a silent conversation that passes between us. I can see a hint of something more in her gaze, a reflection of the same turmoil I feel.

In that instant, I want nothing more than to ask her to stay with me, to share a bottle of wine and see where the night leads. The desire to be with her, to explore this growing connection, is overwhelming. But as quickly as the moment comes, it passes. Isabella gives me a small, somewhat wistful smile before turning to head towards her room.

"Goodnight, Dom," she says softly over her shoulder.

"Goodnight, Isabella," I reply, watching her disappear down the hallway.

I stand there for a moment, the weight of the unspoken words hanging heavily in the air. Then, with a deep sigh, I head into my own room, closing the door behind me.

As I sit on the edge of my bed, I can't shake off the feeling that this fake engagement is becoming something more, something real and complicated. I've always been a man who knows what he wants, but this... this is uncharted territory for me.

Lying back, I stare up at the ceiling, my mind a whirlwind of thoughts about Isabella. The lines between our professional arrangement and personal feelings are blurring, and for the first time, I'm not sure what to do. The idea both excites and unnerves me.

I close my eyes, images of Isabella filling my mind. Her laughter, her intensity, her passion for what she does. She's gotten under my skin in a way no one else has. As sleep finally claims me, one thought lingers—this fake engagement might just be the realest thing I've ever experienced, and I'm not sure I'm ready for what that means.

***

THAT WEEKEND

The Silver Blades and I are on the final stretch to the training camp up in the Cascades, the rugged beauty of the Pacific Northwest unfolding around us. Towering pines and snow-capped peaks dominate the landscape, a picturesque backdrop that never fails to impress.

I'm riding up front with Sam, Isabella's brother, and the conversation takes a turn I'm not entirely comfortable with. Sam's been going on about how stoked he is to potentially become my brother-in-law.

"Man, D, having you officially in the family? That's going to be epic," he says, his enthusiasm genuine.

I feel a twinge of guilt twist in my gut. Here's my best friend, excited about a lie. I steal a glance at his profile, his eyes bright with anticipation, and I mentally bookmark a conversation I need to have with Isabella about how we handle this with Sam. It's one thing to fool the public, but deceiving Sam feels like crossing a line.

"Yeah, man. Epic."

As the bus weaves through the mountain roads, the chatter among the team fades into background noise. My thoughts are a jumble—the upcoming camp, Isabella, and the complex web we've woven.

Suddenly, Sam's voice snaps me back to the present. "Hey, check this out," he says, holding up his phone. "There's a snowstorm brewing. Might hit us tonight."

I lean over to look at the weather app on his screen. Sure enough, a heavy snowstorm is predicted to roll in, potentially blanketing the area in white. A part of me welcomes the challenge—a bit of snow never deterred a hockey player. But another part is wary of the complications it might bring, especially with this Jason Sinclair prick lurking around like a shark.

"We better get settled in fast then," I say, trying to keep the concern out of my voice. "Don't want the team caught out in that."

Sam nods, his focus shifting to the road ahead. "Yeah, good call. This is going to be one hell of a camp."

As the bus continues its ascent, the skies darken, and the first flakes of snow start to drift lazily down.

We pull up to the training camp, the guys are practically bouncing in their seats, ready to hit the ice. The energy is infectious, but I find myself scanning for Isabella, wondering how she's settling in.

I step off the bus into the crisp mountain air, the snow adding a pristine touch to the rustic charm of the camp. Heading towards one of the main cabins, I feel a sense of purpose. This is where the real work begins, where we get ready for the push into the second half of the season.

As I push open the door to the administrative cabin, I'm hit by the sound of raised voices. It doesn't take long to recognize one of them as Isabella's, sharp and firm. The other, I quickly deduce, is Jason Sinclair.

Their argument is heated, with Jason's voice carrying an edge of condescension. He's overstepping, meddling in details that are clearly under Isabella's purview. I can't make out the specifics, but his tone is enough to tell me he's being more than just a regular investor.

Without hesitation, I step into the fray. "Is there a problem here?" I ask, my voice carrying enough authority to cut through the tension.

Jason turns, his expression shifting to one of mock surprise. "Ah, Dom, just the man. Didn't mean to step on any toes here," he says, his tone dripping with insincerity.

"You two already fighting?"

"It's nothing," Isabella fires back, clearly not happy with whatever their conversation had been about.

Jason smirks.

"Don't want to get in the way of lovebirds planning their big day," he says with a sneer, his eyes flicking between Isabella and me. The sarcasm in his voice is almost tangible.

"Yeah, not getting in the way—good idea." Isabella's looking like she wants to rip him apart with her bare hands.

As he strides out of the cabin, a sense of relief washes over the room. I turn to Isabella, my expression filled with concern. "What the hell was that about?" I ask, my voice low but insistent. The look in my eyes is searching, hoping she'll open up about what's really going on with Jason Sinclair.

Isabella brushes off the encounter with a nonchalant shrug. "Just a minor disagreement about logistics. Nothing I can't handle."

I study her for a moment, knowing there's more to it than she's letting on. But I respect her enough not to pry, at least not here, not now.

"Alright," I say, a bit unconvinced. "Just remember, I've got your back in this. Whatever you need."

She offers a small, grateful smile, and we shift our focus to the task at hand—getting the team ready for what promises to be an intense training camp. I can't help but feel a nagging concern about Jason's involvement. Something about him doesn't sit right with me, and I make a mental note to keep a close eye on him. For Isabella's sake, if nothing else.

"Well, now that you're here," she says. "How about we go over the weekend?"

"Works for me."

As we settle into planning the weekend's activities, the conversation flows smoothly between Isabella and me. We're discussing team strategies, but there's an undercurrent of something else, something less tangible.

She nods, slipping into professional mode. Crazy as it might sound, she's sexy as *fuck* when she's like this.

"Practice game's first up," she says.

"Right," I reply. "Looking forward to it. Good way to see where the Blades and Pucks are both at, see where we need improvement."

"Exactly what I was thinking. Then we've got the first drills after that. I'm considering something that challenges their agility," Isabella suggests, her eyes focused on the clipboard in her hands.

"Yeah, agility's key," I agree, leaning in closer to look at her notes. "But let's not forget about endurance. Maybe mix in some long sprints?"

Her eyes meet mine, a hint of a challenge in them. "You planning on showing us how it's done, Mr. Former NHL Star?" she teases.

I chuckle, leaning back against the wall. "Maybe I will. Got to show these young guys they still have a lot to learn."

The air between us crackles with unspoken words. Isabella bites her lip slightly, pondering over the schedule. "We could also do some paired exercises. You know, to foster some team spirit."

"Paired exercises, huh?" I quip, my voice dropping an octave. "Sounds like an opportunity for some... close teamwork."

Isabella smirks, meeting my gaze squarely. "Oh, I'm sure you're all about teamwork, Dom."

For a moment, we're locked in a moment of charged silence, our eyes doing all the talking. The space around us feels smaller, more intimate.

I take a step closer, under the pretense of looking at her notes again. "You know, Isabella, teamwork is all about understanding each other's strengths and weaknesses."

She nods, her breath catching slightly as I hover just inches away. "Understanding is crucial," she replies, her voice a whisper.

Our faces are so close now; I could count the flecks of gold in her eyes. The urge to close the gap, to taste the words right off her lips, is overwhelming.

But just as the tension reaches its peak, the door swings open. Carter, one of the Blades' assistant coaches, enters like a cold splash of reality, abruptly pulling us out of the moment.

"Hey, Dom, Isabella, do we have extra pucks in storage? Some of the guys were asking," he inquires, looking between us expectantly.

"Yeah, there should be some in the main storage locker," I reply, trying to sound nonchalant. "I'll check it out in a bit."

Isabella, who's been unusually quiet, suddenly speaks up, her voice slightly higher than usual. "I, um, I should go check on the team's arrangements," she says hurriedly, avoiding my gaze. "Make sure everything's set for tomorrow."

I nod, watching as she makes a quick exit, her usual composed self seemingly rattled. The coach, still none the wiser, continues with his questions, but my responses are automatic. My mind is still in that moment, the intensity of our near-kiss lingering like a phantom touch.

Finally, seizing a break in the conversation, I excuse myself, claiming a need to sort out some last-minute details. As I step out of the cabin, the cool mountain air does little to ease the heat that Isabella's proximity sparked.

This attraction, it's like a live wire between us, dangerous and unpredictable. I know I need to keep my distance, to maintain the boundaries of our arrangement. But as I walk away, the memory of her so close, the way my name sounded on her lips, haunts me.

I'm playing with fire, and the more I'm around Isabella, the harder it is to ignore the burn. It's a line I can't afford to cross, not just for the sake of our fake engagement, but for everything else at stake. Yet, as I head back to my own tasks, I can't shake the feeling that this is only the beginning.

25

Isabella

RUSHING INTO MY CABIN, a quaint, rustic sanctuary nestled among the pines, I take a moment to catch my breath. The exterior's log walls and the promise of an old-world charm had me expecting something akin to a lumberjack's abode, but inside, it's a different world. Warm, inviting, with plush furnishings and modern amenities skillfully woven into its vintage charm. It's cozy and intimate, the kind of place that would be perfect for a romantic getaway—if only the circumstances were different.

I drop my bag onto the soft, inviting bed and sink down beside it. The soft light from the bedside lamp casts a warm glow across the room, accentuating the fusion of rustic wood and contemporary decor. It's peaceful here, a stark contrast to the whirlwind of emotions churning inside me.

Closing my eyes, I replay the moments in the main cabin with Dom—how close we came to crossing a line. My heart races at the memory, a mix of exhilaration and fear. It's like walking a tightrope; thrilling but dangerous. I'm playing with fire, and I know it. The way his eyes locked onto mine, the heat from his body, the sound of his voice—it's all too much. Too intense. Too real.

I lean back against the pillows, my mind racing. This fake engagement, meant to be a simple business arrangement, is turning into something complex and unnerving. I can't afford to lose focus, not when I've worked so hard to get where I am. Being seen as Dom Steele's fiancée, even if it's all a façade, it's a double-edged sword. On one hand, it's the perfect cover, a shield against any unwanted attention, especially from someone like Jason. But on the other, it's a trap, luring me into a dangerous dance of pretend that feels increasingly genuine.

The cabin, for all its comfort, feels like a gilded cage at this moment. I stand up, pacing the room. The walls adorned with vintage ski gear and framed black-and-white photos of mountain landscapes seem to close in on me. I've always prided myself on my control, my ability to keep personal and professional lives separate. But with Dom, those lines are blurring, and it scares me.

A part of me, a reckless, daring part, wants to give in to this madness, to explore this undeniable chemistry between us. But the rational part, the part that's been my guiding force, screams caution. Dom Steele isn't just any man; he's a former hockey star, a prominent figure with his own set of complications. And I'm a woman who's built her career on being unyielding and focused.

I glance out the window, where the snow is gently falling, blanketing the world in a pristine layer of white. It's beautiful, serene, and for a moment, I let myself get lost in the tranquility of it all. But as the snowflakes dance in the wind, I'm reminded of the storm brewing in my life, a storm that threatens to upend everything I've worked for.

With a deep, steadying breath, I make a decision. I need to put distance between Dom and me, to cool down this simmering tension before it boils over. It's the only way to protect both our careers, and more importantly, my heart. As I lie back down, I vow to keep my guard up, to not let Dom Steele's charm and intensity break through the walls I've carefully built around myself. It's a promise I intend to keep, no matter how hard it proves to be.

Settled in my cabin, I pull out my phone, and right on cue, Jenna's text bubbles up on the screen. Her message is brimming with curiosity, typical Jenna style.

So, how's it going with Mr. Tall, Dark, and fake fiancé? Spill the tea, Iz! her text reads.

I let out a wry chuckle, typing back a response while sinking further into the plush cushions of the armchair. *Everything's fine. Normal, even,* I reply, trying to sound convincing even through text.

Before I can put the phone down, another message from Jenna pops up. *Fine? Normal? This is Dom Steele we're talking about. I give it two days before you two are at it again."*

Her words, meant to be light and teasing, strike a chord. A mix of guilt and denial stirs within me. I start typing a response, a denial loaded with my usual sass, but a sudden wave of nausea hits me out of nowhere. My phone slips from my fingers as I lurch to my feet, a cold sweat breaking out across my forehead.

Staggering to the restroom, the world tilts precariously around me. I barely make it to the toilet before the contents of my stomach revolt, leaving me gasping and shaking. The cool tile against my cheek is the only relief from the sudden, overwhelming sickness.

As the wave of nausea slowly recedes, leaving me drained and confused, a thousand thoughts race through my mind. Stress, maybe? The altitude? Or something I ate? But a nagging voice in the back of my mind whispers other possibilities, ones I'm not ready to face.

I sit back, leaning against the bathroom wall, trying to steady my breathing. My phone buzzes again, likely Jenna with more probing questions or playful assumptions. But right now, I don't have the energy or the desire to dive back into that conversation.

With a deep, shaky breath, I stand up, splashing water on my face and trying to erase the pallor of sickness. Glancing in the mirror, I hardly recognize the woman staring back at me—pale, unsettled, and suddenly vulnerable.

I need to get a grip. This weekend is crucial, and I can't afford any distractions or weaknesses, least of all an unexplained bout of illness. Pushing aside the lingering discomfort and the barrage of questions in my mind, I straighten up, determined to regain my composure.

But as I step out of the restroom, the unease lingers, a shadow I can't quite shake off. It's going to be a long weekend, and I can't help but wonder what other surprises are in store. For now, I need to focus on the training camp and keep my personal turmoil locked away. Whatever this is, it can wait. It has to.

Back in the main room of my cabin, my phone buzzes again. I hesitantly pick it up, expecting more of Jenna's relentless teasing. Instead, what I see on the screen brings an involuntary laugh out of me.

I'll bet you a spa day you're thinking about his abs right now, Jenna's message reads. Classic Jenna—always finding a way to lighten the mood, even when she doesn't know the half of it.

I consider telling her about the nausea, about how off I've been feeling. But I dismiss the thought almost as quickly as it comes. It's probably nothing, just the stress of the situation catching up with me. Or maybe something I ate. I send a quick reply, a light-hearted quip to match her tone, and set the phone aside.

Standing there, in the middle of my cabin, a strange sensation washes over me—the feeling of being watched. I glance around the cozy interior, half-expecting to find someone lurking outside the windows. But all I see is the peaceful snowscape, the trees standing silent and still in the twilight.

"Get a grip, Isabella," I mutter to myself, shaking off the eerie feeling. It's just nerves, nothing more. The events of the day, the close call with Dom, the unexpected sickness—it's all playing tricks on my mind.

Stepping out of my cabin, I pull my coat tighter around me, the crisp late afternoon air snapping me back to the present. I can feel the last remnants of unease slipping away, replaced by a laser focus on the task at hand—the first practice game.

As I stride towards the main lodge, the crunch of snow under my boots grounds me. This weekend is more than just a training camp; it's a showcase of what the StarPucks are capable of. We're here to build a cohesive team, to lay down the foundation of our future successes. It's a chance to really cement my role as their leader and strategist.

I can't let personal distractions cloud my judgment. This is about the team, about our collective goals. It's about proving to Dom, to the Blades, and most importantly, to myself, that I'm more than capable of steering this ship.

As the lights of the lodge grow brighter in the distance, I square my shoulders and quicken my pace. It's time to get to work, to dive into the training camp with all the energy and focus I can muster. Whatever personal turmoil I'm facing, whatever strange sensations are haunting me, they'll have to wait.

Right now, there's a job to do, and I'm more than ready to rise to the challenge.

26

Dom

Stepping out of my cabin, I shove the near-kiss with Isabella to the back of my mind. The memory of her lips tantalizingly close to mine teases at the edges of my thoughts. I want to kiss her, more than I've wanted anything in a long damn time.

But it's not just about desire—there's something about Isabella that threatens to unravel my usual cool composure. I can't afford that, not now. Especially not when it feels like she's edging closer to seeing the real me, beyond the façade.

I shake off these thoughts, I make my way to the rink, feeling the crisp mountain air biting at my skin. The scent of impending snow fills my nostrils, a reminder of the rumored blizzard. A light dusting of snow is already on the ground, crunching under my boots with each step.

As I step into the rink, the familiar chill and echo of the space wrap around me like an old friend. The Silver Blades are already here, scattered across the ice, stretching and prepping. Their energy is palpable, a mix of focus and excitement that I know all too well.

Then, Isabella arrives with the StarPucks, and the atmosphere shifts subtly. She steps onto the ice, all sharp efficiency and commanding presence. Watching her, I feel a surge of something that's not just competitiveness. It's respect, mixed with a dash of something more dangerous.

I initially hang back, watching Rick guide the Blades with his seasoned expertise. The guys are responding well, their movements fluid and focused, but as I watch, a familiar itch begins to take hold. The more I observe, the more I feel that urge to jump in, to take the reins and push the team even harder.

I glance over at Rick, who's deep in his element, barking out instructions with a natural authority. The respect I have for him is immense, but the coach in me is struggling to stay on the sidelines.

"Rick," I call out, striding over to him. "Mind if I step in for a bit?"

He turns, a knowing look in his eyes, and nods. "Go for it, Dom," he says, stepping aside with a wry smile. "Let's see if you still got that coaching magic."

Grinning, I step onto the ice, feeling the familiar thrill of coaching surge through me. I quickly gather the team, laying out my plan with a rapid-fire intensity. The guys nod, their faces lighting up with renewed vigor as I inject my energy into the game.

Across the ice, Isabella is doing the same with the StarPucks, her presence commanding and focused. Our eyes meet for a brief moment, and I can't resist flashing her a smirk. It's a silent challenge, an unspoken acknowledgement of the competition between us that goes beyond this practice game.

The game resumes with me at the helm, and the intensity ramps up. I'm calling out plays, repositioning players, my voice echoing across the rink. The Blades respond with an aggressive zeal, their game elevating under my direction.

Isabella counters with her own strategic moves, her team adapting and responding with equal precision. It's a chess match on ice, each of us trying to outmaneuver the other. Our glances across the rink are filled with a mix of rivalry and something else—a tension that's hard to define but impossible to ignore.

As the game unfolds on the ice, my competitive edge sharpens to a fine point. I'm in my element, the rush of the game coursing through me, awakening that deep-seated desire to win, to dominate. The Silver Blades move with precision, a well-oiled machine under my guidance. But the StarPucks, they're not backing down. Isabella's got them playing a tight game, their strategies countering ours with frustrating effectiveness.

Then it happens—the StarPucks slip one past our goalie, the puck hitting the back of the net with a sound that grates against my nerves. My jaw clenches as the opposing team erupts in cheers. I'm not just irked; I'm fired up, the competitor in me refusing to be outdone.

"Blades, huddle up!" I call out, my voice slicing through the rink's din. The team quickly gathers around me, their faces a mixture of determination and expectation. They're looking to me, their coach, for direction, for that spark to reignite our momentum.

"We're holding back too much," I say, locking eyes with each player. "You're pros, the best in the game. It's time to show these newbies how it's done. No more playing it safe. Let's crank it up and take control of this game."

There's a murmur of agreement, the team's energy shifting, aligning with my own. They're ready, eager even, to escalate the game, to show the StarPucks the full force of the Silver Blades.

I glance across the ice, catching Isabella's gaze. Our eyes lock, and in that moment, there's a silent understanding between us. This isn't just a practice game anymore. It's a battle of wills, a clash of titans. She knows it, I know it. We're both playing for keeps.

The whistle blows, and the game resumes with renewed intensity. The Blades move faster, hit harder, their play a reflection of my own competitive fire. I watch, a predatory satisfaction growing within me as we start to dominate the rink.

Isabella, ever the strategist, adjusts her team's tactics, countering our aggression with cunning plays. But I'm always one step ahead, anticipating her moves, countering with my own. It's exhilarating, this back-and-forth, this test of skill and will.

The game on the ice is a tempest, each player a whirlwind of energy and drive. I'm on the sidelines, but it feels like I'm right there with them, every nerve in my body responding to the clash of sticks and skates. It's not just about coaching anymore; it's about being a part of the action. The urge to play, to feel the ice beneath my skates, courses through me with a ferocity that I haven't felt in years.

The game is in full swing, the intensity palpable. I'm on the edge, my eyes following every move, every play with a hawk's focus. That's when it happens—TJ, one of our best right wingers, takes a hard hit. My heart lurches as he goes down.

Without a second thought, I'm off the bench and onto the ice, my strides quick and determined. As I reach TJ, he's trying to push himself up, his face twisted in pain and frustration.

"Easy, TJ," I say, kneeling beside him. "Let's not rush it."

Isabella skates over, concern etched on her face. We lock eyes for a moment, an unspoken understanding passing between us. This is more than a game; it's about the people who play it.

The medic rushes out, his bag in hand, and gets to work assessing TJ. I stay close, offering a steadying presence. TJ winces as the medic examines his leg.

"Looks like a minor sprain," the medic announces, his tone professional yet reassuring. "You're lucky, TJ, but I'd recommend sitting out the rest of the game."

TJ nods, obviously disappointed but understanding. I help him up, ensuring he's steady on his feet. The concern for TJ is genuine;

these players are more than just members of a team to me—they're like family.

As TJ is helped off the ice, I stand there for a moment, the cold air biting at my skin. I look out over the rink, the players waiting, the game paused. A surge of adrenaline courses through me, a call to action that I can't ignore.

I turn to Rick, the decision already made in my mind. "I'm stepping in," I declare, my voice firm with resolve.

Rick looks at me like I've lost my mind. "You're... *stepping in*? What the hell does that mean?" His eyes go wide as it dawns on him. "No. No way."

I grin. "What better time than now? The team needs a right winger." I sweep my hand over myself. "And here's the best one the ice has ever seen."

"Dom, you're insane. You know you're not cleared to play, not with your knee."

I shake my head, dismissing his concerns. The adrenaline is pumping now, drowning out the voice of reason. "I don't care, Rick. I need to be out there. I'm ready."

Rick tries to argue, but I'm already heading to the locker room. I can feel the weight of everyone's eyes on me, but it only fuels my determination. This is more than just a game; it's a test, a challenge I need to meet head-on.

In the locker room, I quickly gear up, each piece of equipment feeling like a part of me that I've been missing. My heart is racing, not just from the thrill of the game but also from the risk I'm taking. I know my knee is a ticking time bomb, but right now, I don't care. All I can think about is the ice, the game, the need to prove to myself that I've still got it.

As I step back onto the rink, the cold air hits me like a wake-up call. But it's too late to turn back now. I'm committed, ready to face whatever comes, be it triumph or disaster.

I skate onto the ice, the familiar feel of the blade gliding over the surface sending a rush of exhilaration through me. The players look surprised to see me, but there's also an unmistakable spark of excitement. Dom Steele, back on the ice, back in the game.

Rick watches from the sidelines, a mix of concern and resignation on his face. He knows me well enough to understand that once I've set my mind on something, there's no stopping me.

Not now, not ever.

27

Isabella

Stepping onto the crisp, cold ice, I can't help but feel a surge of adrenaline—and not just because of the game. There, fully suited up in his hockey gear, is Dom. He looks like he's just stepped out of a sports magazine cover, all warrior-like and intensely focused. It's a sight both unnerving and undeniably attractive.

"What the hell is he thinking?" I mutter under my breath, my eyes fixed on him as he moves with a grace that belies his size. There's something about a man in hockey gear, the way it outlines his build, that's just... captivating.

I quickly wave Sam over, needing some insight into this madness. "Sam, what's going on? Why is Dom playing? He shouldn't be on the ice with his injury."

Sam shrugs, a wry smile on his face that doesn't quite reach his eyes. "That's Dom for you," he says. "Once he sets his mind to something, good luck changing it. He's playing, and that's that."

I watch, torn between irritation and concern, as the game resumes. Dom's presence on the ice changes the dynamic instantly. He's not just playing; he's dominating, commanding his team with a natural authority that's both impressive and slightly terrifying.

Every check, every move he makes, I find myself holding my breath, half-expecting him to crumble under the strain of his injury. But he doesn't. Instead, he moves with a fluidity and power that speaks of years of experience and a deep, inherent love for the game.

As the puck flies across the ice, my professional admiration for his skill wars with my personal fear for his well-being. He's playing a dangerous game, and not just with the puck.

The tension in the air is palpable, the players from both teams elevating their game in response to Dom's presence. It's as if his stepping onto the ice has flipped a switch, turning a friendly practice match into a high-stakes battle.

And through it all, Dom seems oblivious to the potential consequences, lost in the moment, in the thrill of the game. It's a side of him I haven't seen before, this raw, unbridled passion for hockey. It's captivating and a little bit terrifying.

I force myself to focus on my own team, to provide the guidance and support they need, but my attention keeps drifting back to Dom. Every time he takes a hit or makes a daring play, my heart leaps into my throat.

The game ends with a mix of cheers and exhaustion, the players from both teams showing signs of the intense play. As they leave the ice, I find myself lingering, watching as Dom interacts with his team, laughing and clapping them on the back.

He's in his element, and it's a sight to behold. But as he glances my way, our eyes meeting across the distance, I can't shake the feeling that we're both playing a far more dangerous game off the ice—one that could have consequences neither of us are prepared for.

The rink is alive with action, players from both teams darting across the ice with impressive skill. I'm on my feet, shouting plays, my voice a sharp contrast to the grunts and clacks echoing around me. Despite the tension I feel watching Dom, I can't help but get caught up in the exhilaration of the game.

As I call out strategies, I catch glimpses of Dom cutting through the ice like a knife. He's a force of nature out there, his movements so fluid and precise it's almost poetic. He was a legend in the NHL, and seeing him now, it's clear why. His presence is magnetic, drawing eyes every time he touches the puck.

"Keep your focus, Isabella," I remind myself, shaking off the distraction. But it's hard, especially when he's out there looking like some kind of hockey god, commanding and powerful.

The StarPucks and the Silver Blades are neck and neck, the game a thrilling dance of speed and skill. One of my forwards makes a break for it, slicing towards the goal with the puck. My heart races with anticipation, but at the last second, a Blade swoops in, stealing the puck and turning the game on its head.

"Damn it," I mutter, clapping my hands in frustration. But I can't stay mad for long, not with the game this good.

And then there's Dom. He's everywhere on the ice, a blur of speed and power. With every move he makes, I find myself torn between admiration and concern. The way he plays, it's like he's tempting fate, daring his injury to rear its ugly head.

As the first period draws to a close, Dom makes a breakaway, the puck his loyal companion. He dodges a defenseman with a slick move, and before anyone can blink, he slams the puck into the net. The crowd erupts into cheers, and even though it's just a practice game, the thrill of it is palpable.

"Nice shot," I begrudgingly admit, clapping along with everyone else. There's no denying his talent, and as much as I hate to say it, watching Dom score is a sight to behold.

As the teams regroup for a break, I catch Dom's eye. He's grinning, that cocky, confident smirk that's both infuriating and irresistible. And for a moment, just a moment, I forget about the fake engagement, the complications, and the worries. I'm just a spectator, caught up in the sheer brilliance of his play.

The second period launches with a burst of energy, the players returning to the ice with renewed vigor. Dom and Sam, a dynamic duo, execute an incredible play, slicing through the StarPucks' defense with practiced ease. The puck finds the back of the net, and the Blades erupt in cheers. I can't help but admire their teamwork, even as a knot forms in my stomach.

Not to be outdone, one of my players, Alex "Lightning" Thompson, a speedy winger, seizes an opportunity. He dashes across the ice, a blur of determination and skill. With a deft flick of his wrist, he sends the puck soaring past the goalie. It's a breathtaking goal, one that draws a round of applause even from the Blades' supporters. I punch the air in triumph, pride swelling in my chest.

The tension on the ice is palpable as the final period begins. The game is tied, and both teams are hungry for the win. It's a nail-biter, each team trading possession, neither giving an inch.

Then, with a burst of energy, the StarPucks manage another goal. The cheers from our side are deafening, the players' excitement infectious. We're leading now, but I know better than to get too comfortable, especially with Dom on the ice.

True to form, Dom's competitive fire ignites. He plays more aggressively, cutting through the ice with a determination that's both impressive and terrifying. He gets the puck, and the crowd rises to their feet, a collective breath held in anticipation.

He's unstoppable, a force of nature as he heads towards the goal. Even I, caught up in the moment, find myself cheering him on, the lines between professional rivalry and personal admiration blurring.

But just as Dom is about to score, a sharp cry of pain slices through the air. Dom clutches his knee, the same one he injured years ago, and collapses onto the ice.

The crowd goes silent, the cheers dying in their throats. Players from both teams skate over, concern etched on their faces. I'm frozen in place, shock and fear gripping me.

"Dom!" I hear Sam shout, his voice laced with panic.

I find myself moving before I even realize it, skating over to where Dom lies on the ice, my heart pounding in my chest. He's surrounded by players and the medic, his face contorted in pain.

As I reach him, our eyes meet. There's fear there, and something else—a vulnerability I've never seen in him before. I crouch down, my professional demeanor slipping away, replaced by genuine concern.

"Dom, are you okay?" I ask, my voice barely above a whisper.

He doesn't answer, his jaw clenched as he tries to manage the pain. The medic is already examining his knee, her movements swift and professional.

Time stands still.

28

Dom

PAIN BLINDS ME, A white-hot lance through my knee, as voices and faces blur. The medic's instructions cut through the chaos, sharp and urgent. "On three, we lift. Easy does it," she commands, her tone leaving no room for error.

"One, two, three," she counts, and hands grip the stretcher, lifting me with a jolt that sends a fresh wave of agony through my leg. I can't hold back a groan, my vision narrowing to a tunnel as I fight against the darkness creeping in at the edges.

Isabella's beside me, her face etched with worry. "Dom, stay with me, okay?" she urges, her hand finding mine, a lifeline in the maelstrom.

The world lurches as they load me into the med-truck. Every bump and turn on the way to my cabin is an ordeal, each movement a test of endurance. I'm biting down on my lip so hard I taste blood.

Through the haze of pain, I hear Isabella's voice, steady but laced with an undercurrent of panic. "What do you need? Tell me how to help," she pleads, her fingers squeezing mine.

The medic is a flurry of activity, checking vitals, adjusting supports. "We need to stabilize the knee before we can move him. Keep him conscious," she barks orders, her professionalism a thin veil over the tension.

The world tilts and spins as they transfer me to the couch in my cabin. I'm vaguely aware of Isabella's constant presence, her voice a soothing hum in the background. The medic administers painkillers, her movements efficient but gentle. "This should help with the pain," she says, but her eyes are grim.

Isabella hovers, torn between being in the way and wanting to help. "Ice, we need ice," she says, darting off to fetch it.

I want to tell her it's okay, to put on the brave face I'm known for, but the words get lost in a haze of pain and medication. The world is slipping away, my consciousness ebbing as the painkillers take hold.

The last thing I remember is Isabella's voice, a steady stream of words meant to comfort, to keep me anchored. But the darkness is too inviting, too easy to slip into. I let go, the pain and the fear and the fight all fading away into nothingness.

***

Grogginess weighs on me like a heavy blanket as consciousness slowly seeps back. My eyes flutter open to a blurred world, a dim room lit by the soft, muted glow of a winter afternoon. Snow cascades down outside the window in heavy sheets, painting a tranquil scene at odds with the turmoil inside me.

I try to piece together the fragments of my memory, but they're elusive, slipping away like shadows. Then, as if summoned by my confusion, the door creaks open and Isabella steps in. Her presence is like a break in the clouds, a clarity amidst the fuzziness. She's ethereal in the dim light, her concern etched in the lines of her face.

"How are you feeling?" she asks, her voice tinged with worry.

"Like I've been hit directly in the knee by a truck," I reply, attempting a lopsided grin that doesn't quite reach my eyes. My knee throbs with a persistent ache, a painful reminder of my folly, and my head feels like it's trapped in a vice.

"You've had quite the tumble, Mr. Steele," she says, eyeing my knee with a critical gaze. She carefully checks the bandage, her touch gentle yet firm. "It's a good pull on the knee and a bit of a knock to the head. Fortunately, it's nothing too grave. But, and I mean this," she adds with emphasis, "you need rest. No strenuous activity, especially on the ice."

She pauses, her eyes meeting mine. "And you're lucky it's not worse. You didn't aggravate that old ACL injury, but you were dangerously close. A bad enough injury could have you walking with a limp for the rest of your life. Remember that."

"Understood," I say, the tone of my voice reflecting the gravity of her warning. "I'll take it easy. No heroics."

Isabella's not pleased, her arms crossed as she listens to the medic's assessment. I can see the lecture forming in her eyes, but before she can unleash it, something catches her attention. Her eyes widen in shock, and without a word, she turns and rushes out of the bedroom and into the bathroom, leaving a trail of unanswered questions behind her.

Lying there, I'm left in a stew of confusion and concern, the medic's words echoing in my mind. I've dodged a bullet, but the incident has left its mark. I can't shake the feeling that something's not right, a sense of unease that goes beyond my injuries. And Isabella's sudden exit only deepens the mystery.

As the medic continues her checks, offering advice on pain management and recovery, my thoughts are elsewhere. I'm concerned about Isabella, about the look of alarm that had flashed across her face. What could have possibly caused her to react that way?

The window offers no answers, just the steady fall of snow that seems to isolate us further from the world. I'm trapped in my own body, limited by pain and injury, and now, seemingly cut off from the one person I need to connect with.

The medic wraps up her examination with a final word of advice, her tone stern yet concerned. "Mr. Steele, you need to stay off that knee as much as possible. Rest is crucial for your recovery," she instructs, her eyes scanning mine for understanding.

I nod, absorbing her words while a part of me already schemes ways to get back on my feet.

"However," she continues, sensing my restless spirit, "if you absolutely need to move around, I'll leave a pair of crutches for you. But only for necessary movement, understand? No gallivanting around, especially not back on the ice."

Her words are a clear directive, a non-negotiable order that even my stubbornness can't argue against. "Got it," I reply, a touch of reluctant acceptance in my voice.

"Good," she says, her expression softening slightly. "Take care of that knee. You're no good to anyone if you're permanently sidelined."

With that final piece of advice, she gathers her things and exits, leaving me alone with my thoughts and the unexpected concern for Isabella's sudden departure.

I settle back against the pillows, the painkillers beginning to dull the sharp edges of my discomfort. But they can't numb the worry, the growing sense of unease. Something's up, and I intend to find out what it is.

29

Isabella

HUNCHED OVER THE BATHROOM sink, I rinse my mouth for the third time, trying to rid myself of the lingering taste of my upheaved lunch. My mind is a chaotic swirl of worry for Dom and frustration with him for his reckless behavior on the ice. Seriously, what was he thinking? The nerve of the guy to put himself—and us—in such a situation. Yet here I am, my stomach in knots over him.

A knock at the door startles me from my thoughts. "Come in," I call out, hoping my voice doesn't betray the turmoil inside me.

The door opens, and in walks the team medic, a woman with a kind but no-nonsense demeanor. "Isabella, are you alright?" she asks, concern evident in her eyes.

I straighten up, pasting on a semblance of composure. "Yeah, just nerves, you know. Dom's injury and all," I reply, hoping she buys the half-truth.

She gives me a long, assessing look. "Have you had these symptoms before? Times when you weren't feeling nervous?"

I pause, recalling the unexpected nausea that hit me just the other night, the unease that's been haunting me. "Yeah, a couple of times," I admit reluctantly.

The medic nods, her expression turning thoughtful. "Do you mind if I do a quick checkup?"

A little taken aback, I nod my consent. It's probably nothing, just stress or a stomach bug, but better safe than sorry.

The medic runs through a brief but thorough examination, her professionalism comforting in its routine.

The medic, with a practiced hand, checks my vitals—my pulse, my blood pressure, all the while maintaining a calm, professional demeanor that somehow makes the small cabin's bathroom feel less claustrophobic.

"Your heart rate's a bit elevated, but that could be due to stress," she comments, making notes on her clipboard.

Then, she asks that question, catching me completely off guard. "Can you tell me about your recent sexual activity?"

I stiffen, taken aback. "Why would that matter?" I ask, my voice laced with defensiveness. Why is she delving into my personal life? This is just supposed to be a check on my sudden sickness, not an intrusion into my private affairs.

The medic meets my gaze, her expression unflappable. "It's standard procedure in a checkup, especially with your symptoms," she explains calmly. "We need to consider all possibilities, and it helps to have a full picture of your health. It's just part of the process."

Her explanation, logical and devoid of judgment, diffuses my initial defensiveness. She's right. It makes sense to be thorough, and her professional detachment makes the situation less embarrassing. "Alright," I relent, my cheeks still flushed. "Yes, I've been sexually active recently."

She nods. "I'm going to get some supplies for Dom from the truck. And... let me grab something else, too—assuming I have one in there."

She steps out for a moment, leaving me alone with my racing thoughts. What could she be thinking? It's not like...

She returns with a small box in her hand—a pregnancy test. My heart skips a beat at the sight of it. "Just to rule out any possibilities," she says, handing it to me.

I stare at the box, my mind reeling. Pregnancy? No, that's crazy. But as I think about it, the pieces start to uncomfortably align. The nausea, the fatigue, the way my emotions have been all over the place...

"Take your time," the medic says gently. "I'll be outside if you need anything."

She leaves, closing the door behind her, and I'm left staring at the small, life-altering box in my hands. Could I be pregnant? The thought is both terrifying and absurd. I'm Isabella Carrington, the woman with a plan, the woman who's always in control. And this most certainly wasn't part of the plan.

But as I sit there, the possibility becomes more real, more tangible. And with it comes a flood of questions, fears, and what-ifs. What about my career, my future with the StarPucks? What about Dom and this whole fake engagement mess?

Taking a deep, shaky breath, I make a decision. I need to know, one way or another. With trembling hands, I open the box and follow the instructions, my future hanging in the balance.

The minutes I spend waiting for the result feel like hours, each second heavy with potential consequences. In this brief span of time, a myriad of possible futures flash through my mind—some filled with challenges and others with unexpected joy. But each scenario is tinged with the undeniable weight of responsibility and the overwhelming sense of a life irrevocably changed.

And then it's ready. The test beeps, letting me know it has an answer waiting.

I stare at the positive sign on the pregnancy test, my mind whirling in disbelief. It's as if the world around me has slowed down, every second stretching into an eternity. My thoughts are a jumbled mess of emotions—shock, fear, and a surreal sense of wonder.

The medic knocks and re-enters, her expression turning to one of gentle congratulations as she sees the test in my hand. "Well, looks like congratulations are in order," she says, her tone warm and supportive.

"Thanks," I manage to reply, my voice sounding distant to my own ears. I'm still processing the reality of the situation—I'm pregnant, and everything is about to change.

We move into the main living area of the cabin, where the medic begins to offer me advice on prenatal health care. Her words flow over me, but I'm only half-listening. My mind is elsewhere, grappling with the enormity of what this means for my future, for my career, and for... Dom.

I'm jolted back to the present by the buzz of my phone. It's a text from Rick, informing me that the training for the rest of the day is canceled due to the worsening weather. I glance out the window, where the snow is falling in thick, heavy sheets, blanketing the world in white.

"Someone should definitely stay with him," she says, glancing towards the door that leads to Dom's room. "Given his condition and this storm, it's the best call."

I hesitate for a fraction of a second, then find myself blurting out, "I'll stay." The words tumble out more quickly than I intend, and I rush to justify them. "I mean, I'm his fiancée. It makes sense, right?"

The medic gives me a knowing look, a small smile playing at the corner of her lips. "Of course, it does," she replies, her tone gentle but with an undercurrent of amusement. "Just make sure he rests and takes it easy. I've left some pain medication and instructions, along with some crutches—but make sure he stays in bed as much as possible."

"Got it," I nod, trying to mask the whirlwind of emotions inside me. As she gathers her things to leave, I'm left standing there, suddenly alone with the reality of my situation. Pregnant and about to play nurse to the man who's both the cause of and solution to my current predicament.

In truth, the idea of being alone with Dom, especially now with this news, sends a rush of conflicting emotions through me. But I push those aside, focusing on the task at hand. I need to be there for him, as his fiancée, as his friend.

The medic seems satisfied with my decision and, after giving me a list of prenatal care dos and don'ts, she leaves, wishing me well. I'm left alone in the cabin, the snowstorm raging outside, and the reality of my pregnancy settling in.

I take a deep breath, steadying myself. This is not how I imagined finding out I'd be a mother. In the midst of a fake engagement, in a cabin during a snowstorm, with the father of my child injured in the next room.

Taking a deep breath, I turn towards Dom's room, the fact that everything between us has changed weighing heavily on my mind, along with one question:

When do I tell him?

30

Dom

Isabella steps into the room, and I notice immediately that something's off. Her usual demeanor is replaced by a look of concern, tinged with frustration. I raise an eyebrow, curious.

"What's wrong?" I ask, trying to read her expression.

She hesitates, just for a second, but it's enough to tell me that she's holding back a storm. Then, like a dam bursting, her frustration floods out.

"That... that was incredibly foolish and careless, Dom!" she exclaims, her voice laced with incredulity and rising with each word. "You had no business being out on that ice. You know your knee isn't what it used to be. What if you'd done serious damage? What were you thinking, putting yourself at risk like that?"

Her words hit home, but I can't just admit she's right. Not when my pride is on the line. "I'm not a child, Isabella," I shoot back, my tone stubborn. "And you're not my mom. I don't need someone hovering over me, worrying about every move I make."

Her face changes at the mention of 'mom,' a flicker of something deeper passing over her features, but she quickly shifts gears. "It's not about hovering, Dom. It's about being responsible. You have a whole team relying on you, a business to run. You can't just throw caution to the wind for the sake of an adrenaline rush."

I wince inwardly. She's not wrong, but admitting that feels like conceding defeat. "Look, I know my limits. I've been playing this game my whole life," I argue, trying to sound more confident than I feel.

Her expression softens just a fraction, but there's still a fire in her eyes. "It's not just about the game, Dom. It's about thinking ahead, about not making rash decisions that could impact more than just you." She pauses, taking a deep breath.

Her face changes at the mention of 'mom,' a flicker of something deeper passing over her features, but she quickly shifts gears. "Training's cancelled for the day because of the storm," she announces, her tone business-like. "I'm staying here to take care of you."

I can't resist the opportunity for a joke, even now. "Oh? Did the team medic leave a sexy nurse's outfit for you?" I ask, a playful smirk on my lips.

Isabella's response is immediate and without words—she grabs a pillow and hurls it at me. I catch it with a laugh, appreciating her fiery spirit even in the midst of our disagreement.

Her frustration is clear, but there's a hint of something else in her eyes. Concern, maybe? It's hard to tell with Isabella.

Isabella collapses into the chair with a huff, her gaze fixed on me with a mixture of frustration and concern. "You're lucky, Dom," she says, shaking her head. "This could have been much worse. Maybe then you would've realized what a dumb thing you did."

I attempt to shrug it off, but the sternness in her voice keeps my attention. "The medic said it's a minor ACL sprain and a slight concussion," she continues, using the medical terms with an ease that suggests she's familiar with the lingo. "You need to take it easy, at least for the rest of the day. Maybe this storm is a small blessing in disguise."

I scoff at the idea, the restlessness already building within me. "I'm fine, Isabella. I don't need to be coddled—" I start, trying to push myself up from the bed.

But she's at my side in an instant, her hands firmly pressing me back down onto the mattress. "Don't even think about it, Steele," she says, her voice firm but laced with a hint of playfulness. "You're staying put. Doctor's orders."

I look up at her, about to argue, but the fire and passion in her eyes stop me in my tracks. There's something about the way she's looking at me, a mix of irritation and genuine concern, that makes me pause. For a moment, I'm caught in her gaze, and the world around us seems to fade away.

With a sigh, I relent, sinking back into the pillows. "Fine, Nurse Carrington," I grumble, but there's no real heat in my words. "I'll stay put. For now."

She gives me a satisfied nod, a small smile playing on her lips. "Good. That's what I like to hear."

Settling back into the chair, she crosses her arms, her eyes never leaving me. It's clear she's not going to let me out of her sight, not until she's convinced I'm really okay. And as much as I hate to admit it, there's a part of me that's grateful for her presence, for the unexpected care she's showing me.

The room grows quiet, the only sound the howling wind outside as the storm picks up intensity.

Isabella's phone buzzes again, breaking the quiet tension in the room. She glances at the screen, her eyebrows knitting together in concern. "It's Rick," she says, looking up at me. "The storm's worse than they thought. Roads to the camp are closed, and everyone's advised to stay put for the night."

I let out a low whistle, peering out the window at the swirling snow. "Looks like we're snowed in then," I remark, a hint of amusement in my voice despite the situation. "Good thing these cabins are well-stocked. We might as well make the most of it."

There's a moment of silence as the reality of the situation settles in. We're isolated here, cut off from the rest of the world by a blanket of snow. It's an unexpected twist, but not necessarily an unwelcome one.

Isabella stands up, a determined look on her face. "Well, in that case, I guess I should make us dinner," she offers, her tone taking on a lighter, more playful edge.

I raise an eyebrow, pleasantly surprised. "You? Cook for me? Now that's an offer I can't refuse."

She rolls her eyes but there's a smile on her lips. "Don't get too excited. It's not going to be anything fancy. Just... you know, food."

I chuckle, watching as she moves towards the kitchen area. "Food sounds perfect, Isabella. I'm at your mercy."

As she busies herself in the kitchen, I find myself watching her, a sense of contentment washing over me. Despite the pain in my knee and the throbbing in my head, there's nowhere else I'd rather be. Trapped in a snowstorm with Isabella Carrington—it's like the setup to a story I never knew I wanted to be a part of.

The sound of pots and pans clanging and the aroma of cooking food fills the cabin, adding to the cozy ambiance. Isabella moves around the kitchen with a grace and efficiency that's captivating, and I realize that I'm seeing a new side to her, one that's more relaxed and domestic.

"Need any help?" I call out, half-joking.

"I think I can handle it," she replies, not taking her eyes off the stove. "You just rest and keep that knee safe."

I lean back, resigned to my role as the patient for the evening. The thought of Isabella taking care of me, cooking for me, it's oddly comforting. And as the storm rages outside, I can't help but feel a sense of warmth and safety here with her.

Maybe being snowed in isn't such a bad thing after all.

31

Isabella

"YOU EAT LIKE YOU'VE been starved," I tease, watching him attack the meal.

Dinner is an uncomplicated yet cozy affair, the kind that suits a snowbound evening perfectly. I opt for a classic—grilled cheese sandwiches with a side of tomato soup. It's comfort food at its best, simple but delicious, and just right for the snowy night outside.

He looks up, his eyes twinkling with mischief. "Hey, I'm in recovery mode. My body needs it." He takes another spoonful, his appreciation evident.

The cabin is quiet except for the sound of the crackling fire and Dom's satisfied eating. Once he's polished off the plate, he wipes his mouth with a napkin, looking contented.

"I want to sit by the fire," he announces, pushing the plate away.

I raise an eyebrow, my protective instincts kicking in. "You're supposed to be resting. Moving around isn't a good idea with your knee."

"It's just a few feet to the living room," he counters, a hint of challenge in his voice. "And didn't the medic leave crutches somewhere?"

I sigh, knowing there's no arguing with him when he's set on something. "Fine, but I'm helping you."

He grins, a boyish charm in his expression that's hard to resist. Carefully, I help him out of bed and onto the crutches. As he leans into me for support, I'm acutely aware of his presence—the solid weight of his body, the warmth radiating from him, and that unmistakable scent of his that's a blend of cologne and something innately Dom.

My heart skips a beat as I feel his muscles tense and flex under my hands. There's a raw strength to him, a primal energy that's both intimidating and incredibly attractive. I steal a glance at his face, finding his eyes already on me, a silent communication passing between us.

We move slowly towards the living room, each step a careful dance. I'm hyper-aware of his proximity, the heat of his body seeping into mine. It's a strange juxtaposition—Dom Steele himself leaning on me for support.

As we settle by the fire, the warmth envelops us, a cozy cocoon against the storm raging outside. The flickering flames cast dancing shadows across the room, adding to the intimacy of the moment.

We sit there, side by side, watching the snow fall outside and the flames dance in the fireplace. It's a serene, almost picturesque scene, but my mind is a whirlwind. The news of my pregnancy is still sinking in, a shockwave that's reverberating through every part of me. And right here, beside me, is the father—Dom.

Then, breaking the silence, Dom chuckles. "Can't wait for this knee to heal up. I've still got some game left in me," he says, a playful grin on his face.

His words ignite something in me, a fuse that's been burning since I saw him on the ice. "You think this is a joke?" I snap, turning to face him. "You were reckless out there, Dom! You could've seriously hurt yourself—for what? A game?"

He raises an eyebrow, his smile fading. "Easy, easy—just a joke. And besides, you don't need to baby me. It's not like you're my *real*..."

"Don't you dare," I cut him off, feeling a surge of anger and protectiveness. "Just because this engagement is fake doesn't give you the right to be irresponsible with your health. You're not invincible, Dom."

He looks taken aback by my outburst, his usual cocky demeanor faltering. "Isabella, I..."

"No," I interject, my voice rising despite my efforts to stay calm. "You don't get to brush this off. I've seen what happens when athletes push themselves too hard. You're not playing just for yourself anymore."

I stop, suddenly aware of the double meaning in my words. My hand instinctively goes to my stomach, a protective gesture that feels both foreign and instinctive. A rush of emotions floods through me—fear, uncertainty, and an overwhelming sense of responsibility. My gaze drops to the floor, unable to meet Dom's questioning eyes.

"You're not just risking your career, Dom," I continue, my voice shaky. "There are people who care about you, who... who depend on you." The words hang in the air, heavy with unspoken implications.

He watches me closely, his usual bravado replaced with something more tender, more concerned. "Isabella, if there's something going on, you can tell me. We're in this together, right?"

I let out a frustrated sigh, feeling the weight of the secret I'm carrying. How do I tell him? How do I admit that our fake engagement has led to something so real, so life-changing?

"It's not just about the game, Dom," I say, struggling to keep my emotions in check. "It's about being responsible, about thinking of the future. You can't just live in the moment when others are... are involved."

I try to continue, to let out more of the frustration and worry that's been building up inside me, but it's like a dam has broken. Suddenly, I'm overwhelmed by everything—the baby, Dom, the sheer enormity of the situation. Tears start streaming down my face, emotions I've been trying to keep in check finally spilling over.

Dom, seeing my distress, doesn't say a word. He just wraps his arm around me, pulling me into his embrace. I find myself sobbing into his shoulder, his strong presence offering a surprising comfort. In this moment, he's not the cocky, infuriating man I've been sparring with; he's just Dom, caring and solid and unexpectedly tender.

As I cry, letting out all the fear and uncertainty, I realize that he's giving me exactly what I need right now. Support. Care. And maybe, just maybe, something that feels a lot like love. It's a strange thought, one that I never expected to have about Dom, but in his arms, it feels undeniably true.

Gradually, my tears subside, and I pull back slightly, sniffling and trying to regain some semblance of composure. Dom clears his throat, breaking the silence that had settled between us.

"Isabella," he starts, his voice low and gentle, "I owe you an explanation. About today, about why I did what I did."

I look up at him, my eyes still red from crying, but curious. Despite everything, I want to understand him, to know what drives him. It feels important, more than just a need for clarity on today's recklessness. It feels like a step towards understanding Dom, and maybe, understanding us.

He looks into my eyes, his own reflecting a depth of sincerity I haven't seen before. "I'm listening," I say quietly, ready to hear what he has to say.

32

Dom

Where the hell to begin? Talking about myself, my past, doesn't exactly come easy to me.

I lean back, letting the memories wash over me. "You know, my dad passed away when I was eight, but I clearly remember many things about him. He was the kind of guy who believed if you're doing something, you do it full tilt. No half measures," I say, a half-smile playing on my lips.

"Hockey wasn't just a game in our house; it was more like a religion. Dad put a stick in my hand practically before I could walk. I won't lie, I hated it at first. Felt like I was being forced into something." I shake my head slightly, the image of a frozen pond and my dad's stern face flashing in my mind.

"But there was this one game in high school. It was a real nail-biter, you know? We were down, the clock was ticking, and something just... switched on inside me. I remember grabbing the puck, feeling like I was flying across the ice. Scored the tying goal, and then bam!

Nailed the winner in overtime." I tap my fingers on my knee, lost in the moment.

"That night, something changed. I didn't just play hockey; I felt it, in every part of me. Suddenly, it wasn't my dad's dream; it was mine. And man, I was good... I wish he'd been there to see me. I thought I was going to be the greatest, you know? And maybe for a minute there, I was." My voice trails off, a mix of nostalgia and regret coloring my tone.

Leaning forward, I run a hand through my hair, the memories vivid and raw. "You see, Izzy, hockey wasn't just what I did; it became who I was. When I was on the ice, I felt alive, invincible. It defined me, gave me purpose."

I pause, a shadow crossing my face. "Then came that game. It was routine, just another day at the office, until it wasn't." My voice tightens as I recall the moment. "One wrong move, a twist, a fall, and everything changed. The ACL tear... it was more than an injury. It was the end of a dream."

"After the surgery, I was in denial, big time. Kept telling myself it was temporary, that I'd be back on the ice, better than ever. But reality hit hard. The doctors, they were clear. My days in the NHL were over." The words still sting, even after all this time.

"I didn't handle it well. Threw myself into this playboy lifestyle, partying, fast cars, faster women. It was all a blur, a way to fill the void. But truth is, I never wanted any of that. It was just noise, a distraction from facing the truth." I shake my head, the bitterness evident in my voice.

"I had to find a new purpose, reinvent myself. It's been a hell of a ride, but sometimes, like today, I still chase that ghost. Trying to prove to myself, or maybe to my old man, that I'm still that guy. The one who could make the impossible happen on the ice." My gaze drifts away for a moment, lost in thoughts.

"But I'm not that guy anymore. And maybe that's okay. Maybe there's more to me than just hockey. It's just... hard to let go, you know?" I look back at Isabella, a mix of vulnerability and resolve in my eyes

Continuing, I let out a deep sigh. "I know, what I did today... it was stupid. But letting go of hockey, it's like losing a part of myself. Sometimes, I fool myself into thinking I can still play, that I can go back to who I was. But then reality slaps me in the face, and I'm back to square one."

I finish speaking and turn to face Isabella. Her eyes are fixed on me, an intensity in her gaze that I haven't seen before. There's understanding there, maybe even admiration. I chuckle awkwardly, trying to lighten the mood. "Sorry, I didn't mean to bore you with all my personal shit."

But as I look down, I realize our bodies are still pressed together, the warmth and closeness a stark contrast to the raw emotions I've just exposed. For a moment, we both seem to pause, the air charged with unspoken words and pent-up feelings.

Then, without a word, our lips meet. The kiss is slow at first, a tentative exploration, but it quickly deepens, driven by all the tension and emotion that's been building between us. It's a kiss that says more than words ever could, a mingling of past pain and present desire. For a brief moment, everything else fades away, and it's just us, lost in a world of our own making.

33

Isabella

THE FIRE CRACKLES SOFTLY in the background, casting a warm glow over the room. As our lips meet, there's a deep sense of connection that transcends the physical. Dom's kiss is tender, a stark contrast to his usual cocky demeanor. His strong arms hold me gently, mindful of his injury, yet his embrace is reassuring and safe.

Our banter fades into a comfortable silence, filled only with the sound of our breathing and the occasional pop from the fireplace. We move slowly, each touch and glance laced with a growing awareness of each other. He looks at me with eyes that reflect a myriad of emotions—vulnerability, desire, and something that might just be the beginnings of love.

As he carefully removes my sweater, his fingers brush against my skin, sending a shiver down my spine. I return the gesture, my hands sliding over the contours of his muscular arms, feeling the strength that lies beneath. There's a moment where our eyes lock, and everything else fades away—it's just Dom and me, wrapped up in our own little world.

In this moment, I see the man behind the confident façade, the one who has faced loss and uncertainty, and it draws me to him even more. Our movements are slow and deliberate, a dance of discovery and care.

As we lay nestled by the fire, I can't resist a little teasing. "So, Mr. Tough Guy, how's the knee feeling? Need me to kiss it better?" I ask with a playful smirk.

Dom chuckles, his eyes twinkling with mischief. "I wouldn't say no to that, but I'm more worried about you. I'm supposed to be the one sweeping you off your feet, not the other way around."

I raise an eyebrow, my lips curving into a sly smile. "Oh, I don't know, I think you're doing just fine. But if you need to prove your strength, I could think of a few ways," I reply, my voice dropping to a sultry whisper.

He grins, the confidence returning. "Is that a challenge, Ms. Carrington? Because you should know, I never back down from a challenge."

Leaning in closer, I playfully poke at his chest. "Just be careful. I wouldn't want you to strain yourself. After all, we can't have Seattle's hottest hockey executive out of commission."

Dom's laugh is rich and warm, filling the space between us with ease and comfort. "Trust me, Isabella, I'm just getting started. And as for being out of commission... well, let's just say I've got a few moves left in me."

His arms wrap around me, pulling me closer, and I can't help but feel a surge of excitement. His injury hasn't diminished the strength in his embrace, and the heat of his body against mine is intoxicating.

The heat from the fireplace wraps around us, mirroring the warmth growing inside me. I'm acutely aware of every point where our bodies meet, the heat of his skin against mine. His hand finds its way to my hair, fingers gently weaving through the strands, a touch so full of tenderness it makes my heart swell.

As the fire casts a warm glow across the room, the space between Dom and me diminishes with every breath. The playful banter fades into a charged silence, our movements speaking louder than words. With careful fingers, I begin to slip his shirt off, revealing the broad expanse of his shoulders and the impressive contours of his arms. There's a raw strength to him, an undeniable power that's accentuated by the intricate tattoos snaking up his forearm, telling stories of their own.

He watches me intently, his gaze never leaving mine as I continue to undress him. The muscles in his arms flex under my touch, and I can't help but admire the definition, the way they speak of discipline and physical prowess. His injuries haven't dulled the strength that's evident in every line of his body.

Next, I reach for his belt, my hands slightly trembling with a mix of nervousness and excitement. As I unbuckle it, his hands find their way to my waist, pulling me closer. The proximity sends a thrill down my spine, and I'm acutely aware of the heat radiating from his body.

His pants join his shirt on the floor, and there it is—his perfectly sculpted backside, a testament to years on the ice. It's hard not to stare, not to touch. I allow my hands to explore, tracing the lines of his muscles, feeling the solid strength beneath his skin. He's a sculpture come to life, a masterpiece of athleticism and raw masculine beauty.

Dom, in turn, gently peels away my clothes with reverence. His touch is confident yet tender, as if he's cherishing every moment, every revelation of skin. His hands move to undress me, and there's a tenderness in his touch that belies his rough, alpha exterior. He carefully slides the straps of my dress down my shoulders, his fingers grazing my skin with a feather-light touch that sends shivers down my spine. When my dress falls to the floor, I'm left standing before him, feeling both vulnerable and empowered under his gaze.

"You're beautiful," he says, his voice a low rumble that resonates deep within me. His eyes roam over me, not missing an inch, and I feel a flush creeping up my cheeks.

I try to brush off his compliment with a self-deprecating joke. "This is just what a diet of coffee and stress gets you. Not much time for the gym," I quip, attempting to lighten the mood.

But Dom isn't having any of it. He steps closer, his hands finding my waist, pulling me into him. "Don't," he says softly but firmly. "Don't dismiss what's clearly there. You are stunning, Isabella. Every part of you."

His sincerity catches me off-guard, and for a moment, I'm at a loss for words. It's not often that someone sees me—really sees me—beyond the sharp, sassy manager. But here, with Dom, I feel seen in a way that's both unsettling and exhilarating.

He trails his fingers gently down my arm, then back up to cup my face. "I mean it," he insists, his eyes locked with mine, conveying a depth of feeling that words can't fully capture. "You're not just beautiful. You're strong, you're smart, and you're incredibly sexy."

As our kisses deepen, the world around us fades into a blur of sensation and emotion. There's a synchronicity in our movements, a dance of desire that's as natural as it is intoxicating. Dom's hands are everywhere, exploring, igniting fires that race through my veins.

He travels down, down along the length of my legs, his eyes smoldering as he locks gazes with mine. I'm shivering with anticipation, goosebumps breaking out all over my body as his big, rough hand moves over me. I look him over, taking in the sight of his thick arms, his narrow middle, his heaving chest.

God, he's something else.

Dom lowers himself down, kissing my neck as his hand finds my cunt. I gasp through the kiss, waves of pleasure spreading out through my body as he teases me down below, his fingertips dancing over my lips. It feels so goddamn good, but I want *more*. My hand covers his, pressing it down, guiding him without words to give me what I crave.

But Dom lifts up, giving me a grin that says, "you get what I give you, when I want you to have it."

"Tease," I say, pleasure still radiating from down below.

"It's more fun that way," he replies. "Trust me."

I want to trust him. I *do* trust him. I want to release, to give myself over to Dom and let him take me in only the way that he can. Finally, mercifully, he spreads my lips and turns his attention to my clit. I gasp as he touches me, the anticipation making it far more intense than it otherwise would've been. He makes slow circles and I squirm, my hips pushing against his touch.

Dom kisses me hard, his lips moving down, down, along my neck and to my breasts, where he gives each of my nipples slow, luscious attention before continuing over my belly and to my thighs. He flashes me a sexy-as-fuck grin before placing his tongue on my clit.

"Oh... oh *God*."

He knows just how to please me, just how to give me what I need. He licks me long and slow, his fingers penetrating me, my walls gripping them, wetness flowing over his touch. It doesn't take much of this, much of this touching before he's brought me to a slow, roiling orgasm. I gasp, my back arching as I pull in sharp gasps of air, each wave of pleasure rushing through me.

When he's done, Dom raises up, his lips glistening with my juices.

"Can't think of anything that tastes as sweet as you, lover." He flashes me one more grin before wiping away my arousal with the back of his wrist, then coming in for a kiss.

"Such a charmer," I say.

"I do my best."

"Now, as much as I love a good tease..."

He laughs, low and throaty and sexy. "Don't worry—I'm about to lose my mind if I'm not inside you."

"That makes two of us."

I glance down at his thick, hard cock, watching as he lowers himself between my thighs. He positions his manhood at my entrance, and by this point I'm so wet and ready that I practically bring him in myself. His familiar thickness, his sensual hardness, fills me in the way I crave, and all I can do is bit my lower lip as he bottoms me out.

Dom wraps his arms around me, each thrust slow and deep, intentioned for me to feel each bit of him move in and out, in and out. He opens his eyes and I meet his gaze and right away I see the love there, see the passion. This isn't just sex, this is something *more*.

I wrap my legs around his hips, my hands finding that perfect, athlete's ass of his, and I push him down. His glutes tense underneath my touch and he's picking up his pace, the power and depth behind every thrust making it clear he's on the verge.

Then he stiffens, his cock erupting into me. It's enough to make me come hard too, my eyes closed and my hand on his rear as I focus on the orgasm and the sensation of his cock pulsing inside.

In the aftermath, we're a tangle of limbs and heavy breaths, the heat of our passion slowly giving way to a gentle, glowing warmth. I rest my head on Dom's chest, listening to the steady rhythm of his heart. It's a sound that speaks of life, of vitality, and in this quiet moment, it's profoundly comforting.

Dom's arm wraps around me, holding me close in a protective embrace. There's a peace in this closeness, a sense of safety and belonging that I hadn't realized I was seeking. His touch is gentle, a stark contrast to the intensity we just shared, but it's no less impactful.

We lie there in silence, the crackling of the fire and the soft patter of snow against the windows creating a cocoon around us. It's a rare moment of stillness in our otherwise tumultuous ruse, a chance to breathe and just be.

34

Dom

I WAKE UP TO the morning light filtering through the curtains, casting a warm glow over the room. Isabella is still asleep next to me, her face peaceful, a stark contrast to the storm of emotions we weathered last night.

I can't help but watch her, taking in the soft rise and fall of her chest, the way her hair fans out on the pillow. She's beautiful, and for a moment, I let myself just appreciate her, forgetting the chaos that's unfolded around us.

Carefully, I shift, planning to test my knee. It feels surprisingly better, like the rest did it some good. Maybe I can...

"Don't even think about it, hotshot," Isabella's sleepy voice cuts through my thoughts. I look over, meeting her eyes. There's a playful sternness in them, a hint of a smile tugging at the corners of her mouth.

"I feel fine," I protest, but even as I say it, I know it's a half-truth. I'm eager to get back on my feet, to regain some sense of normalcy, but the concern in her eyes stops me.

Isabella sits up, the sheets pooling around her waist, her gaze fixed on me. "You might feel better, but that doesn't mean you're healed. Use the crutches until you're fully recovered," she insists, her tone brooking no argument.

I can't help but smirk at her insistence. "Yes, ma'am," I reply, a touch of mock salute in my voice. "But you have to admit, I'm a pretty resilient guy."

She rolls her eyes, but I can see the affection behind the gesture. "Resilient or stubborn, I'm not sure which," she quips back.

As I reach for the crutches leaning against the bedside table, Isabella helps steady me, her hands gentle yet firm. I'm struck by the care in her touch, the way she seems to balance strength with tenderness.

"Thanks," I say. "And, uh, not just for the help standing. It's for everything - for staying with me, for taking care of me, for being here despite this mess."

"You're welcome," she replies, and there's something in her voice, a depth that suggests it's about more than just this moment.

As I steady myself on the crutches, I realize that despite the uncertainty of our situation, there's something real between us. Something that goes beyond fake engagements and public facades. It's a thought that both excites and terrifies me, but I know it's one I can't ignore. Not anymore.

The buzz of my phone draws my attention away from the serene morning. I grab it from the nightstand, reading a message from Rick. The training camp is starting back up, and he's inviting me to join in, if I'm up for it. A surge of energy courses through me at the thought of getting back out there. Despite my injury and everything that's happened, I can't deny the pull of the ice, the game, the life I've always known.

But there's something else stirring inside me, something unfamiliar yet powerful. It's a sensation that's been building since Isabella and I crossed a line we can't uncross. Could it be... something more than just physical attraction? The thought is both exhilarating and terrifying.

"I'm ready to go," I tell Isabella, the words carrying more weight than just my eagerness to return to the rink. She pauses, her expression conflicted as if she's wrestling with something on her mind. I can sense there's more she wants to say, something important, but she's holding back.

"Is everything okay?" I press, trying to reach out to her, to bridge the gap that's formed between us. She looks at me, her eyes searching mine for a moment, and I can almost feel the weight of her thoughts.

"It's nothing," she finally says, sliding out of bed with a grace that's all her own. But as she walks past me, she squeezes my butt playfully, a mischievous glint in her eye. It's a simple gesture, but it's loaded with unspoken words, a shared intimacy that's both comforting and confusing.

I can't help but laugh at her boldness, the tension of the moment easing slightly. "Watch it, Coach," I tease back, the familiar banter a welcome respite from the complexities of our situation.

She shoots me a sassy look over her shoulder, the kind of look that's become a signature of our interactions. "Just making sure you're still in one piece, Steele," she quips, the corners of her mouth curling into a smile.

We dress, bundling up for the cold weather that no doubt awaits us.

Stepping outside, the world is a winter wonderland, blanketed in fresh snow, aside from the paths carved out by the snow plows. The camp is alive with energy, despite the early hour. Some of the team members are already up, stretching their legs with morning jogs, their breath misting in the crisp air.

Isabella and I walk side by side to the cafeteria, our easy banter from earlier continuing. The playful flirting feels natural, a comfortable rhythm we've fallen into despite the complexity of our situation. I can't help but steal glances at her, admiring the way the morning light plays off her hair, the easy grace in her step.

As we enter the cafeteria, a familiar figure catches my eye, and my mood darkens. Jason Sinclair is here, his gaze fixed on us with an unsettling intensity. He looks like he's got a secret, and I don't like it one bit. His presence is a stark reminder of the underlying tension in this whole charade.

Trying to shake off the unease Jason's presence brings, I focus back on Isabella. But the atmosphere between us shifts, turning more serious as we both seem to ponder the same question—what does last night mean for us?

"So, about last night..." I start, my voice trailing off as I search for the right words.

Isabella looks at me, her expression a mix of vulnerability and strength. "Yeah, about that," she replies, a hint of uncertainty in her voice.

I pause, unsure how to articulate the whirlwind of emotions that last night stirred up in me. "I mean, we can't just pretend it didn't happen, right?" I say, trying to gauge her reaction.

She nods, her eyes meeting mine. "No, we can't. But Dom, what does this mean for us? For this whole... arrangement?" Her voice is steady, but there's an undercurrent of concern that I can't ignore.

I take a deep breath, feeling the weight of her question. "I don't have all the answers, Isabella. But I know that what happened between us, it was real. More real than anything I've felt in a long time."

She bites her lip, considering my words. "I feel the same way," she admits softly. "But we need to be careful, Dom. We can't let whatever this is... complicate things more than they already are."

I nod, understanding her caution. "I agree. We'll take it one step at a time, figure it out as we go."

As we join the line for breakfast, the tension between us eases slightly, replaced by a quiet understanding. We're in uncharted territory, both professionally and personally. But as I glance over at Isabella, I can't help but feel a sense of excitement for the unknown path we're embarking on together.

35

Isabella

THE MORNING SUN CASTS a golden glow over the rink as I oversee the StarPucks running through their drills. Their energy is high, their movements sharp and precise. I can't help but feel a surge of pride at how far they've come. My mind briefly wanders to the upcoming end-of-training game against the Blades. It's going to be a great test of our progress, a chance to really see what my team can do.

I find myself occasionally glancing towards the Blades' side of the rink, where Dom is. Even from this distance, his presence is commanding, and my heart gives a little flutter remembering last night. But I shake off the distraction; I have a team to focus on.

During a brief pause in the drills, I pull out my phone and send a quick text to Jenna. I can't keep the pregnancy a secret from my best friend. My fingers fly over the screen, typing out the news. Almost instantly, Jenna's response comes through, a flurry of excitement and questions. She's thrilled for me, but her immediate question hits hard: "What does this mean for you and Dom?"

I stare at the message, the weight of the question heavy in my mind. I don't know, I type back. It's the truth. I'm not sure what this means for the fake engagement, for Dom, for me. Everything feels like it's in a state of flux.

Before I can delve deeper into the conversation with Jenna, a shadow falls over me. I look up to find Jason Sinclair approaching, his confident stride and well-tailored suit making him stand out among the athletes.

"Bella," he greets me, a hint of something unreadable in his tone.

I straighten up, tucking my phone away. My heart starts to race, not from excitement, but from a mix of wariness and irritation. What does Jason want now?

"So, how's the future hubby?" he asks, a smirk playing at the corner of his lips.

I force a smile, keeping my voice neutral. "He's fine, Jason. Focused on the training, like all of us here."

As Jason's gaze lingers, a discomfort settles over me.

"And the training camp... are you getting my money's worth?" he asks, his tone deceptively casual.

I resist the urge to roll my eyes, instead returning his gaze, maintaining a professional demeanor. "It's going well. The team's really pulling together, showing great progress."

"Good to hear," he replies, though his eyes suggest he's more interested in something else. "And how are you managing with the... added responsibility of your engagement? Must be a lot to juggle."

His question, edged with insinuation, makes me bristle. "It's fine, Jason. Dom and I are managing just fine."

He nods, but there's a probing intensity in his eyes. "Must be quite the change, right? Spending so much time together, sharing... everything."

I force a smile, even as irritation bubbles within me. "We're professionals, Jason. We know how to balance our personal and professional lives."

His smile widens, but it doesn't reach his eyes. "Of course, of course. Just curious, you know. After all, engagements can bring out so many... new dynamics."

The way he stresses 'new dynamics' sends a clear message—he's digging for something more, something beneath the surface of my and Dom's relationship. I stiffen, my guard up.

"Is there a point to all these questions, Jason?" I ask, my tone firm.

He leans in slightly, a conspiratorial glint in his eye. "Just making conversation, Isabella. It's not every day you see two high-profile individuals like you and Dom getting together. People talk, you know."

I straighten up, my patience wearing thin. "People talk, huh? What exactly are they saying, Jason? And why are you so interested?" My voice is sharp, cutting through the facade of casual chit-chat. "This feels like more than just idle curiosity."

He pauses, letting the tension thicken around us. The rink, with its echoes of skates and pucks, feels miles away. Jason leans in, his voice lowering. "I have reason to believe that you and Dom aren't quite the lovebirds you're pretending to be."

The air seems to still around me. His words, so blunt and accusing, send a shockwave through me. How much does he know? And more importantly, why does he care? My mind races, trying to piece together his angle.

I straighten up, my instincts kicking in. "I don't know what you're talking about, Jason." My voice is steady, but inside, a storm is brewing. "Dom and I are engaged. That's all there is to it."

Jason raises an eyebrow, his smirk widening. "Really, Isabella? That's all there is to it?" His tone drips with skepticism. "You expect me to believe that? You two have barely known each other, and suddenly you're engaged. It doesn't add up."

I feel a flash of irritation. "What's it to you, Jason? Why are you so hung up on my relationship with Dom?" I ask, trying to steer the conversation away from dangerous waters. "And why do you care so much about Dom's business ventures? It's not like it affects you." My voice is firm, trying to establish boundaries in this increasingly uncomfortable conversation.

Jason's expression hardens, his eyes narrowing as he leans in closer. "Let me be blunt, Bella. Apex Arena, Dom's brainchild, it's more than a minor inconvenience for my plans. It's a direct threat."

I raise an eyebrow, trying to keep my voice level. "And why is that your concern?"

He smirks, the gesture devoid of any warmth. "Because, dear, it's not just about a stadium. It's about control, influence. Dom's expansion into the West Coast with this project is a power move. It could shift the balance in our industry, and I can't have that."

I feel a surge of indignation. "So this is about your ego? Your need to be the top dog?"

Jason chuckles, a sound that grates on my nerves. "It's about business, Isabella. And in business, you either lead or get left behind. Dom's project could overshadow my ventures, attract my clients. I can't allow that."

I cross my arms, trying to maintain my composure. "Then discuss it with Dom. I'm not involved in his business decisions."

He chuckles, a sound devoid of humor. "Oh, but you are, Bella. Whether you like it or not. Your engagement is part of his public image now, part of the narrative he's selling to his investors."

I frown, not liking where this is going. "What are you implying?"

"I'm done implying," he says. "I believe your marriage is a farce. And I'm going to make it known, one way or another."

Anger flares within me. "You're threatening me?"

"It's not a threat, it's a proposition," Jason replies smoothly. "Think about it. End this charade with Dom. And maybe... consider a real relationship. One with someone who can appreciate you fully."

His insinuation sends a chill down my spine. "You mean... with you?"

He smiles, but it's cold and calculating. "Why not? We have history, Bella. And I can offer you stability, a real partnership."

I shake my head in disbelief. "I don't believe this. You're trying to blackmail me into a relationship?"

"Blackmail is such a harsh word," he says with a shrug. "I prefer to think of it as guiding you towards a better choice. You have until the speeches tonight. Make the right decision, Bella."

He begins to turn, glancing over his shoulder for one parting shot.

"Oh, and you'd be surprised at what you can learn just by keeping your ears open in these cozy little cabins. It's amazing the secrets they can reveal, especially about... certain deceptions."

His words hang in the air, heavy with implication. The idea that he's been eavesdropping, that he knows about our fake engagement, sends a wave of panic through me. I stand there, speechless, as he walks away with a self-satisfied smirk, leaving me to grapple with the enormity of what he's just implied.

With that, he turns and walks away, leaving me standing there, reeling from the encounter. How could I possibly expose the truth about my and Dom's relationship without causing a scandal? And what would that mean for the Apex Arena, for Dom's career... for my own?

I feel trapped, caught in a web of Jason's making. The idea of succumbing to his manipulations repulses me, but the alternative could bring everything crashing down. I need to think, to plan, but time is running out.

As I watch Jason's retreating figure, a sense of dread settles over me. Tonight's speeches could change everything, and I'm not sure I'm ready for the consequences.

36

Dom

THE EVENING DESCENDS ON the training camp, bringing with it a buzz of anticipation and an unexpected flurry of activity. I've been so caught up in the day's events that I haven't had a chance to catch up with Isabella. But as the hour for the evening speeches approaches, I feel a knot of unease tighten in my gut. Something's off, and I can't quite put my finger on it.

The event tonight is more than just a casual gathering; it's a significant joint conference between the Silver Blades and the StarPucks. The main cabin, usually echoing with the sound of skates and pucks, has been transformed into a venue befitting the occasion. Rows of chairs face a small, makeshift stage, and banners of both teams hang proudly in the background.

As I weave through the crowd, I can sense the electric mix of excitement and nervous energy. Tonight's event isn't just a celebration of the training camp's success; it's a platform for some key members of both teams to make speeches, highlighting the camaraderie and competitive spirit fostered over the weekend so far. There's also an undercurrent of anticipation for the rest of the season ahead, a chance to set the tone for what's to come.

Rick, the Silver Blades' manager, and a couple of the senior players are slated to speak, along with Isabella and some of the StarPucks' leadership. It's a moment for motivational words and team-building sentiment, a capstone to the intense training we've all undergone.

I should be focusing on the speeches, perhaps even practicing my own speech, but my mind is elsewhere. I'm scanning the crowd for Isabella, hoping to catch her eye, to gauge her mood. But she's nowhere to be seen. Instead, my gaze lands on Jason Sinclair, chatting amiably with a group of investors. His smile looks fake, and there's something calculated about his demeanor that sets me on edge.

The hall is more crowded than I expected, buzzing with journalists and even a few notable faces from the investment team behind Apex Arena. The air is charged with excitement and expectation, a stark contrast to the turmoil brewing inside me. As I scan the room, my eyes land on Isabella. She's across the hall, her posture rigid, her expression a mix of conflict and stress. Next to her now, almost like a shadow, is Jason Sinclair, looking far too smug for my liking. Something about the way he's watching her sets off alarm bells in my head.

I start to make my way over to Isabella, intent on getting to the bottom of whatever's going on. But before I can reach her, the press descends on me like vultures, their questions a cacophony of curiosity and intrusion. They're all eager to hear about Apex Arena, and of course, the engagement. I plaster on my best public smile, answering their inquiries with practiced ease, but my attention is divided, my gaze continually drifting back to Isabella.

As I parry questions about the arena's features and the impact it'll have on the league, I notice Jason whisper something in Isabella's ear. Her reaction is subtle, but I know her well enough to see the brief flash of panic before she masks it with a neutral expression. Whatever

Jason's game is, it's clear he's playing for keeps, and Isabella is caught in the middle.

The speeches are about to start, and I finally manage to extricate myself from the press. I make a beeline for Isabella, but before I can reach her, Jason steps up to the microphone. The room falls silent, all eyes on him. There's a gleam in his eye that I don't trust, a sense of triumph that has no place here. Jason, the one paying for this whole weekend, is the first one to speak.

Jason clears his throat, commanding the attention of the room with an ease that speaks of years in the limelight. "I want to take a moment to talk about the values that drive us in this sport," he begins, his voice smooth and practiced. "Teamwork, integrity, honesty. These aren't just words; they're the pillars upon which we build our careers and our lives."

I shift uncomfortably, sensing the direction this is heading. There's a deliberate cadence to his speech, a buildup that feels more theatrical than genuine. The room listens intently, hanging on his every word, unaware of the undercurrents swirling beneath the surface.

"As we stand here today, celebrating the success of this training camp and looking ahead to a promising season, it's vital we remember the importance of these values." Jason pauses, his gaze sweeping across the room before settling pointedly on Isabella and me. "Integrity and honesty. Without them, what do we have? Just a hollow shell of what could have been a meaningful pursuit."

The cold dread in my stomach grows heavier, a sinking realization of what's coming next. Jason's words, laced with insinuation, hang in the air, a prelude to the storm about to break.

"And speaking of honesty," Jason continues, his gaze locking with mine. "I think it's important that we address the elephant in the room. The so-called engagement between Dom Steele and Isabella Carrington."

Shit.

37

Isabella

THE ROOM FALLS INTO a hushed silence, the atmosphere thick with anticipation. I can feel the tension rising, a tangible force that grips the room in its hold. Jason's smile is calculated, the smile of a man holding the winning hand.

"Many of you have been following the news of their engagement. A heartwarming story, isn't it? Two professionals at the top of their game, finding love amidst the competitive world of hockey." His tone is dripping with sarcasm, each word a calculated strike. "But what if I told you that this engagement is nothing more than a facade? A charade played out for the sake of publicity and personal gain."

The murmurs start almost immediately, a ripple of shock and disbelief spreading through the crowd. The press, sensing a story, lean in eagerly, their cameras and recorders poised to capture the moment. Beside me, Isabella looks stricken, her face pale with shock.

Jason leans into the microphone, his voice steady and clear. "Yes, ladies and gentlemen, you heard me right. This engagement is a sham.

A well-orchestrated lie designed to manipulate public opinion and further their own careers."

The moment Jason's words hit the air, a cacophony of whispers and gasps ricochet around the room, each one like a dagger to my heart. I should've told Dom about Jason's threat, about the twisted ultimatum he posed. But fear and indecision had held me back, and now, it's all unraveling in the worst way possible.

Jason's standing there, smug and victorious, as he declares to the room, "I have proof, ladies and gentlemen, that their so-called love story is nothing but a farce. A deceitful play for public sympathy and personal gain."

I can see Dom from where I stand, his face contorted in a mix of shock and fury. He moves with a predator's precision, his body language screaming intent as he storms towards the stage. There's a dangerous edge to him, a raw, untamed energy that's both terrifying and magnetic.

He's about to reach Jason when my voice cuts through the chaos, a desperate plea that somehow finds its target. "Dom, stop!" My voice is louder than I expected, echoing off the walls, commanding attention. It's enough to halt him in his tracks, his clenched fists trembling with barely restrained rage.

The room falls silent, all eyes on us. The media, with their cameras and recorders, are capturing every moment of this implosion, their lenses trained on our faces, searching for guilt, for shame, for any crack in our facade.

Jason, seeing his opportunity, presses on with his revelation, his voice oozing false regret. "It's a shame, really. To think that such respected professionals would stoop to such deceit. But the truth always finds a way, doesn't it?"

I feel like I'm in the middle of a nightmare, unable to move, to speak, to escape the judgmental stares piercing through me. This isn't how it was supposed to go. This partnership with Dom, this fake engagement, it was a means to an end, a strategy, not a scandal.

But as I watch Dom, standing there seething with anger and betrayal, I realize the gravity of what we've done. Our little arrangement, born out of convenience and ambition, has spiraled into something far more damaging. We've played with fire, and now we're getting burned.

I need to do something, to say something, to salvage what little dignity we have left. But the words elude me, stuck in my throat like a lump of coal. All I can do is stand there, frozen, as the reality of our situation sinks in.

38

Dom

THE ANGER IS A hot, pulsating thing in my chest, threatening to burst out with every stride I take away from the chaos Jason's just unleashed. I'm halfway to my cabin, the cold, crisp air doing nothing to cool the fury that's boiling inside me. My phone, a relentless source of buzzing and pinging in my pocket, is a cacophony of texts from investors, all echoing the same sentiment—betrayal, confusion, and threats to pull out of the Apex Arena project.

I'm furious, not just at Jason for his underhanded tactics, but at myself for not seeing this coming, for not being prepared. And then there's Isabella. Why didn't she warn me? Did she even know? My mind races with accusations and questions, each one a sharp jab to my already frayed nerves.

I stop abruptly, my breaths coming out in visible puffs in the cold air. The snow underfoot feels like the only thing grounding me to the moment, to the reality that my world is possibly crumbling around me. I run a hand through my hair, trying to make sense of it all, but it's like trying to grab at smoke.

And then, there's her voice, cutting through the turmoil.

"Dom!" Isabella calls out, her voice laced with a mix of urgency and something else I can't quite place. I turn, and there she is, her figure a stark contrast against the white landscape, her expression a tumult of emotions.

In her eyes, I see a reflection of the storm that's raging inside me, a storm of fear, uncertainty, and something deeper, more personal. For a moment, all the anger, the frustration, the sense of betrayal, it all takes a back seat as our gazes lock, communicating more in silence than words ever could.

This isn't just about the business, the investors, or the arena. This is about us, about what's been growing between us, something I've been too stubborn, too afraid to fully acknowledge. But here, in this moment, it's undeniable, a force just as powerful as the anger and the betrayal.

I take a step towards her, my resolve faltering. The need to confront, to accuse, to demand answers is still there, but it's waning, tempered by the realization that whatever this is between us, it's not something that can be ignored or pushed aside. It's real, and it's right here in front of me, in her eyes, in her presence.

As Isabella approaches, the snow crunching under her feet, I brace myself. For what, I'm not sure. An explanation, a confrontation, a confession? Whatever it is, I know that this moment, this conversation, it's going to change everything. And as much as it terrifies me, I know it's a change that's been a long time coming.

Fury boils inside me as I confront Isabella, my words sharp and my tone seething with accusation. "Why didn't you warn me about Jason? You knew he was up to something!" I can feel the heat of my anger radiating off me, a wildfire threatening to consume everything in its path.

"You let me walk into that blind," I continue, my voice rising, edged with betrayal. "You knew he had something on us, and you said nothing!" The words tumble out, each one laced with a mix of hurt and disbelief. How could she keep this from me?

Isabella stands there, her expression a mixture of shock and hurt, but I'm too far gone in my own turmoil to stop. "Do you have any idea what you've done? The investors are bailing, and this... this could ruin everything!" My hands are balled into fists at my sides, the tension in my body mirroring the chaos in my mind.

But even as I unleash my frustration, a part of me recoils at the intensity of my own emotions. It's not just anger at the situation; it's the raw fear of losing what we've built, of losing Isabella.

As I draw a ragged breath, ready to continue my tirade, Isabella's voice cuts through the air, stopping me dead in my tracks.

"I'm pregnant," she says, the words soft but carrying the weight of the world.

I freeze, every muscle in my body tensing as those two words sink in. Pregnant. It's as if the ground has shifted beneath my feet, the entire world tilting on its axis.

My anger, once a roaring inferno, is instantly snuffed out, replaced by a stunned, overwhelming silence. I'm suddenly aware of the rapid beating of my heart, the rush of blood in my ears.

And I've got no idea what the hell to say next.

39

Isabella

THERE HE STANDS, DOM Steele, the epitome of confidence and control, rendered utterly speechless by my revelation. It's a side of him I've never seen, and in this moment of vulnerability, he seems more real than ever.

I take a step forward, my voice trembling slightly as I try to explain the whirlwind of emotions and decisions that led to this moment. "Dom, I... I was overwhelmed," I begin, my words faltering. "Finding out about the baby, seeing you hurt on the ice, and then Jason's threats... It was all too much."

I can see him struggling to process my words, his expression a mix of shock and hurt. "I didn't know how to handle it. The thought of everything changing, of losing the life I've worked so hard for..." My voice trails off as the gravity of the situation weighs on me.

The silence between us stretches, filled with unspoken fears and uncertainties. "I know it was a mistake not to tell you about Jason," I continue, mustering as much courage as I can. "But it was a human mistake. I was scared, Dom. Scared of losing you, scared of what the future holds."

I pause, taking a deep breath as I prepare to lay my heart bare. "I can understand if you can't forgive me for this. But I need you to know, this wasn't about deceit. It was about trying to protect what little control I thought I had left in my life."

As the words leave my lips, I feel a sense of release, as if admitting my fears and flaws to Dom has lifted a weight off my shoulders. But the fear of his reaction, of what this means for us, remains a gnawing presence in my mind.

I stand there, vulnerable and exposed, waiting for Dom to say something, anything. The future of our relationship, of our family, hangs in the balance, and all I can do is hope that the man I've come to care for so deeply can see the sincerity in my eyes and the love in my heart.

I stand frozen, his words washing over me like a tidal wave. "Are you crazy?" Dom's question hangs in the air, a mix of disbelief and something else—something warmer.

"Crazy?" I repeat, my voice a shaky whisper. How can he not see the mess I've made?

But then, he smirks, and it's like a ray of sunshine piercing through the storm clouds in my mind.

"Yeah, crazy," he says, and there's a gentleness in his voice that I've never heard before.

He steps closer, and it feels like the world around us fades into nothingness. "You think you need to apologize to me? If anything, I should be the one begging for your forgiveness," he says, his eyes earnest and intense. "After all, I've been a goddamn coward."

I'm speechless, my heart pounding in my chest. "You've been a *coward*?" I whisper, unable to grasp his meaning.

Dom nods, his gaze never leaving mine. "I've been terrified of how real this has become. Terrified of admitting that what started as a facade has turned into the most genuine thing I've ever felt." His voice is a low rumble, filled with emotion.

As Dom stands there, his eyes locked onto mine, there's a vulnerability in him that I've never seen before.

"I love you, Isabella," he says, his voice resonating with a sincerity that takes my breath away. "I love the way you challenge me, always pushing me to be better, to think harder. You don't just accept things as they are; you question, you fight, you strive for more. And that... that's incredible."

I can feel my heart racing, a mix of surprise and joy as he continues. "I love how you care about your team, how you put their needs above your own. You're not just their manager; you're their leader, their protector. The passion you show, the dedication... it's inspiring."

His words wash over me, painting a picture of all the little things he sees in me, things I never realized he noticed. It's overwhelming, this flood of affection and admiration coming from Dom Steele, it's more than I ever expected. But here he is, laying his heart bare in front of me, confessing his love in a way that's so raw and real.

"And your passion," he adds, his eyes sparkling with emotion. "It's like a fire, Isabella. It burns bright and fierce, and it draws people in. You don't just do things; you put your soul into them. And that's... it's just beautiful."

I'm struggling to find words, to respond to this outpouring of love and admiration. It's as if he's peeled back the layers of our fake engagement, revealing something true and profound beneath. This isn't just Dom Steele, the hockey legend and businessman; this is a man who sees me, truly sees me, and loves what he sees.

In that moment, any doubts, any fears I had about us, about what we are to each other, they just melt away. Here, in front of me, is a man who loves me for who I am, who sees my strengths and admires them. How can I not forgive him? How can I not love him back?

"And God, the baby," he continues, his voice softening further, "it just makes everything more meaningful, more precious."

He reaches for my hands, his touch sending a current of warmth through me. "I'm asking you to forgive me, Isabella. For not treating you how you deserve, for not realizing sooner what you truly mean to me."

His eyes search mine, laying his soul bare. "I love you, Isabella Carrington. You're extraordinary, and I want to be there for you, for our baby. Every step of the way."

In that moment, with his heartfelt words, the barriers around my heart begin to crumble. He's not just the cocky, bad boy jerk I thought I knew—he's more, so much more. His declaration of love, his promise of commitment, it's what I've yearned for without even knowing.

"I love you too, Dom Steele," I finally manage to say, my voice quivering with emotion. "And I forgive you. We have a future to build, for us, for our baby. And I can't think of anyone else I'd rather build it with."

As we stand there, holding each other, the world outside our bubble doesn't matter. It's just Dom and me, and the promise of a new beginning. A beginning filled with love, hope, and a shared future.

40

Dom

I WAKE UP TO a world bathed in sunlight, the kind of morning that screams potential. But right now, all I can think about is the hour ahead. It's time to face the music with Isabella by my side.

We're going public about Jason's bombshell, holding an impromptu press conference to set the record straight. The internet's been a buzzing hive since last night, and it's up to us to calm the swarm.

Isabella looks nervous, a rare crack in her usually unflappable armor. I lean in, whispering, "Hey, we've got this. Together." My words seem to bolster her, a faint smile breaking through.

"Thanks, Dom. I needed that," she says, her voice steady.

We walk hand in hand to the main cabin, where the press, our teams, and the investors are gathered. It feels like walking into the lion's den, but I'm ready. Ready to fight for us, for our future.

The cabin is packed, a sea of expectant faces turning towards us as we enter. Camera flashes ignite like a storm of lightning, and the murmur of the crowd swells to a crescendo. I squeeze Isabella's hand, a silent message of solidarity.

We take our place at the front, standing side by side. The room falls silent, waiting for us to speak. I clear my throat, feeling every eye on me.

"Good morning, everyone. Thanks for coming on such short notice," I start, my voice calm and clear. "I know there's been a lot of speculation since last night, and we're here to set the record straight."

I glance at Isabella, giving her an encouraging nod. She steps forward, her presence commanding the room.

"We want to address the claims made by Jason Sinclair," she begins, her tone confident. "Yes, it's true that our engagement began as an arrangement. But what started as a strategic move evolved into something real. Something neither of us expected."

I take a deep breath, feeling the weight of every eye in the room fixed on me. This is it, the moment of truth. No more hiding, no more games. My heart is pounding in my chest, a rhythmic reminder of what's at stake. But as I look out at the sea of faces, something steadies within me.

"I know this might come as a surprise to many of you," I begin, my voice strong and clear, ringing out in the hushed room. "Life, as I've learned, rarely follows a script. It's full of twists and turns, unexpected journeys, and surprises. And this," I gesture between Isabella and me, "this is one of those astonishing turns."

I pause for a moment, letting my words sink in, feeling every beat of my heart as if it's a drum leading me forward. "Isabella," I continue, turning slightly towards her, "she's been the most wonderful, unexpected turn in my life. I started this journey with a plan, a strategy. But what I didn't plan for was falling for this incredible woman standing beside me."

The room is still, a captive audience hanging on my every word. "She's not just someone I'm in a contract with, or a partner in a business deal. She's become my confidant, my support, and my unexpected joy. I've found in her a strength, a passion, and a heart that I never knew I was missing."

I take another breath, feeling a wave of emotion rise within me, raw and honest. "In Isabella, I've found more than just a partner; I've found a reason to rethink what I thought was my path. She's changed everything, and for the better."

The room remains silent, but I can feel the shift, a change in the air. It's as if my words have bridged a gap, turned skepticism into understanding.

"We've faced challenges, yes, but we've also discovered a love that's real and powerful. And now, we're starting a new journey together, one that's about more than just us." I glance at Isabella, her presence a source of strength and certainty.

"And there's more," I continue, my gaze softening as I turn to Isabella. I gently pass the baton to her, letting her share this part of our story.

She steps forward, a radiant glow on her face despite the nerves.

"We're expecting a baby," she confirms, her voice filled with a mixture of pride and joy. The news sends a ripple through the crowd, a chorus of congratulations and excited murmurs.

As I conclude my speech, a hush falls over the room. I look around, meeting the eyes of the press, the investors, and the team. "I lied to all of you," I admit, my voice steady with the weight of my confession. "We both did. And for that, I am truly sorry. But if it meant having Isabella in my life, I'd make the same choice a million times over."

Turning to face her, I take her hands in mine, feeling their warmth, their strength. "I love you, Isabella. More than I ever thought possible." The words feel like a release, a truth that's been waiting to be acknowledged.

Tears glisten in Isabella's eyes, reflecting the depth of emotion that has grown between us. "I love you too, Dom," she says, her voice thick with emotion. It's a moment of pure, unguarded honesty, and it feels like the world outside this room has faded away.

As we exit the cabin, a buzz of excitement follows us, the press and photographers eager to capture every moment. But all I can focus on is the woman beside me, the woman who has become my everything.

Out of the corner of my eye, I catch the eager lenses of the cameras, the reporters jostling for a better view. I chuckle, a sound born from the absurdity and the beauty of this moment. "Looks like we've got an audience," I say to Isabella, my heart light with joy.

She smiles, a radiant, stunning expression that captures all the love and chaos of this journey. "Then let's give them a show," she replies, her eyes shining with love and mischief.

With a laugh, I pull her close, and our lips meet in a passionate kiss. It's a kiss that speaks of love, of forgiveness, of new beginnings. Around us, the cameras click and flash, but they fade into the background, insignificant against the power of what we share.

As we part, breathless and exhilarated, I know that this is just the beginning. There will be challenges ahead, questions to answer, and paths to navigate. But with Isabella by my side, I'm ready for anything. The press might be clamoring for more, but for us, this moment is enough. It's a promise of a future filled with love, partnership, and the joy of the unexpected.

We step back, hand in hand, ready to face whatever comes next. But for now, this moment is ours—this one, and all the moments to follow.

Epilogue

ISABELLA

TWO YEARS LATER

"WATCH DADDY, ALEX!" I encourage our little boy, who's perched on my hip, his wide eyes following every move on the ice. Despite being just over a year old, Alex already shows signs of being as enthralled by the game as his father. He claps his chubby hands together, a babbling cheer that melts my heart.

The StarPucks and Silver Blades are deeply immersed in their final practice game, a fierce yet friendly rivalry that has become the highlight of our now-annual training camp. It's surreal to think it's been two years since Dom and I publicly declared our love. Our journey from a fake engagement to building a family feels like something out of a fairy tale.

Dom, now a respected coach for the Blades, commands the ice with the same intensity he used to play. It's inspiring to see how he's redirected his passion for the sport into molding future hockey stars. His love for the game is a legacy he's already passing down to Alex.

Our life is a delicate balance between New York and Seattle. While I continue my role with the StarPucks, Dom is putting the final touches on the Apex Arena. His dream project is nearing completion, promising to be a landmark in the world of hockey.

As the final practice game reaches its peak, the energy on the ice is palpable. Amid the flurry of activity, my gaze often finds Sam, my brother, slicing through the defense with an ease that speaks of his rising status. It's no secret in the NHL circles; Sam's quickly becoming one of the hottest players in the league, his talent and dedication shining through in every game.

Jason Sinclair, the man who once threatened to unravel our lives, has disappeared from the public eye. His attempt to discredit us only served to disgrace himself. I sometimes wonder where he ended up, but those thoughts are fleeting. He's a chapter of my life I've turned the page on.

"Goal!" Alex's excited shout draws me back to the present, just as one of the Blades scores an impressive goal. The team erupts into cheers, and even the StarPucks can't help but appreciate the skill on display.

As the game concludes, the players gather at center ice, their camaraderie a testament to the spirit of the sport. Watching them, I feel a profound sense of pride and achievement.

Dom skates over, his smile infectious as he reaches out to take Alex. "Did you see that, little man? Mom's team is pretty awesome, huh?"

Alex reaches for his dad, babbling in his baby language, which Dom seems to understand perfectly. I watch them, my heart swelling with love for my two boys.

"We're a great team, aren't we?" Dom says, looking up at me with eyes full of love and a future of endless possibilities.

Jenna weaves through the crowd, two steaming cups of coffee in hand, her trademark sassy grin lighting up her face. "Here," she says, handing me a cup. "Figured you'd need this. Watching all this testosterone on ice must be exhausting." Her quip brings a laugh, the kind only a best friend can draw out.

Before either of us can say another word, I glance up to see Sam skating over. "Hey, Isabella, I was wondering if..." Sam starts, his confident stride slowing as he approaches. But then he catches sight of Jenna. His voice falters, trailing off into silence. There's a brief moment where they just look at each other, an unspoken conversation passing between them.

Jenna, never one to shy away from a moment, breaks the ice. "Hi, I'm Jenna, Isabella's partner in crime and occasional voice of reason," she introduces herself, extending her hand.

Sam, recovering from his initial surprise, takes her hand, his own grin matching hers. "Sam, Isabella's overprotective big brother and, apparently, admirer of her friends," he replies, a playful tone in his voice.

They share a quick, slightly awkward handshake, both trying to mask their mutual interest.

"Nice to meet you, Sam," Jenna says, pulling her hand back but her eyes linger on him, a spark of interest clear in her gaze.

"Likewise," Sam responds, his eyes still locked with Jenna's.

"Only good things, I hope," Jenna quips, her smile widening.

"Nothing but the best," Sam assures her.

It's so damn cute that I have to restrain myself from breaking out into a big, stupid grin.

The moment stretches out, a palpable tension in the air, before Sam, looking slightly flustered, breaks the eye contact.

"Well, I'll let you two get back to it." He smiles one last time at Jenna before skating off to join the rest of the team.

As he leaves, I lean in, a mischievous glint in my eye. "Well, well, Jenna. Seems like someone's got a crush on my brother."

Jenna rolls her eyes playfully, trying to play it cool. "Please, he wishes," she says, but her flushed cheeks betray her true feelings.

After the game, the energy and excitement of the day gradually fade into the peaceful quiet of the evening. Dom and I, along with our little Alex, retreat to our cabin – the same cozy haven where I took care of him after his knee injury. With Alex soundly asleep in his room, we find ourselves in front of a roaring fire, the warmth and crackle of the flames echoing the comfort and serenity in our hearts.

We sink deeper into the comfortable couch, a blanket draped loosely over us, as we reminisce about the day's events. Our conversation naturally drifts to the incredible journey we've been on together. From our first contentious meeting to the tangled web of our fake engagement, and now, to this moment, where everything feels so real, so right.

There's laughter as we recall some of the more absurd moments, the early clashes, and the unexpected turns that somehow led us here. We share memories, like snapshots of a life that's been anything but ordinary. Every story, every shared experience, adds another layer to the warmth that envelops us, a warmth that extends far beyond the crackling fire in the hearth.

The quiet of the night wraps around us, a peaceful backdrop to our shared reflections. In these moments, with Dom by my side, I feel a contentment that goes deeper than I ever imagined possible. It's in his laugh, the way his eyes light up when he talks about our future, the gentle way he holds my hand as we talk – it all speaks of a love that's grown stronger, more profound with each passing day.

As the conversation lulls, Dom's expression grows more serious, yet tender. He reaches for my hand, holding it gently. "Isabella," he begins, his voice filled with emotion, "these last two years have been an incredible journey. From a crazy, fake engagement to building a beautiful, real family with you and Alex... it's more than I ever hoped for in my life."

He pauses, taking a deep breath, and I sense the weight of his words, the significance of this moment. "But there's one thing missing," he continues, his grip on my hand tightening reassuringly. Before I can voice my question, he pulls a small box from his pocket.

Kneeling before me, he opens the box to reveal a stunning ring, sparkling in the firelight. "Isabella Carrington," he says, looking up at me with eyes full of love, "will you make this real? Will you marry me, not as part of a ruse, but for real, for love, for a lifetime together?"

Tears spring to my eyes, a mixture of joy and love overwhelming me. "Yes, Dom, yes!" I manage to say through my tears.

The cabin, our secluded world, fills with the sound of our laughter and happiness as he slips the ring onto my finger. We embrace, a perfect moment of love and commitment, far away from the world's eyes, intimate and deeply personal.

We break apart, our eyes meeting in a shared understanding of the depth of our love. "A real engagement," Dom says with a playful, loving grin, "no theatrics, just us."

I gaze into those gorgeous green eyes of his.

"Just us. Now and forever."

Life with Dom and Alex is a dream come true. It's laughter and love, challenges and triumphs, dreams shared and a future filled with endless possibilities. As we step into this next chapter, hand in hand, I know we're ready for anything life throws our way.

And as I look up at Dom, his eyes shining with love and pride, I realize that this is just the beginning. Our happily ever after is a promise, a commitment to a lifetime of loving and growing together. And I wouldn't have it any other way.

Epilogue 2

DOM

YEARS LATER

THE GRAND OPENING OF the Apex Arena is a symphony of light and sound, a culmination of dreams and relentless effort. As we step into the sprawling, state-of-the-art facility, I feel a rush of excitement tinged with pride. The Blades and the StarPucks, poised for their opening game of the season, add to the electric atmosphere.

The Apex Arena? Man, it's like stepping into the future. The outside's all sleek curves and glass that catches the light just right, making the whole place sparkle like it's part of the game. Inside, we're not just talking seats with a view; we're talking about every seat being the best in the house. It's all high-tech too—holograms, interactive stuff for the fans. The place is like something out of a sci-fi movie.

And the rink, it's perfect, like a sheet of ice waiting for legends to be made. The way the sound system's set up, every cheer from the crowd, every hit against the boards, it's like you're right there on the ice with the players.

We hit a rough patch at the start, yeah, with the investors and all. But Isabella, with that sharp mind of hers, and a bit of my never-back-down attitude, we turned it around. Got back most of our original backers and even roped in some new ones. They saw what we were building here wasn't just another arena; it's a game-changer.

Alex, now four, clutches my hand, his eyes wide with awe. "Daddy, it's huge!" he exclaims, his excitement contagious. The arena buzzes with the energy of thousands of fans, a heartwarming sight after the uncertainty of the past years.

I make my way to the stage, feeling Isabella's supportive gaze on me. The crowd quiets as I clear my throat, ready to share my heart.

"Good evening, everyone," I begin, my voice echoing through the arena. "Today isn't just the opening of a building. It's the celebration of a journey—a journey of determination, passion, and teamwork."

I pause, letting my gaze sweep over the crowd, feeling the weight of this moment.

"Five years ago, the Apex Arena was just a dream, a vision of creating a home for hockey that would bring together players, fans, and communities. There were times when this dream seemed too distant, too challenging. But here we are, thanks to the relentless spirit of the Silver Blades, the StarPucks, and every single person who believed in us."

I smile, thinking of the struggles and victories along the way.

"I want to thank our amazing teams, our devoted fans, and, of course, our investors—both old and new—for your unwavering faith. Your support has been the backbone of this project."

Then, my eyes find Isabella and Alex in the crowd, and my heart swells.

"Most importantly, I want to thank my family. Isabella, your brilliance and strength have been my guiding stars. And Alex, my son, you remind me every day why we strive to build a better future."

The crowd erupts in applause, a sound that fills me with gratitude and hope.

"Tonight, as the Blades and the StarPucks take to the ice, we celebrate not just a game, but the spirit of unity and ambition. The Apex Arena is more than a venue; it's a promise of great things to come."

As I step down from the stage, the roar of the crowd follows me. Not going to lie—I love it, love being in the spotlight.

The evening progresses smoothly, the atmosphere electrified with excitement and celebration. Alex, our little dynamo, takes the crowd by storm, his youthful energy and infectious smile winning hearts left and right. Isabella, the embodiment of grace and poise, moves through the throng of guests, her presence commanding respect and admiration. Together, we're a force, a duo that's weathered storms and come out stronger.

As the festivities start to wind down, Isabella catches my eye and gestures towards a quieter section of the arena. Jenna gives us a knowing smile as she scoops up Alex, promising him a grand tour.

But the moment we're alone, Isabella's eyes hold a mischievous glint as she delves into her purse, retrieving a small package wrapped with meticulous care.

She hands it to me, her lips curling into a playful yet enigmatic smile. "For you," she whispers, her voice a soft melody that dances in the air between us.

I take the package, feeling its lightness, my curiosity piqued. "What's this, Izzy?" I ask, my tone teasing, yet touched with a hint of wonder.

"Just a little something," she replies, her eyes sparkling with unspoken secrets.

I carefully unwrap the gift, revealing the tiny pair of hockey skates. They're so small, so delicate—a stark contrast to my big, rough hands.

My heart skips a beat as the realization dawns. I look up at Isabella, searching her face for confirmation. "Are you...?"

She nods, a radiant smile spreading across her face. "Yes, Dom. We're going to be parents again."

The words send a rush of warmth through me, a wave of love and joy that's almost overwhelming. I gently set the skates down and pull her into my arms. "Isabella, this is... it's amazing. I can't believe we're doing this again."

Her arms wrap around me, her body fitting perfectly against mine. "I know," she murmurs, her voice laced with happiness. "I couldn't wait to tell you."

I lean back, cupping her face in my hands, marveling at the love I feel for this incredible woman. "Every moment with you is special, Izzy. You've given me a family, a purpose... everything."

She reaches up, her fingers trailing along my jawline. "And you've given me the same, Dom. I love you so much."

Our lips meet in a kiss that's gentle yet filled with all the passion and promise of our life together. The world around us fades away, leaving only the two of us, lost in our love and the excitement of the new life we're about to welcome into our world.

I pull Isabella close, my heart pounding with a mix of excitement and tenderness. Our journey together, from a ruse to real love, from partnership to parenthood, has been nothing short of extraordinary. And now, we're embarking on another chapter, one that's sure to be filled with as much love and adventure as the last.

"Isabella, this... this is incredible," I manage to say, my voice thick with emotion. "I love you, and this little one already."

She rests her head against my chest, and I wrap my arms around her, feeling the future growing inside her, a new life we've created together. As I stand there, holding her, the noise and celebration of the Apex

Arena fades into the background. In this moment, it's just us, our family, and the promise of another beautiful journey ahead.

Stepping back into the thick of the celebration, I can feel the shift in the air, the charged excitement that comes with our secret now ready to be shared. Alex, our little champ, is the first target of this news, buzzing around Jenna like a pint-sized whirlwind of energy.

"Hey, sport," I say, dropping to a knee to catch his attention. His bright eyes, so like his mother's, lock onto mine with curiosity. Isabella, always radiant, is right beside me, her hand finding its way to my shoulder.

"What's up, Daddy?" Alex's voice is all eagerness, a mirror of my own anticipation.

Isabella's smile widens, and there's a sparkle in her eye that always hits me right in the heart. "You're going to be a big brother, buddy," she says, her voice carrying a warmth that fills the entire space.

The words land like a comet in the midst of our little gathering, sparking a round of cheers and excited chatter. Alex's face lights up, the realization dawning on him, and his reaction is pure gold—a mix of awe and joy that only a kid his age can muster.

We stand back up, turning to face our friends, our family, the world. It's more than just a celebration of the Apex Arena now. It's a celebration of us, of this growing family, of a love that's just getting stronger.

As the news spreads, the congratulations and back-slaps come rolling in. The whole thing turns into a dual celebration—one for the arena, sure, but even more for the new life we're about to welcome into our world.

I look around at the faces of our friends, our family, and it hits me—this is just the start. Our journey, our story, it's nowhere near done. It's growing, just like our family. As I pull Isabella in close, feeling her against me, I know deep down that every challenge, every victory, every moment—it's all leading us here, to this moment, and the many more to come. Our happily ever after isn't just a storybook ending; it's real, it's ours, and it's just getting started.

THE END

***

A NOTE FROM THE AUTHOR

Dear Reader,

If you enjoyed Dom and Isabella's journey, you'll *love* 'Pucking My Off-Limits Billionaire Boss'!

Scan this QR code to get your copy of 'Pucking My Off-Limits Billionaire Boss":

Scan me

A Sneak Peek is just one page away...

Now, a quick favor: Please give this book a star rating on Amazon when prompted. And if you have a few minutes, scan this QR Code to go *directly* to the review section of its Amazon page and share your thoughts. Your words can help others find their next read!

Scan me

Thank you!

Let's continue our literary adventures, one page at a time.

Love,

Livvy

Pucking My Off-Limits Billionaire Boss

AN ENEMIES TO LOVERS SECOND CHANCE ROMANCE

Marrying my small town's hottest billionaire seems like a fairy tale.

But little do they know, it's all a charade...

Struggling after my dream coffee shop in Seattle crashed
and having my heart broken by my ex,
I flee to my hometown, determined to buy back my former café and rebuild my life.

Back in Cedarwood, I face a double blow: my possessive ex tracked me down,
and someone just beat me to buying 'Mocha Memoirs'—*by a day*.

Worse yet, that *someone* is none other than Jake Rogers—my best friend's brother and my old flame,

whose body is one hot chiseled masterpiece with well-defined muscles, sculpted underneath bronzed skin.

To shield me from my psycho ex, Jake agrees to play my fake fiancé, and I work for him in return.

Jake's protection is my ticket back to caffeine glory.

No strings. Except the heat simmering between us is hotter than a double espresso.

He wants a second chance—but trusting him burned me once.

Now, we're brewing more than lattes—it's steaming chemistry, danger, and a fake romance that smells suspiciously real.

Will I survive a possessive past, a scorching present, and the biggest gamble of my life?

Scan this QR code to get your copy of 'Pucking My Off-Limits Billionaire Boss':

Scan me

SNEAK PEEK

1

Lucy

It's my best friend's wedding, but you'd never know it by the way Jake freaking Rogers is stealing the spotlight.

I lean against the polished bar at the Cedarwood Hotel, champagne flute in hand, watching the spectacle unfold. The reception hall is abuzz with laughter, clinking glasses, and the vibrant beats of a DJ spinning contemporary hits. The atmosphere is electric, with a lively crowd moving to the rhythm of Dua Lipa's "Don't Start Now," a song that's got everyone on the dance floor, showcasing their best moves.

Lights twinkle like stars caught in the grand chandeliers, casting a warm glow over the happy chaos. It's the kind of shindig that makes you believe in fairy tales, if only for a night.

And Jake Rogers, Cedarwood's golden boy, is right in the thick of it. He's surrounded by a cluster of admirers, his easy smile and confident stance drawing them in like moths to a flame. I take a sip of my champagne, the bubbles tickling my nose, as I watch him regale the crowd with tales of his impending return to hockey with the Los Angeles Lancers.

Max, his best friend and the groom, is egging him on, adding his own exaggerated flourishes to the story. The two of them are a double act; Max's loud guffaws are the perfect counterpoint to Jake's sly wit.

As I take another sip, I can't help but roll my eyes. Jake always had a way of commanding attention. It's like he has his own gravitational pull, and right now, he's the center of the universe. But hey, it's his sister's wedding; he's entitled to a little limelight, I guess.

I'm about to take another sip when Hailey Rogers, the bride herself, waddles over to me. Six months pregnant and absolutely radiant, she flops into the chair beside me with a sigh of relief. "Luce, what's up with the wallflower routine? Not like you at all," she chides, her eyes sparkling with mischief.

I shrug, a small smile playing on my lips. "Someone's gotta witness the madness, right? Plus, you know me, I'm just here for the free booze and the chance to see you in that gorgeous dress."

Hailey laughs, her hand resting on her pronounced belly. "Well, you're missing out. Jake's on fire tonight. Did you hear about his new contract with the Lancers? He's moving to freaking *LA*. Can you believe it?"

I nod, glancing back at Jake. He's now animatedly describing a play, his hands moving through the air as if he's back on the ice. "Yeah, I heard. Good for him."

Hailey gives me that look, the one that only a best friend can muster. It's a piercing, all-seeing gaze that cuts right through the facade, probing for what's really bubbling underneath.

"You're *not* just here for the free booze, are you?" Hailey asks, her voice soft but probing. "Is this about your big move? Opening the second location of Mocha Memoirs must be nerve-wracking."

I let out a wry chuckle, shaking my head slightly. "Man, you've always had a way of seeing right through me, huh?"

She laughs, a warm, melodic sound that fills the space between us. "That's what best friends are for, Luce. So, spill it. What's really going on?"

I sigh, picking at the label of my empty beer bottle. "I'm excited, I really am. It's just... I'm feeling a bit overwhelmed. With the new store opening, there's so much riding on it. It's like every decision is make-or-break. And then, seeing everyone here, moving forward in their lives... it's a lot."

Hailey's expression softens. "Lucy, you're about to do something incredible. You've always been the one to take on challenges head-on. Don't let the pressure dim your shine."

I smile, comforted by her words. "You're right. I need to focus on my own journey, not get caught up in everything else. It's just a big step, you know?"

"Of course, I do," Hailey says, squeezing my hand. "But if anyone can make it in Seattle, it's you. You're going to be amazing."

Chiding myself internally for being so glum on Hailey's big day, I give her a sheepish smile. "Sorry for being a bit of a downer at your wedding. Anything I can do to make up for it?"

"See? That's the spirit!" Hailey beams at me, her eyes crinkling in amusement. "Actually, yes, there is something. How about you go over there and make nice with Jake? And while you're at it, maybe take him down a peg for hogging all the attention." She follows up her words with a sly wink.

I grin, a spark of mischief lighting up my eyes. "Taking down your full-of-himself brother down a notch? Now that's something I can do. Consider it my wedding gift to you."

We hug, then I take a deep breath, bolstered by Hailey's encouragement, and make my way through the crowd towards Jake.

There he is, Jake Rogers, in all his infuriatingly handsome glory. He's standing there, the epitome of charm, with his normally shaggy dark hair slicked back just enough to add a hint of roguish sophistication for the wedding. It suits him, giving him an air of James Dean cool that's impossible to ignore.

He turns, and I catch a glimpse of his sparkling blue eyes, alive with that mischievous twinkle that I've known since we were kids. They're the kind of eyes that don't just look at you; they see right through you, leaving a trail of fluttering hearts in their wake.

As he laughs at something Max has just said, those infamous dimples make their appearance, etching deep into his cheeks. They lend him a boyish charm that's in stark contrast to the powerful, athlete's body he carries so effortlessly, a body that's no doubt the result of countless hours on the ice. It's all hidden now beneath the sharp lines of his tuxedo, but the broad shoulders and the way the fabric clings to him leave little to the imagination.

And that smile. That damn smile that's disarmingly sincere and just a tad too cocky. It's a smile that could sell a fortune in toothpaste. It's the kind of smile that you remember, the kind that sneaks into your thoughts at the most inopportune times.

Pain in the butt he is, I have to admit—he looks good. Not that I'd ever tell him that. He doesn't need any more ammunition for that ego. But as I make my way over to him, weaving through the sea of guests, I can't help but acknowledge the simple truth: Jake Rogers has always looked good. And standing here now, all dressed up and beaming with confidence, he doesn't just look good.

He looks like every dream I've told myself I don't have.

He's in the middle of a story, his audience hanging on every word. I sidle up to the edge of the group, waiting for the right moment to jump in.

"Hey, Jake," I call out, loud enough to cut through his tale. "You planning on leaving any attention for the rest of us, or are you just going to keep hogging the spotlight all night?"

The crowd chuckles as Jake turns to face me, a broad grin spreading across his face. "Lucy Marks," he says with mock surprise. "I was wondering when you'd come over to bask in my glow."

"Oh, believe me, it's hard to miss," I retort, waving a hand as if trying to clear away his so-called 'glow.' "But seriously, Jake, try to leave some room for the rest of us mere mortals to shine, will you?"

Jake chuckles, stepping closer. "Lucy, if I knew you were craving the spotlight, I would've shared it with you. After all, what are old friends for?"

I raise an eyebrow, taking a step to meet him halfway. "Shared? Please, Jake, we both know you love the spotlight too much to share it with anyone."

The small crowd around us is eating up our exchange, their laughter and smiles encouraging our playful banter.

That's when Max, the groom and Jake's best friend, steps in with a mischievous glint in his eye. "Alright, you two, there's only one way to settle this little spat of yours."

Jake and I turn to him, both of us echoing, "And what's that?"

Max grins, pointing towards the dance floor. "A dance-off. Right here, right now. Let's see who really deserves the spotlight tonight."

The suggestion sends a new wave of excitement through the onlookers, and I can't help but accept the challenge. "You're on, Rogers. Prepare to be owned."

Jake's smile widens as he offers his hand, accepting the challenge. "Let's see what you've got, Marks."

As the music kicks up a notch, Jake and I face each other, a silent agreement passing between us. The crowd circles around, their excitement palpable. It's showtime.

"Alright, Rogers," I say, my voice laced with challenge. "Let's make this interesting. If I win this dance-off, you're making a grand announcement congratulating Hailey and Max. Let's put the spotlight where it belongs, on the newlyweds."

Jake's eyes light up with the thrill of the bet. "And if I win, Lucy Marks, you have to join me for a drink later. A chance for us to catch up properly. Deal?"

I nod, a sly smile playing on my lips. "Deal."

The DJ, sensing the mood, cues up a track that's impossible to resist—Bruno Mars' "24K Magic." Its infectious beat fills the room, and the crowd instinctively moves closer to the dance floor, their anticipation palpable.

Jake doesn't waste a moment. As soon as the funky, upbeat intro hits, he's in his element. He starts with a smooth, confident glide across the floor, reminiscent of his days gliding on ice. His movements are surprisingly rhythmic for a guy better known for his hockey prowess than his dance skills. There's a natural, easy charm to his steps that draws whoops and hollers from the crowd.

Not to be outdone, I tap into my own repertoire. The vibrant beats of the song are the perfect canvas for my dance moves. I start with a sassy shimmy, letting the rhythm flow through me, my feet moving in time with the pulsing bass. I throw in a series of spins, my dress twirling around me, then transition into some quick, sharp footwork that echoes the song's energetic vibe.

Jake watches, an eyebrow raised, and then meets my challenge head-on. He mirrors my footwork, adding his own flair—a couple of fancy spins and a slide that ends with a playful bow in my direction. The crowd cheers, loving the friendly rivalry.

We're both grinning now, the sheer joy of the music and the challenge sparking between us. Our moves become more playful and exaggerated, a silent conversation of dance. He steps forward, I spin away; I beckon him closer, he comes in with a mock-serious tango pose. It's a dance battle that's less about winning and more about the shared exhilaration of the moment.

As the song reaches its bridge, the tempo picks up, and we match it, our movements becoming more frenetic and fun. The crowd is clapping along now, fully invested in our impromptu performance.

By the time the final chorus rolls around, Jake and I are both breathless, our playful competitiveness giving way to a mutual respect for each other's hidden talents. The song ends on a high note, with both of us striking an exaggerated pose, arms spread wide, basking in the applause and laughter from our friends and family.

The applause is thunderous, the guests clearly enjoying the spectacle. But as Hailey steps up, it's clear there's no easy way to declare a winner.

"It's a tie!" she announces, and the crowd seems to agree, their cheers echoing her verdict.

True to his word, Jake grabs a microphone from the DJ and steps up to the center of attention. He clears his throat, and his voice booms through the speakers, echoing around the hall.

"Alright, everyone," he begins, his tone a perfect blend of charm and humor. "While I know you've all enjoyed my incredible dance moves and dazzling personality," he pauses for a laugh, "let's remember why we're really here tonight."

He turns towards Hailey and Max, his expression softening. "To celebrate the love of an amazing couple, Hailey and Max. Let's give it up for them—the real stars tonight. Here's to a lifetime of happiness, love, and all that other good stuff!"

The crowd erupts into laughter and applause, their focus shifting back to the beaming newlyweds. Hailey and Max, their smiles wide and genuine, stand up to acknowledge the cheers, the love in the room palpable.

As the applause dies down, Jake hands off the mic and bounds over to me, a playful glint in his eye. "So, about that drink..."

I roll my eyes, but I can't suppress the smile tugging at the corners of my mouth. "Fine, you've earned it. But just one drink, Rogers. Don't get any ideas."

2

Jake

Walking away from the dance floor, I can't help but grin, replaying the dance-off in my head. Lucy Marks, of all people, had just given me a run for my money. I've got to admit, I didn't see that coming. She's always been fiery, but tonight, she's like a firecracker—full of surprises and twice as explosive.

I find her at the bar, nursing what looks like her third glass of champagne. "You know, Lucy," I begin, leaning casually against the counter, "I always knew you had rhythm, but I didn't realize you were hiding those dance moves. Were you planning on joining a salsa competition I don't know about?"

Lucy turns, her eyes sparkling with that familiar sass. "Please, Jake. I was just trying not to outshine the bride. Someone has to keep their ego in check around here," she retorts, nodding subtly in my direction.

"Oh, come on. You love my ego. Admit it, it adds to my charm," I say with a wink, enjoying the easy back-and-forth we've always had, ever since we were kids.

She rolls her eyes, a smile tugging at the corners of her mouth. "In your dreams, Rogers. It's going to take more than a few dance moves and a wink to impress me."

I laugh, taking a sip of my drink. "Is that a challenge, Marks? Because you should know, I never back down from a challenge."

Lucy leans in, her tone playful yet edged with a challenge. "Oh, I know all about your 'challenges,' Jake. Remember the time you tried to outdo me in Mrs. Henderson's English class? How did that end again?"

I feign a pained expression. "Okay, okay, no need to bring up ancient history. Let's focus on the present. Like your big move to LA."

Her laughter rings out, genuine and unguarded. "Come on—it's just LA. No big."

"Just Seattle, she says," I mimic, raising my eyebrows. "You're taking on a new city, opening a new store. That's pretty damn impressive, Lucy."

She shrugs, a hint of vulnerability flashing in her eyes before she covers it with her usual bravado. "Well, someone's got to show the big city how it's done. And who better than me?"

"That's the spirit. And hey, if you need a ruggedly handsome, incredibly charming coffee taster, you know where to find me," I offer with a cheeky grin. "Just hit the Pacific Coast Highway and head down."

"Ruggedly handsome?" Lucy scoffs, but I can tell she's fighting back a smile. "Keep dreaming, Rogers."

We fall into a comfortable silence, sipping our drinks. I can't help but admire her—Lucy's always been a force to be reckoned with, but tonight, there's something different about her. She's more confident, more radiant. It's captivating.

"So, Lucy," I say, breaking the silence. "Now that you've conquered the dance floor, what's next on your list? World domination?"

She laughs, shaking her head. "For now, I'll settle for conquering Seattle. But who knows? World domination could be next."

I nod, impressed. "Well, when you take over the world, remember the little people. Like me."

"You little? Never," she says, her tone teasing. "You've always been larger than life."

Our eyes meet, and there's a spark—something electric, something that's been simmering under the surface for years. I've always known Lucy Marks was special, but tonight, it's like I'm seeing her for the first time.

The playful edge to our conversation slowly gives way to something more profound, like we're peeling back layers to reveal parts of ourselves that the other hasn't seen. It's strange, this sudden shift in our dynamic, but not unwelcome.

"So, Lucy," I start, my tone less cocky, more contemplative. "Seattle's a big move. You ever get scared, diving into something new like that? God knows I'm a little nervous."

She looks at me, clearly surprised by the question. "You, nervous? I thought nothing scared you."

I shrug. "Everyone gets scared, Lucy. I may not show it, but yeah, there are things that worry me. Like leaving everything I know behind for LA, starting up my hockey career after putting it on ice for a few years. It's a big step, even for me."

Lucy's expression softens. "I guess we're both jumping into the unknown, aren't we? It's terrifying but exciting. And nice pun, by the way."

I laugh. "Yeah, the unknown," I agree, feeling an unexpected kinship with her. "But you know, sometimes you've got to take the leap, see where you land."

She nods, her eyes thoughtful. "Exactly. And who knows, maybe we'll both land on our feet."

The conversation drifts to our dreams, our fears, and everything in between.

As I sit across from Lucy, the ambient glow of the bar highlighting her features, I can't help but be struck by her—again. I've always known Lucy was beautiful, that's never been up for debate. But tonight, there's something different about her. It's as if she's shed some invisible armor, revealing the vivid intensity of her presence.

Her long auburn hair, usually tied back when she's working at her coffee shop, cascades in waves, catching the light every time she moves, framing her face in a way that makes her bright green eyes even more striking. They're like two emeralds, full of life and dancing with the reflections of the dim bar lights, captivating in their depth.

Her figure, often hidden beneath the apron she wears at work, is revealed in the soft contours of her dress, hugging her curves gracefully. There's an effortless elegance about her, a natural allure that's both subtle and overwhelming. She moves with a confidence that's undeniably sexy, each gesture and glance carrying an air of sophistication and an understated sensuality.

There's a natural grace in the way she holds herself, a confidence that's not just surface deep. It's in the tilt of her head when she listens, the easy way her smile spreads across her face, genuine and unguarded.

As we talk, the chemistry between us grows, a tangible current in the air. It's like we're both aware of it, yet neither of us is ready to acknowledge it just yet.

As the conversation meanders through the nooks and crannies of our past and flutters over our hopes for the future, I notice the party's energy has begun to wane. The laughter and music that had filled the room seem to have quieted down, the crowd thinning out as the night draws on. Time has flown by while we've been lost in our own world, and it's a bit startling to realize how much the room has emptied.

I catch a glimpse of Max and Hailey, the newlyweds, sneaking out with those eager, mischievous smirks that newlyweds wear—the kind that say they've got much better things to do than say proper goodbyes to lingering guests. I elbow Lucy gently, nodding towards the escaping couple.

"Looks like the party's losing its stars," I say, my words laced with amusement. "Might be our cue, huh?"

Lucy follows my gaze, and a knowing smile spreads across her face. "Seems like the perfect time to make our own escape then."

I nod, the idea forming fully now. "You know, my bar is just down the block. Everyone who'd be there is here, so we're closed for the night. How about we get out of here and continue this chat there?" The invitation hangs between us, equal parts question and challenge.

Lucy pauses, her eyes holding mine in a gaze that's both intense and a little uncertain. Then, as if coming to a decision, she gives me a nod that sends a jolt of anticipation through me. "Yeah, I'd like that," she agrees, her voice steady but her eyes betraying a flicker of excitement.

We leave the reception together, walking side by side down the block to Cedarwood Tavern. The night air is cool and refreshing, a stark contrast to the warm buzz of the wedding reception.

As we reach the bar, I unlock the door and let us in. The place is empty, the dim lighting creating an intimate atmosphere. I lead her to a cozy booth at the back, feeling a mix of excitement and nervousness.

"So, this is your empire, huh?" Lucy says, looking around with an appreciative eye.

"Yeah, this is it. Not much, but it's mine," I reply, feeling oddly vulnerable under her gaze.

In the dimly lit corner of Cedarwood Tavern, the world outside seems to fade away, leaving just Lucy and me in our own little bubble. I pour us a couple of drinks, the clink of the glasses echoing softly in the quiet space.

"So, we're both heading out of Cedarwood, huh? What are the odds?" I say, a half-smile playing on my lips.

Lucy takes a sip of her drink, her eyes meeting mine. "Seems like fate has a sense of humor. Both of us leaving town, but staying on the same coast."

I nod, leaning back in the booth. "Yeah, it's a new chapter. But leaving the bar in someone else's hands? Feels like sending my kid off to college."

She laughs, the sound warm and genuine. "I know the feeling. Handing over Mocha Memoirs to my team? Terrifying. I half expect to come back and find they've turned it into a nightclub."

Our eyes lock, and there's a moment of silence, heavy with everything we're not saying. It's like we're both on the edge of something, a precipice that's both thrilling and terrifying.

Then, without warning, I let slip the words that have been sitting on the tip of my tongue all evening. "You know, you look incredible tonight, Lucy. Not that you don't always look great, but tonight there's something..." I trail off, realizing that I've crossed an invisible line.

The air shifts between us, charged with a new intensity. The playful banter that has been our dance all night suddenly feels like a prelude to something much more profound. It's as if a floodgate has opened, and all the unspoken attraction and tension come rushing out.

Lucy's expression changes, the playful smirk giving way to something deeper, more vulnerable. She moves closer, and I can feel the heat of her body, the faint scent of her perfume.

The air between us crackles with unspoken tension, and I can feel the pull, an irresistible force drawing me towards her. It's a sensation that's both exhilarating and terrifying in its intensity.

Then, almost as if drawn by a magnet, our heads lean in closer, the space between us disappearing. When our lips finally meet, it's like a spark igniting a fire. The kiss is tentative at first, but soon deepens, fueled by years of unexplored chemistry.

Her lips are soft against mine, and I can taste the champagne she's been drinking. My hand finds its way to her cheek, and she leans into the touch. The kiss is everything I didn't know I was missing—passionate, consuming, and right.

We break apart, our breaths mingling, our eyes locked. There's a shared understanding, a recognition of something that's been simmering under the surface for far too long.

As our lips part, the air around us seems charged with electricity, each breath heavy with unspoken desire. Lucy's eyes, shining with a mix of passion and anticipation, meet mine, sending a shiver down my spine. Her hand slides from my cheek down to my chest, tracing a path that sets my skin ablaze.

"Jake," she whispers, her voice a sultry melody that resonates deep within me. The way she says my name, it's like a key unlocking something primal inside me. I pull her closer, our bodies pressing together in a dance as old as time.

Our kisses become a language of their own, telling stories of longing, of missed opportunities, and newfound possibilities. Her fingers tangle in my hair, pulling me deeper into the kiss, each movement igniting a fire that had been smoldering within us for far too long.

Lucy's eyes dance with mischief as she looks up at me, a sly grin playing on her lips. "So, Mr. Hockey Star, think you can keep up with me off the ice?"

I chuckle, leaning in closer, our noses nearly touching. "I don't know, Ms. Coffee Connoisseur, I've been known to be pretty quick on my feet. But I'm more interested in seeing if you can keep up with me."

Her laugh is light and flirtatious. "Oh, I have a few tricks up my sleeve. You might be surprised."

I raise an eyebrow, intrigued and more than a little excited by her playful challenge. "Is that a promise or a threat?"

"It's a guarantee," she retorts, her fingers tracing the collar of my shirt. "But be warned, I don't play fair."

I grasp her hand gently, bringing it to my lips for a soft kiss. "Neither do I. I think that's something we have in common."

Her breath hitches slightly as I kiss her hand, her eyes locked onto mine. "Then let the games begin," she says, her voice a sultry whisper that sends a thrill down my spine.

I lean in, whispering in her ear, "You better be ready, because I plan on winning."

She pulls back, her eyes sparkling with excitement and desire. "Then game on."

We go right back into kissing, our tongues probing for one another, her taste like nothing else. Bit by bit, we strip one another out of our clothes. Her body's perfect, with ripe, round tits and hips that I want to sink my teeth into.

Lucy, on the other hand, has her eyes locked onto my manhood. I'm spear-straight, ready to plunge inside of her. Lucy's tongue snakes over her lips as she takes in the sight of me.

"You want my cock?" I ask.

She nods. "So damn much."

"You're going to have to work for it."

She grins, biting down on her lower lip. "Tell me what kind of work you have in mind."

I stand up, coming over to her and putting my hands onto her hips. I pull her close, pressing her against my stiffness. I reach between her thighs, feeling her warmth, feeling her sensual wetness.

God, I want her. Truth is, I've always wanted her, ever since we were teenagers, ever since she was nothing more than some gawky redhead my sister was best friends with. She's anything but gawky now, all curves and tits and lips.

"Turn around."

She flashes me a smirk before turning, pointing that luscious, round ass at me.

"Take hold of the desk."

"Bossy, bossy man."

Scan this QR code to get your copy of 'Pucking My Off-Limits Billionaire Boss' now!

Scan me